BROKEN PRINCE

R.G. ANGEL

Broken Prince – Cosa Nostra book 1
By R.G Angel
Copyright © 2021 R.G. Angel

Cover: Sarah Kil Creaive Studio
Formatting: Pink Elephant Designs
Editing: Editing by Kimberly Dawn

"She was never afraid of his darkness or the demons who danced in his eyes. He thought no one could ever love him if he revealed what lurked inside. He always knew he was different, how could anyone understand? But she was never afraid of his darkness or the beast within the man." -

Unknown

PROLOGUE

Tires screeching, fear, screams, and pain...so much pain. A pain I thought was the worst I experienced until I opened my eyes and looked in her unblinking dark ones.

I realized as I slipped slowly into unconsciousness as I stared into their lifeless eyes and mangled bodies that they were dead, taken away from me. I could not move, could not speak, could not breathe. All my mind could scream was, "Please let me die with them."

I should have known better than to expect any reprieve from life—now was time to live in my hell, my purgatory...my penance.

1

CASSIE

They say everybody wants to be famous, be on the covers of the newspapers. That any press is good press, but that is a load of crap!

The press had been nothing but a curse for me and my little brother, Jude. We were Cassandra and Jude West, the children of the Rivertown Murderers.

These people... My parents used their small investment firm to embezzle the retirement funds of more than fifteen thousand people in ten years and they had also murdered thirty-two elderly people in an attempt to cover their tracks.

My face, half hidden behind my messy red hair as I walked out of the court during the trial, even made the first page of our regional paper and I had wanted to disappear on that day. I was not going to court to support them. I was going there—I was not sure why I was going there.

Maybe part of me hoped they would have the decency to apologize to me and Jude for destroying our lives and making us pariahs because the stigma we were carrying was a heavy cross to bear.

I let out a sigh of relief when my father was sentenced to life without parole and my mother to forty years I was there to make sure this whole nightmare would finally end and they would end their lives behind bars.

I didn't miss the glares directed my way by the families of the victims every time I took my seat in the back of the room. People didn't believe that the twenty-year-old daughter of these two sociopaths didn't know something was wrong, and even if I genuinely had no idea, I couldn't help but feel guilty. Had I missed anything? Were there signs?

When I exited the court after the verdict, I looked at my watch and groaned. I only had one afternoon with Jude per week and this final day of trial stole two precious hours from it.

It has been four months since my life—our lives—spiraled into hell. We had no other family and social services declared I was not fit to take care of my brother and I couldn't deny it. I was broke; I had to drop out of nursing school, and I was now sleeping on the uncomfortable futon of our old maid who was one of the only people showing me a little compassion.

I rushed to catch the bus. I had to get to the Home soon as visitation ended at five p.m.

Seeing my baby brother only an afternoon a week was breaking me. I missed him so much and I was worried sick; he was only ten, way too young to have to deal with all of this.

No one should be dealing with all of this.

When I arrived, Amy, the social worker dealing with Jude's case, was pacing in front of the door.

"I thought you would not make it," she said, pulling me into the visitation room.

"I know!" I gasped breathlessly. "Thank you for waiting."

She gave me a small smile. "You deserve someone cutting you some slack," she said gently, bringing tears to my eyes.

I was so unused to kindness recently. I had been lucky when she had been assigned my brother's case. We'd been in the same high school even if she had been a senior when I joined and it created a sort of kinship that I was beyond grateful for.

She opened the side door and spoke to someone; the door opened wider and my brother rushed in.

"Cassie!" he shouted, running into my arms.

I hugged him tightly. He was so short and frail. He might have been ten, but he didn't look older than seven. He was my little man though; our parents had always been emotionally distant. It has always been Jude and me.

"I'm sorry. I didn't want to be late," I told him, caressing his dark-blond hair softly.

He kept his arms around me and lifted his eyes, looking at me with his big, sad green eyes—much too weary for a little boy his age.

"Are we okay now?" he asked with a small voice.

I nodded. "Yes, we are. They're not coming back." I frowned, noticing the small bruise on his jawline. "What's that?" I asked, brushing my fingers on it.

"Nothing." He shrugged. "I fell."

I looked up to Amy who looked at us with so much sorrow it cracked my heart open even more. I had to get him out of here.

"I'll take you home as soon as I can, li'l man. I swear I will."

"I know, Cassie. It's okay. I'm okay here."

No, you're not. You're miserable, but you're trying to be strong for me when you shouldn't have to, I thought. "I know but I miss having you with me so I want to get you back as soon as possible." I forced a smile I hoped looked genuine. "Who's supposed to help me sample brownies now, huh?"

He nodded. "Yeah, I'm sort of an expert."

I chuckled. "Yes, you are."

Amy sighed. "I'm sorry, guys, but Jude has to go back now."

I looked up and she looked really crestfallen. I was

sure she had a soft spot for Jude, but then again, who didn't?

I nodded. "I'll see you next week and we can video chat this week sometimes," I said before throwing a quick look at Amy who nodded. She did that every week for us, using her own phone to allow Jude and I to talk for a few minutes. That woman really was a godsend and at least she helped us make this horrible situation just a little better.

"Love you to the moon and back," he said, hugging me tightly again.

"Love you to the sun and back," I replied, kissing the top of his head, already feeling the burn of my unshed tears at the back of my eyes.

After he left, Amy turned toward me.

"What really happened?" I asked, knowing full well that Jude's bruise was not an accident.

She sighed, shaking her head. "Kids have been tough on him," she admitted reluctantly. "Being related to…" She winced. "It's a heavy cross to bear."

"I know. I'm planning to change our name as soon as I can get him back." I sat on one of the uncomfortable orange chairs lining the visitation room.

I knew I had to leave. There was no reason for me to still be here; the center was now closed to the public, but I just needed a few minutes.

A few minutes with someone who looked at me, not as an accomplice to the monsters my parents were, but as one of their victims.

"I'm just not convinced that day will ever come," I admitted, and saying it out loud hurt more than I anticipated.

"So they refused to take you back, huh?" she asked, coming to sit beside me, gripping my hand in hers.

I nodded. "Yes, I can't blame them though. The hospital had a hard time justifying my presence there and since nursing school kicked me out." I shrugged. "What was the point of me working there anyway?"

"We can fight their decision, you know. I looked into it and they had no grounds for dismissing you."

I shook my head. "What's the point? No one wants me there. The students look at me like I am a monster, the teachers too. And even if I force it, I need hospital training and no hospital will offer that to me."

"Yeah." She nodded with resignation. "What about your living situation?"

"Still squatting on Mrs. Broussard's futon." I'd never been more grateful in my life. Mrs. Broussard had been working for my parents since I was five years old and when everything turned to shit, she'd been the only one offering me the helping hand I desperately needed despite her own children's advice. "I need to give her back her space and stop eating her food." I looked heavenward. "Nobody is willing to hire me in this town but—" I looked at the door connected to the living quarters my little brother occupied. "I just can't leave; he needs me."

"You remember Ms. Lebowitz, don't you?"

I looked at her with confusion at the change of subject. "The high school career counselor?"

She nodded. "She retired but I know she's working part-time for the temp agency by the pharmacy." Amy shrugged. "She always had a soft spot for her old students. Why don't you go see her?"

Ms. Lebowitz had been an older lady, an eccentric hippy, but she'd always seen more than she let on. She had known even then that I'd been the one caring for Jude. She was the one who suggested nursing school after seeing my caring nature.

"I like her. It's worth the shot." I looked at my watch; it was much past the time and I didn't need Amy to get into trouble and have Jude removed from her care due to her involvement with me. "What about Jude and his bruises?"

"Don't worry, I've moved him into a room with younger kids. He's okay now." She answered my unspoken thoughts.

I threw her a grateful look. "I need to go now. I have to grab my bus."

"Let me drive you home, please."

I nodded. The bus ride to Mrs. Broussard's was going to take more than forty-five minutes, and I had to admit that, after the draining day I had, I was more than grateful to accept.

9

"Why are you so nice to me"? I asked Amy as we took to the road. "Not that I'm not eternally grateful but—"

She shrugged. "Call it empathy. I've seen you before at the hospital; you genuinely cared about the patients, and the way your brother talks about you? You're his whole world. I've seen a lot of mean, heartless people in my line of work and you're not one of them. You're caring and loving and so obviously unaware of your parents' monstrosities" She threw me a quick look full of concern. "You don't deserve to be treated the way you are so if I can help ease this injustice just a little…I will."

I looked away, blinking back my tears. Her words somehow gave me hope. Maybe others would see it too. Maybe others would cut me some slack and help me get Jude back.

Yes, tomorrow was another day and I would turn the tide, no matter the sacrifices.

For Jude.

2

CASSIE

I woke up to the sound of Mrs. Broussard humming in the little kitchen area and the smell of freshly brewed coffee.

I sat up and winced at the soreness of my back left by the metal bars of the thin futon. I would never say anything though; she'd given me shelter when everyone turned their back on me. She'd been my savior.

"Ma Cherie." She smiled, putting a plate on the counter for me. "I made a little extra for you." Her amber eyes were sad despite the brightness of her smile.

"What would I do without you?" I asked, rubbing my eyes and padding barefoot in my flannel pajamas, then sitting on a stool.

"You'll be fine, Cherie. You're a good person; you always have been. Life will come around, you'll see."

"I hope you're right," I said, taking a bite of pain perdu. "I'm going to the temp agency today in town. If God, karma, or whatever is out there and ever wanted to grant me a favor, today is the day."

"I can speak with Camille."

I shook my head. Camille was a junior doctor at Hospital Central and she was not a fan of me and the trouble she thought I was putting her mother into.

I could not blame her though. Her mother had worked tirelessly for my family, who treated her no better than a piece of furniture. She'd worked that hard just to buy herself this tiny apartment in an over-fifty complex and I was now living on her meager income.

I was no better than a leech but that was stopping today. I would get a job no matter what.

"That's not necessary. Let's see how it goes today."

Amy had assured me that as soon as I had a steady job, a place to live big enough to get Jude, and a little savings, she'd do everything in her power for me to get him and once I had him back we would leave, change our names, and start fresh. Just the two of us.

Mrs. Broussard looked at the clock. "Do you want me to drive you there? I have a little time."

I smiled but shook my head, my mouth full of pain perdu. "I'm fine, don't worry."

She cocked her head to the side. "I'm allowed to worry about you, Cassie. I've watched you grow."

I reached for the newspaper on the counter, and she rested her caramel hand on top of mine.

"Maybe you shouldn't, Cherie."

I sighed. "Believe me, there's nothing they can say I have not read before."

She hesitated for a second before lifting her hand with a sigh. "Nothing good will come from this," she said with defeat, before turning around and putting her plate in the small dishwasher on the counter.

I was glad she was not looking at me as I couldn't help but wince at the first page title.

'Riverside Monsters - jailed for life!' The main title appeared in black letters but instead of a picture of them, it was me on the front page of the Riverside Herald, standing alone on the steps of the court-house, my unruly red hair flying around my face. I looked grim, defeated, and I was. My life had taken a turn for the worse, but I was not defeated because of their sentencing. No, that had been the only good thing in all of this.

My parents had always been emotional terrorists, using me and subsequently Jude for their own horrible schemes. It had been hard finding out in court that Jude was conceived via insemination not because they were dying for another child but because I'd been growing up and didn't look that cute anymore and therefore didn't inspire that much trust anymore.

What I'd always taken as nothing more than the lack of parental instinct and a busy work life had been, in fact, so much worse than I could have ever imagined. We had been toys, props, nothing more.

I hoped that Jude would never find out he had been nothing more than a means to an end. A card added to the table without any feeling involved.

I also hoped I loved him hard enough to make up for all the scars inflicted on him by the monsters who had put us in this world.

I forced a smile when I met Mrs. Broussard's concerned eyes and put my plate in the dishwasher before going to rummage in the two little suitcases I've been allowed to take with me.

I prayed I had something suitable to go see Ms. Lebowitz because when I left home, I'd expected to go back eventually. I hadn't expected everything to last that long.

When the FBI had shown up at our house, I had been happy that Jude was at school. Tens of agents just took over the place, turning the house upside down, and informed me that the house was now under Asset seizure.

No one wanted to tell me what happened and even if I suspected my parents may have embezzled money, I never would have imagined the true horror.

After a moment an agent had come up to me, a

big terrifying man, and barked that I had thirty minutes to pack what my brother and I would need for a few weeks.

I packed two suitcases for me and one for Jude as quickly as I could under his watchful eyes. Was he expecting me to hide something? Did he think I was involved in whatever my parents had done?

The agent then mentioned me toward his big black SUV.

"Can I take my car?" I had asked, pointing to the Toyota my parents had bought me earlier this year. It had not been a heartfelt present; they just needed me to chauffeur Jude around and do all the shopping they were not bothered to do.

He shook his head. "No, all assets owned by Martha and John West are now seized by the federal government of the United States." He opened the back door of the car. "Where will you be staying?"

I froze at that moment. Where would I be staying? I'd been so busy with nursing school and taking care of Jude, making up for all my parents' shortcomings, that I didn't really have friends, at least no one close enough to give me a place to stay.

"She'll stay with me, won't you, Cassie?"

I'd turned around and let out a little tearless sob of relief when Mrs. Broussard came toward me already dressed to leave.

"I need to go pick up Jude—"

"Jude West will be picked up by social services." The agent tried to grab the suitcase I made for Jude.

I'd tightened my hold on the handle and took a step back. "I have to talk to him; he'll be scared. Please, sir. He's just a little boy," I begged, my voice breaking at the thought of my little brother scared and alone.

He had looked at me for a second and sighed. "Social services will be going to school in the next thirty minutes or so; you can go wait there."

And I went with Mrs. Broussard, swearing to my terrified little brother that I was going to fix everything soon, but I was four months in now and I was not a step closer to getting him back.

The assets were still frozen and all my parents' belongings were to be sold for the compensations the victims' families were awarded. I couldn't care less about the house, cars, and bank accounts—I didn't want anything. I would never consider enjoying anything they acquired with the literal blood of other people, but I would have loved being able to go get more clothes and other things for Jude and me.

I sighed, rummaging through the clothes and settling for my pair of dark jeans and a long-sleeve green shirt, hoping it would look professional enough.

"See you later!" Mrs. Broussard shouted from behind the bathroom's door as I jumped into the shower.

Once she was gone, I could finally let go of my strong facade and I cried as the warm water hit my face, my tears mixing with the water. I didn't even try to contain my sobs as more and more tears ran down my face.

I cried for my little brother and the abuse I could not protect him from. He was the loveliest little boy, with a heart so big he could fit the world, and I could only imagine how the hate received was affecting him.

I had a hard time with it myself…death threats, insults, ostracized. It was a heavy cross to bear for me, I could not even start to comprehend how heavy it might be for him.

Once the water turned cold and my tears dried up, I got out of the shower, put my unruly hair in a bun, and put on some makeup for the first time in months.

I didn't feel even remotely ready to face the world today with my face plastered all over the newspapers in this town, but some things were more important than my own comfort and it was getting my brother back and leaving Riverside.

I looked at my bank account and despite my meager savings, I decided to indulge in an Uber for once. I didn't think I could face the curious, angry, and judgmental looks of the bystanders who were still wondering if I had been in on it with my parents.

When I made it to the agency, I was happy to see

that Ms. Lebowitz's desk was closer to the door and that except for the younger blond girl behind the other desk, the agency was empty.

She had not changed one bit since high school, with her gray hair halfway down her back, her flowy boho dress, and kind brown eyes. I could almost smell her patchouli perfume from behind the door.

When I walked in, the young woman's eyes widened and it was obvious she knew who I was with just one look. I was a local celebrity now... *Yay me.*

Ms. Lebowitz looked up and smiled brightly at me. That hadn't happened for a while and it felt nice.

"Miss West!" She beamed, clapping her hands, making her numerous bangles chime in the so familiar sound that reminded me of high school. "What brings you here?"

I straightened my shirt, trying to give myself a certain presence. "Good morning, Ms. Lebowitz, long time no see."

"Please call me Patty; school's been over a long time." She gestured to the seat across from hers. "What can I do for you?"

I sat and sighed. I was not sure if I should even fake at all. She had always been so perceptive of students; maybe that was what made her so great at her job. "I need a job."

She nodded. "Yes, of course." She started typing

on her computer as I chanced a look at the other woman.

She was not even pretending not to eavesdrop anymore. She had left the telephone off the hook and was staring at us, her elbow on her desk, chin in hand.

Ms. Lebowitz looked at her screen for what seemed like forever before turning toward me, her previous genuine smile replaced by a fake one I'd never seen on her face before.

"Ummm, you know, Cassie, it's not the right time of the year and jobs are quite sparse these days." Ah, yes, I saw where that one was going.

"I'll take anything." Yep, I was not above begging at this point. "You know I've done nothing wrong," I said in desperation.

"Of course, I do!" She gasped, resting her hand on her chest. "You had to be one of the most mature and caring students I ever encountered." She shook her head. "How people like them had a daughter like you is beyond me." She sighed.

"I need to get Jude out. People are unkind to me and it's okay, but him…" I pursed my lips and shook my head. Now was not the time to burst into tears. "I just need money, fast."

She cocked her head to the side, her eyes filling with sadness. "Cassie—"

"There's always Hartfield Manor," the other woman piped up, making Ms. Lebovitz tense.

She turned her head slowly and glared at the blond woman. I didn't think I'd ever seen Patty Lebowitz glare at anyone before. "I don't think that is the solution, Karin. Why don't you go back to your work?"

I frowned, even more intrigued now. "What's Hartfield Manor?" I asked, looking directly at Karin.

She turned toward me, blowing her blond hair over her shoulder as a silent 'fuck you' to Patty, but I was too desperate for a job to care right now.

"It's a full-time live-in housekeeper job," she replied with a voice much too sweet to be honest. She was not trying to help, not really, but my need for money superseded any warning bells going on in my head.

"Okay..." I glanced toward Ms. Lebowitz who was throwing daggers at Karin. "I can't say I've much experience in the field. I've been to nursing school for two years out of my three but—" I winced. "Also, I'm Cassie West, I'm not sure anyone—"

She waved her hand dismissively and scoffed. "They're desperate. They'll take anyone we'll send them. It's four times the average hourly governess salary." She shrugged. "You said you needed money fast, so I thought—"

"You thought *nothing*, Karin—only about your commission," Patty snapped before turning toward me "Listen, Cassie, sweetheart." She sighed. "This is not the job for you. This job, I'm not sure who the owner is, but all seven housekeepers we sent quit in less than six weeks! Seven, Cassie."

I bit my bottom lip; it was true that it didn't look good but at the same time... "What's the salary?"

"Cassie..." Ms. Lebowitz trailed off wearily, probably knowing she'd lost me.

"Please." My voice broke.

She sighed with defeat. "Fifteen hundred dollars a week."

"Fifteen hundred dollars a week?" I shrieked. With that amount of money I could secure a place and enough savings to get Jude back in like four to six months.

Amy had promised that once I secured a two-bedroom apartment, a steady job, and enough savings to ensure financial security in case of a drawback which we estimated at around ten thousand, I could get Jude back.

The city was expensive but the suburb was okay, and it was far enough from Riverside for us to be able to start fresh; however, I needed money and lots of it. This job could be my saving grace.

"I'll take it. I can work every day except for Thursday afternoons." It was the only day I was allowed to see Jude.

Karin's smile widened. "Excellent. I'll make the call."

"Please, Cassie, I'm not sure this is the best move—"

"Do you have anything else to offer me?" I asked a little colder than I intended. Clearly, it was not the ideal job, but it was a shitload of money, and if blond bitch was right, they were desperate enough to not care I was the daughter of the Riverside monsters.

She shook her head. "The man is mean. The other candidates were terrified."

I shrugged. "At least they made it out alive; it's more than what my parents did to people. And seriously, the way these people raised me? They were mean, cold, dismissive. I'm equipped and desperate enough to deal with a horrible old man. What's the name of the tyrant?"

She leaned back in her chair, knowing she had lost the battle. "We don't know. We were hired by a conglomerate based in the city." She shook her head. "The other women never stayed long enough to meet him and…" She shrugged. "Frankly, I assume it's an old and half-demented shareholder they want to keep hidden."

I grimaced. "That's a lovely picture."

"I would like you to reconsider, Cassie."

I shook my head. "I can't, this is too important."

She nodded before turning toward Karin who was just hanging up.

"They approved your Thursday afternoon. You get your Sundays as well. They are expecting you tomorrow at nine a.m. sharp."

I nodded. It was earlier than I expected, but the sooner I started, the better it would be.

"Patty will print you the address and the job description. Try not to run away."

Bitch. "I'll do my best."

Mrs. Lebowitz lost all joviality as she printed the documents and took my details, including a copy of my driver's license and social security number to prepare all the paperwork.

"I'll be okay," I told her once we were done. "It's not forever."

She gave me a small smile. "It's just—you're just a sweet girl, Cassie, and I heard this man is a beast."

I shrugged. "Who's better than the daughter of monsters to deal with a beast?" I took the folder and quickly skimmed the never-ending list of obligations before looking at the address. "Ridgepoint?" I couldn't help but ask.

I didn't even know there were houses that high up. It was in the mountains, far from everything. It was a little problem as it would take me a good thirty minutes just to go back into town to see Jude. "That's far..." I admitted, suddenly not so sure anymore.

"You've got access to a car," Karin quickly explained, seeing my resolve waver. "You can take it whenever you need it."

I took a deep breath. "Okay, no problem. I'll have my friend drive me in the morning." I looked at Karin. "Thank you for your help," I added quite reluctantly, knowing that her actions had been driven by a hefty commission and nothing more.

"I'll keep on looking for you," Ms. Lebowitz continued stubbornly. "As soon as I find something suitable, I'll give you a call."

I could have told her not to bother, that as soon as I could get my brother back, I would leave this town forever and never look back, but she was a lovely woman and I didn't want to worry her more than she already was. "Perfect, yes, let's do that. I'll see you soon."

"Call me if you need anything!" she shouted just as the door closed behind me. I waved her goodbye and walked a lot lighter now to the bus stop, the folder secured against my chest.

I had a job, with an astronomical salary and no living expenses. It was almost too good to be true! And what if the man was a beast? Ms. Lebowitz had been mistaken; the innocent girl I had been before my parents' arrest was dead and gone. I was not soft anymore. I'd taken so much hate in the past months… It was enough to make me as desensitized and strong as I needed to be.

I scoffed internally. *Bring it on, beast; this girl can take it!*

3

CASSIE

"I'm not sure I like this, Cassie." Mrs. Broussard leaned forward on her seat and tsked, looking at the austere black metal gate and oversized, moss-covered gray wall.

The estate was so big, we could barely make the dark gothic Victorian manor at the end of the gravel driveway.

It looked just as austere and uninviting as the gate and the man who lived in it.

"It's okay, it's only an old man." I hadn't told her the whole story, that I didn't know who my boss was, or that seven women had run—kicking and screaming—from the house.

"You can stay with me longer, you know. There's no rush," she insisted.

I couldn't though. Of course, I couldn't. I couldn't continue being a weight on her and having people treat her poorly just because she was showing me kindness. I also had to move on and do what I could for Jude now before he lost the little innocence he had left.

"I'm good. It is a chance for me." I hoped my smile looked genuine as I reached for the door handle. "I better ring that bell before it's too late."

As soon as I rang the bell, the camera attached to the wall turned to me.

"Yes?"

"I'm Cassie West. I'm here f—"

"Please take your belongings and make your way to the entrance; you will be escorted inside." The voice was young, sharp, commanding. Not the type of voice I expected for some reason.

I turned toward the car and Mrs. Broussard who was still looking at me curiously. "My friend gave me a lift…" I started.

"Your friend is not allowed on the grounds, only you are. Take your belongings and proceed to the side door." The command in his voice didn't leave any room for argument.

"Of course." I turned to the car with a smile on my face.

I opened the passenger door and leaned in. "I'm going to take my suitcases now and walk there, okay?"

She frowned. "It's far, Cassie, and your suitcases are not small."

I sighed. I had to be honest with her. "They're quite high on security; they don't want to let you in."

Her frown deepened. "Why not?"

I shook my head. "It doesn't matter. I need this job and if they are tight on security, who can blame them?"

She sighed in surrender. "Promise me to come back if anything happens. I don't care that you foolishly think you're a weight for me. You're not."

"I promise. I'll call you."

I grabbed my two suitcases from the trunk and rolled them to the small side door which opened as soon as I stopped in front of it.

I turned around and waved to Mrs. Broussard before rolling my suitcases on the white pebbles. I was grateful I was wearing flats because the long way and the pebbles getting stuck in the wheels of my suitcases made it so much harder for me to pull them.

By the time I reached the gray stone stairs and black doors, I was a breathless, sweaty mess.

I rang the bell and the door opened immediately by an older man with gray hair with a black suit.

Was he waiting for me behind the door?

"Miss West." He moved from his spot at the door, inviting me in with a gesture of his hand. "Leave your suitcases in the hall; they will be taken to your room."

This man sounded quite older than the man who had answered at the gate.

"I will give you a tour and reiterate a few rules which you should already have been made aware of. Remember them."

"Okay, but I could always ask you again, no?" That man was as stuck up as they came but having a safety net, no matter how thin it was, was better than nothing.

"No, I'm not working here. I was just placed here as it seemed...difficult to find a new live-in house-keeper. I shall depart as soon as we are done."

He seemed pleased with that and I could not blame him if the inside of the house, which was just depressing, reflected the people living in it. If I was not desperate, I would be leaving too. It looked too much like a horror movie to my liking, but desperation was a funny thing; it made you disregard a lot of things.

Jude needs you to get this $6k salary a month!

I sighed. "Okay, I'm ready to drink in your words."

He threw me a side glance but kept on walking. "You are free to go in any room on the ground floor and the first floor. Rooms that you are not to access are locked. However—" He stopped walking and turned toward me. "You are *never* to go to the second floor, under *any* circumstances." If I thought he looked stern before, it was nothing compared to how he looked now.

"Why? What is on the second floor?" I asked, throwing a curious look toward the dark wooden staircase covered with red carpet.

"Nothing of interest to you." The dark warning in his voice made me shiver. "Let's continue." He gestured me forward.

We entered a kitchen, which despite being spacious, was smaller than I had anticipated for such a big house. It had a homey feel that was not reflected in the halls and a couple of rooms he had pointed out to me.

The kitchen was square with an island in the middle and a rectangular wooden kitchen table with six chairs.

It was a lovely kitchen—don't get me wrong—with a gigantic American fridge, two ovens, a six-fire cooker, and more wooden cabinets that I couldn't count right now, but I liked the feel of this kitchen. It was warm, with white and yellow splash-proof tiles with a sunflower pattern surrounding the whole left side. Huge windows looking out on a gigantic garden brought so much light to the room.

"It's a lovely kitchen," I commented, knowing that I would enjoy spending time in this room.

The older man nodded. "Indeed." He pointed to the left at the door by the fridge. "You have the pantry, utility room, and door to the garden this way. Please look at what you need; food deliveries come on the same day as the cleaning crew—Tuesdays and Fridays."

"So, we don't have much contact with the outside." It was genuinely weird to witness how reclusive this old man could be. "Is there any other live-in staff?"

"The security detail, yes. Not something I'm at liberty to discuss with you."

I frowned. Security detail? "I've not seen anyone."

He straightened up. "And that's the way it should be. Another critical rule to respect: do not engage with the master unless he engages with you. Do not make your presence a nuisance, and do not interact with him or any of his security detail."

"And who is the *master*?" Saying this word was hard; it sounded as if I'd just stepped in some kind of Victorian show. "Does he need any particular attention? Medical or otherwise?"

The butler or whatever... Let's call him 'Stuck-up Jim' eyed me critically. "This is again not something pertaining to your role. You are here to ensure the good functioning of the house. That the cleaning crew are doing their job, that the house is stocked in food, that should anyone come to the property, you deal with them and any request made to you through the HCS."

Was I dumb or was he doing it on purpose? "HCS?"

He sighed. "Have you *read* the package given to you?"

I nodded. "Yes, but it was only yesterday and it—" It was my turn to sigh. *Cut me some slack, man.*

"Home communication system." He pointed to the screen on the wall by the entrance. "Any requested tasks that are not prescribed in your typical day-to-day schedule will be available here. There is another one on the first floor. It works both ways. Should you need anything or if there is an emergency, you can contact the master who will reply if appropriate. Please only use the system if absolutely necessary. Do not make a nuisance of yourself; do not speak to the master or security detail unless directly spoken to," he repeated.

Like in 1683? I nodded. Could it get weirder? "Is the *master*"—*yep, still weird to say*. "Aware of my need for Thursday afternoons off?"

"Yes, this has been approved." He gestured me out of the kitchen. "Please, let's continue the tour. I will need to leave soon, it is a long drive back to the city."

I followed him silently to a room that seemed to be part library, part dining room. "You are free to read any book you wish to read," he said, probably noticing my eyes locked on the floor-to-ceiling shelves full of books. "But only when the door is unlocked and outside of dining times." He glanced at his watch. "You will cook meals and serve dinner at eight p.m. sharp. Not seven thirty, not eight thirty.

Once dinner is served"—he pointed to the red switch to his left— "you turn on this switch before exiting the room. It will inform the master that dinner is served and will turn on a light outside the door. You won't be allowed back into the room until the light is off again."

I nodded, wondering why the secrecy was so crucial.

"You will need to cook for four. The other portions are to be kept in the kitchen for the security detail, should they wish to partake." He took another look at his watch. "Lunch has to be served at one p.m. sharp."

"Let me guess, not twelve thirty, not one thirty." I was not sure why I was trying humor on a man who was most likely dead inside.

Maybe that's why he can stand this house. I thought, taking in the room once again. Everything was dark there—dark wood, dark furniture. Everything was expensive and old but so...lifeless.

Stuck-up Jim ignored my comment, already exiting the room. "Come to the first floor, please."

We walked up the massive staircase, and I couldn't help but look up when we reached the first floor, curiosity sinking its talons in my brain.

The staircase up to the second floor looked completely identical to the one I just took. I wasn't sure what I expected after such an ominous interdiction. Dragons? Rabid dogs maybe?

Jim cleared his throat, bringing my attention back to him.

He was standing in front of a door where my suitcases were resting, looking at the staircase. "I advise you against it; this is what cost some of your predecessors their jobs."

"I was not going to."

"Uh-huh." He gestured to the door. "This is your room. I must leave now. You are not expected to work until dinnertime. Please ensure you follow the rules, be aware of the HCS, and there shouldn't be any issue." He bowed his head. "Good day."

He turned around and left me there, in front of the closed door. He seemed to be eager to leave, again not something I could blame him for.

When I opened the door to my bedroom, I was surprised by what I found. It was like stepping into another house.

I expected dark furniture, dark walls…basically a nun's cell.

But this room was bright. Two big windows looked out to the gardens. The walls and furniture were cream, and there were peach curtains and a bedspread as well as a comfy-looking peach armchair on the side of the room, facing a fireplace.

The room was not overly big but fresh, clean, and joined to a small walk-in closet and a matching bathroom made of white marble and peach tiles.

I let my hand trail over the clawfoot bathtub in

the middle of the room and then to the giant walk-in shower big enough for two.

I pulled my suitcases into the room before sitting on the soft mattress, looking out the window.

I decided that it wouldn't be so bad if I kept to the rules and that in a few short months, I'd be able to get Jude back.

But the question I couldn't let go of was, who the hell was the master of this house?

4

LUCA

I ignored the rasping on my door, looking out the window at the run-down gazebo in the garden. It was strange how things could run down fast for lack of care.

I let out a humorless laugh, stroking the scars on my left cheek with my forefinger. It was not only true for objects; I was run-down too.

The door opened and I sighed. Only Dom would dare come in uninvited.

"Please make yourself at home," I said with heavy sarcasm, not bothering to turn around.

"Did you send her a message to thank her?"

"Did you ask for my opinion when you gave her the best guest room?"

Dom sighed and I heard the sound of leather as he

took a seat across my desk. He was here to stay. *Fuck it*. I took a sip of my Macallan Millennium 50-Year-Old Single Malt Scotch Whisky. I had not been a big drinker before but things changed. At least now I was a drunk with taste.

"This house has fourteen bedrooms, Luca. Only you and I are living here. How many guests did we get in twenty-seven months? Oh, that's right. Zero. So, excuse me for trying to make it better for her. We don't want this one to run."

"Why not? Having you around is already too much, and now you want me to chitchat with the girl?"

"She seems nice."

Yes, she did, young and fresh but also haunted. I knew who she was, the Riverside monsters' daughter, and maybe that would make her desperate enough to stick around for a while. My uncle was fed up with having to hire people.

I sighed and finally turned around in my chair, finding my former best friend and current head of security detailing me critically but also with a concern he didn't manage to hide no matter how much he wanted to, and it aggravated me. I didn't deserve or want his concern.

"I'm busy."

"You're busy doing what?" He looked pointedly at my empty desk. "Wallowing in self-hatred and self-pity?"

"Don't forget self-destruction," I added, taking a large sip of my drink. "It's a full-time job."

He leaned forward. "It's ten a.m., Luca." He reached for my glass. "It's not a bit early to destroy your liver?"

I growled, moving my hand away from him. "It's my body, my life. I'll do what the fuck I want. You're my head of security, not my brother nor my friend. Remember. Your. Place," I snapped.

The hurt that flashed in his dark eyes added to the agonizing weight of guilt I already carried around every day.

"We used to be," he replied almost wistfully.

"Things change, people change." Lord knew I had. I was not even remotely the man I'd been and I liked it that way. I went from the terrifying, gorgeous, and adulated Gianluca Montanari, underboss of the East Coast's most powerful Mafia family—maybe even the country—to the clinical alcoholic beastly wreck of a man—human garbage wishing that each of his breaths would be the last.

He sighed, standing up. "I think I'll go thank her if you don't."

I cocked an eyebrow at him. "And I should care because?" I scoffed with a mocking smile. "Is Domenico crushing on Snow White?" I sighed, shaking my head in fake contrition. "If she is as inno-cent as she seems, I highly doubt she's for you. Your kinks are...hard to swallow." I added, smiling into my drink and finishing it in one gulp.

His previous concern and pain turned into anger. *"Mangia merda e muori!"* he barked.

Eat shit and die...how original. I reached for the bottle on the floor and filled my glass. "I'm working on it. Bye now."

He swirled around and exited the room, slamming the door behind him for good measure, in case I didn't know how angry I was making him.

It was always the case these days. Actually it had been like that for the past few years. Fighting with Dom was much easier than acknowledging the extent of my fuck-ups.

I shook my head and looked at the closed laptop on my desk...my window to the world and to Cassandra West. She'd been here three days now and she'd been the only one following the rules, and I had to admit her cooking is delicious.

I rolled my eyes. *Fuck you, Dom!*

I opened the laptop and logged in to the HCS.

'Thank you for the meals; they've been delicious. Especially the strawberry tart.' I let my finger hover on top of the send button. Should I do that? She was paid for it and handsomely, I might add. Why would I need to thank her for something that was literally her job? I moved my finger to the delete button, but somehow, I couldn't press it.

I rolled my eyes and pressed 'send' before thinking better of it. *Why did I even listen to Dom?*

The reply came almost immediately like she'd been waiting in front of the screen. Maybe she was bored.

'Thank you. I wasn't sure what you'd like. So glad you enjoyed it. I'm getting the grocery list ready; is there anything else you would like to eat?'

I shook my head. The old Luca would have answered *'your pussy'* in a heartbeat and saw where that led us…which I was positive would have been her, naked and wet, on the kitchen table and me eating her like she was my last meal.

My dick stirred and I looked down, surprised. It had been a while since my dick stirred from its long-term coma. It was usually on life support—just like me, not feeling anything except my constant self-hatred. That was what happened when you were a bona fide walking dead.

'Anything, I don't care.'

'Oh, okay. You've got a lovely house and the gardens are amazing. I've been exploring.'

I knew that; of course, I did—there wasn't anything happening on this estate that I wasn't aware of.

I sighed and stood up, staggering on my feet a little. I was not going to chat with her. I barely handled chats with Dom—it was not to chat with Astraea, goddess of innocence.

I scratched at my beard as I turned toward the window, and for the first time I noticed my reflection. I'd taken down all the mirrors I had access to—I didn't need the reminder of who I'd become. How long had it been since I'd seen myself now? Six months? A year? I wasn't sure, but not long enough.

The beard and long hair didn't hide who I was, what I'd done. I wore my shame, my sins on my skin, and there was no forgetting, no moving on from that —not that I wanted to.

Arabella. My heart squeezed as a wave of nausea hit me. Was it the alcohol or the guilt? I was not sure —probably a bit of both.

My phone beeped on the desk. I'd forgotten to turn it off after ordering a case of whisky.

'I'm sending Savio.' I guessed ignoring my uncle for six weeks had been pushing it.

Fuck. Me.

Savio, my asshole cousin, the newly self-proclaimed underboss of the family. My uncle's perfect brawn. He'd always been envious, jealous, and angry—just like the rest of us—but he was too stupid to go for what he wanted.

After my accident that had incapacitated me in more ways than one and my father's murder a few months later, my uncle Benny stepped up as head of the *famiglia* and I could not have cared less who took over. The whole famiglia could have disappeared for all I cared. Savio was now the underboss and a pain in my fucking ass.

I would not deal with all his fake solicitude and shitty Hallmark shit. *'Time heals all wounds, Gianluca'*, *'They are immortal in your memories'*... Fucking blow my brains out and spare me more TED talk.

I picked up the phone and called my uncle.

"I knew that text would get your attention," he announced gravely.

"What do you want? I don't like being threatened."

"You take a visit from your cousin as a threat?" He let out a low chuckle. "That's not very nice."

"I'm not nice. What do you want? I've things to do." *Drink myself to sleep.*

"is that a way to talk to your uncle?" he asked, coldness tainting his tone.

I knew that he wanted to say, 'Is that a way to talk to your boss?' But he couldn't because no matter what happened, I was still the legitimate heir. I could walk over there and throw him off the throne if I wanted to—only I didn't care, not even a little. He could keep it.

I simply sighed. I was not going to entertain him or his ego. I was just going to wait until he said his piece.

"I just wanted to remind you not to scare that one away. We've scraped the bottom of the barrel with that one. She's barely grown-up. If this one runs, I'm not sending Stewart anymore. You'll have to fend for yourself," he warned me.

Did he really think I cared? "Understood."

I suddenly heard some music in the background for a couple of seconds and I knew he was not in the usual Montanari offices but in the strip club's office. I rolled my eyes; that was Uncle Benny to a T.

"Anything else?"

"The famiglia's meeting next week—it would be good if you joined."

I had to laugh at that. It was not joyous but dark and cold and broken—just like me. "God, I can't think of anything worse! Let's not and pretend I did." I shook my head. Half the family hated me; the other half pitied me.

"At least think about it, *figlio*."

I wanted to tell him that I was not his son, I was an orphan—mostly by my own hand.

I sighed again. It seemed to be my only way of communication these days. "I won't. And please only call when it's important. Bye."

I hung up before he attempted any further useless chatter.

I exited my office, walking barefoot back to my room. I was not even sure why I bothered leaving my room during the day. I took a few steps out and stopped. Frowning, I walked softly to the side of the stairs and listened.

She was humming. I didn't recognize the tune but

it felt like a lullaby—sweet, soft, comforting, just like this little woman with a sweet voice probably was.

I knew she'd taken the job out of desperation. I was sure that after the seventh nosy bitch left the place, I was done for, and it took weeks to find a replacement and then she came along.

She didn't belong here, in the middle of the ghosts, the pain, and the guilt, but here she was, reviving a spark of life I wasn't sure I deserved.

Don't be absurd. If she saw you, she'd run away. Like number three did...or was it four? I shook my head. Dom had been certain it had been my beastly attitude that made her run and not my beastly looks. I was not certain and I didn't care; this house was not for the faint of heart.

Tell me, Cassandra West, are you here to stay?

5

CASSIE

One thing was certain, by expecting the worst about that job, I was actually pleasantly surprised.

It was true that I felt immensely lonely in this big house but at least it was not the hellhole Ms. Lebowitz was convinced it was and I'd called her to tell her that. I'd also called Mrs. Broussard too to reassure her and have some human contact.

It really felt like this house was working on a different plane. I'd seen the security details from far away in the garden as they were touring the grounds. I'd also seen one of them around the house a couple of times, but it was just glimpses. All I knew was that he was tall and muscular, with dark hair and a goatee.

I'd even been happy when I saw the car of the cleaning crew pull in on Tuesday, thinking we could bond and chat, both being house staff, but that had also been a mistake.

The four women had just come in and went straight to work. If it wasn't for the quick hellos, I would have thought I was invisible. They were efficient, moving around with military precision, having done the whole house, including my bedroom, in under four hours.

But today I was happy. I was going to see Jude, and I wouldn't have to face people as I was allowed to take the staff car, a cute little Chevrolet Spark.

I missed my brother so dearly, and despite the little calls that Amy helped us sneak here and there, I lived for these Thursday afternoons.

I was ready to go, shouldering my handbag, but stopped by the HCS. That had been the only rule I broke. I was messaging him, the mysterious owner of this gloomy house. He had not replied since that first time and yet I kept messaging him. I wasn't sure why. The more I did it, the less I believed he would answer, and yet I hoped. I was just so lonely that any kind of connection—even through a screen—would be welcome.

He had not yet told me to stop bothering him so part of me thought he liked getting my random messages and that made me smile, especially since I'd bothered him for a couple of hours yesterday telling him how I would love to redo his garden and that gardening had always been a passion of mine.

'*I'm going to see my brother. Do you need me to bring you anything?*'

The two ticks appeared, received, and read. I waited a minute.

'*I'm going to the candy store and buy my weight in sweets and I will shamelessly eat them in my bedroom. Do you want some?*' The double tick appeared with still no reply. '*Okay, that's fine. I'll pick for you. I'll be back around six. I'll bring some takeout too, so you don't have to cook for yourself.*'

All the thoughts of the isolated manor and the hermit owner vanished when I parked at the Home where Jude was staying.

"You look well," Amy announced as she came to get me from reception.

I nodded. "I've got a job now. It pays very well. I should be able to get Jude soon."

"Yes, I'll help you. Your brother's always speaking so highly of you. Every time he talks about you, it's clear to me and the other social workers that you've always been a mother to him." She smiled. "I don't think getting him back will be a problem once you can prove financial autonomy."

She directed me to the visitor room and gestured me to one of the plastic chairs.

I looked around the room, with its white walls, posters that belong more in an eighties' waiting room than here, the neon orange plastic chairs I was sure were created to make you so uncomfortable so you wouldn't extend your welcome.

"Do you think I'll be able to take him out soon?"

She gave me a small smile. "I applied for it, but you know. As long as you're not entirely cleared by the authorities—"

"But—" I shook my head, taking a deep breath. I couldn't take my frustration out on Amy; she'd been on our side from the start. She'd told me that her main goal was to keep our family united and keep Jude in the system for as little as possible. "They told me I was cleared; they even apologized." Which I knew was uncommon.

She nodded. "Yes, they did. It's obvious you didn't do anything, but bureaucracy…" She rolled her eyes. "Once the report hits my boss' desk, I promise I'll get it to the family judge as a priority to get you more rights." She smiled at me. "I've got to admit supervising your visit though is the highlight of my days. So much love."

My heart squeezed painfully in my chest. Jude was the person I loved the most in the world.

"We'll be right back," she said before disappearing behind the door.

I walked closer to the door, somehow not wanting to lose another second with Jude by sitting down at the end of the table.

As soon as he walked in, his face filled with the

same glee I sure was reflecting on my face at seeing him.

He ran to me and hugged me tightly.

"How are you, buddy?" I asked him, running my hand in his silky hair.

He looked up, keeping his arms around me and I studied his face. The bruise from last week was gone and there weren't any new marks on him.

"I'm okay; it's not so bad here. School's good. We're doing a volcano in science."

"Are you?" I asked, trying to put as much excitement in my statement as I could. I should have been the one helping him with his science experiments. *No, it should have been your parents' job, you know, the sociopathic killers.*

He nodded, finally letting go of me, and I leaned down to kiss the top of his head.

"How is work?" he asked as we sat side by side. It was not a question that a ten-year-old should care about, but he knew what a good job meant for us.

"It's good, really good." *At least not as bad as I thought.* "Oh, I brought you something you're going to love!" I reached for my bag and retrieved the three books I borrowed from the house library. I would be able to buy him lots of books once I got my salary. Fifteen hundred dollars a week! I could still hardly believe it. "I borrowed them from work; I'll bring you others next week."

"Cool!" He took them eagerly and quickly went through them.

My eyes filled up with tears. Jude was always content with so little. He was the best kid there was.

I looked up and blinked back my tears. I only had a couple of hours with him; I couldn't waste them crying.

"Did you know that the infinity sign is called a lemniscate?" he asked, resting his hand on top of the books.

"No, I didn't but now I do. Thank you."

Jude beamed. My brother loved words, and everything that has to do with words. The doctors had said he was on the autistic spectrum, very low on it, but using words and word games were his coping mechanism. My parents had been angry at him when they'd found out my brother was 'broken.' It was rich coming from sociopathic killers.

I took a deep breath, trying to chase the thoughts of my parents away. I didn't want to let them spoil one more minute of my life.

"So, what do you want to play with today?" I asked him, looking at the small brown shelves against the wall containing well-used board games.

"Scrabble?"

I smiled and nodded. Which ten-year-old would choose Scrabble? My little brother, lover of words.

We played for over an hour as I listened to him talk about his new friends and the school. It was somehow good to know he was not as miserable as I feared he was.

Amy just sat in the background silently, playing on her phone.

And once again my time with Jude finished much sooner than I'd hoped. Time always flew by when I was with him.

It was always so hard to let him go, putting my brave face on. I missed him so much.

"I love you, Cassie. Thanks for the books," he said, hugging me.

I kissed the top of his head. "I love you too, Jude bug. Be good, okay?"

He gave me a wide smile, showing me the adorable gap between his front teeth before disappearing into the living quarters.

I sat back down, letting go of my bravado for a minute.

"I promise, he is fine," Amy said reassuringly, coming to stand beside me, squeezing my shoulder. "I'm not saying he doesn't miss you, because that would be a lie, but he is okay."

I nodded. "He's used to being content with little. Our parents never loved us, never doted on us." I sighed. "Jude shouldn't be used to that."

"You're making up for it, tenfold."

"I hope so."

"So, your job…"

I turned a questioning look at her. It sounded tentative, uncomfortable...so unlike her.

"Yes?"

"Ms. Lebowitz told me you're working as a live-in housekeeper for Hartfield Manor."

I frowned. "I declared that to social services... I've been told to get a job; is this job not suitable?"

"No, no, it is!" she rushed out, raising her hands in surrender. "I'm not asking that as a social worker but more as a concerned friend."

Friends? I thought that was a bit of a stretch, but she did so much for us that I could not say anything.

"Okay..." I trailed off, standing up and crossing my arms on my chest.

"It's just there are a lot of rumors about the place. I'm not sure how much of it is true but..." She shrugged. "I'm worried about you."

I rolled my eyes. It felt like I was discussing ghouls and ghosts with Mrs. Broussard all over again. "What have you heard?" To be fair I wanted to know because I still wanted to figure out who my recluse employer was.

"Mafia," she said, her cheeks reddening at the absurdity of her words.

"Mafia?" I repeated. Okay, that was not something I expected.

She winced. "That's what has always been said and you know the Reststop?"

I nodded. The Reststop was a small panoramic

cafe that was on the side of the road when you went to the top of Ridgepoint. It was lovely there. The Reststop was made of glass, giving you a breathtaking view of the mountain and the lake below.

"The owner says he used to see expensive black cars with tinted windows going up there, and a couple of times, men stopped at the café—dressed in designer suits and wearing sunglasses." She shook her head. "You can't tell me that's not weird."

"No," I admitted. "But the key words here are 'used to.'" I sighed. "I've only been there a week but there's nothing to say; the place is boring as hell." This also made no sense since I woke up on the first day with an NDA on the kitchen table I needed to sign and leave beside his lunch on that day.

"Yeah." She waved her hand dismissively. "It's probably just stupid stories."

"Yes." *Probably.* I looked at my watch. "I've got to go back; I need to do some shopping and I have quite a drive."

She walked me to the door silently. "I'll call you with Jude this week."

"Thank you, Amy, really."

As I stopped at the pizzeria to pick up dinner and at the Sweet Shop using the petty cash there was for me at the house, I couldn't stop thinking about what Amy told me.

Maybe it was true; maybe my boss was an old Mafia guy. It would explain the security at the house.

I just hoped that if it were true, it would not stop me from getting Jude back.

I went back to the empty, quiet house and put the pizzas in the oven to heat up while I ate quite an unhealthy number of sweets.

I was not sure what type of pizza he would like so I set a platter with a few different ones, even giving him two slices of my favorite—ham pineapple. I hoped he wouldn't be mad about the dinner; technically I was not to provide him any food on Thursdays or Sundays.

I left the food in the room but realized only after I pressed the button to call him for dinner that I'd left the book I was reading on the side table.

I sighed, rushing into the kitchen to have my own dinner. I looked around the kitchen, considering yet again what Amy had told me about this house.

It was true that despite this luminous sunflower-decorated kitchen and my bedroom, every room I'd been in was all darkness and gloom, the gardens painfully bare, and the gazebo in the middle chipping and rotting away. But all of this said neglected old family house, not Mafia.

I rolled my eyes. Here I was, Cassie, the Mafia expert. what was a Mafia house anyway? I'd seen *The Godfather* one too many times.

I finished my second slice of pizza and realized that the kilo of sweets I ate before had been a mistake.

Ah, more for the security, I suppose.

I went back to the sitting room and was surprised to see the light already out. He'd never eaten so fast before.

I walked in and stopped as soon as I closed the door behind me. The atmosphere in the room was heavy; my stomach filled with lead… I was not alone.

"I don't accept thieves in my house."

I gasped, turning toward the deep gravelly voice. I could barely make him out from the shadows between the fireplace and the bookshelves, but he was tall and wide, wearing a black hoodie, with the hood up, making him part of the shadows.

I took an instinctive step forward.

"Stay where you are!" he ordered coldly, making my heart thunder in my chest with fear and apprehension. I couldn't afford to run away and yet, the need to run was almost overwhelming.

I took a small step back.

"Give back what you stole."

I shook my head. "I-I didn't steal anything."

"The books," he continued, his tone even and yet so cold it cut me like a knife.

"What books?" I was so anxious now I could barely think. I felt cold sweat forming at the back of my neck and running down my spine. It was a level of anxiety I had not felt since that day with the FBI.

"Today, you left with three books. Where are they?"

"I was told I could use this library as I saw fit." I turned toward the table and the copy of *The Kite Runner* was gone.

"Use doesn't mean steal, sell, or... I'm going to have to let you go."

Despite the fear I felt now facing this terrifying shadow, it was nothing compared to the despair I felt at the idea of losing this job. It was not an option; it was my only rapid solution to get Jude back.

"No, please, sir. I need this job." I hated how my voice cracked as my eyes filled with tears. "I didn't steal those books; I borrowed them. You see, my little brother is with social services and he loves to read. He's obsessed with words and these books were in old English. I'm getting them back next Thursday, and I won't bring any to him anymore." I let out a sob and Lord, was it embarrassing. "I'm not a thief."

"It runs in your blood."

Ah, he knew who I was, and he was a giant asshole.

His mean comment somehow switched my fear to anger. That was a petty low blow.

"Am I fired then?" I asked, crossing my arms on my chest.

He remained silent for a while, just being a ghostly shadow in the corner.

"Stop breaking the rules."

"Even messaging you?" I tried.

"Especially messaging me. I thought my lack of

reply would show my lack of interest." He turned around to leave.

"Wait, can I have the book back?"

He stopped, keeping his back to me. "No, this book is mine."

It was a well-read copy of *The Kite Runner*; it was a mainstream book. Nothing special about it.

"But I was—"

"I said no," he replied before exiting the room.

Prick!

But now I knew that the owner was neither old nor frail. I couldn't see much of him, but he looked tall and wide even in the darkness and his deep, gravelly voice was the same I heard on the first day and that was a really attractive voice.

I rolled my eyes. I really didn't have the time to find anyone attractive, especially not the hermit, an obviously damaged man who signed my checks.

6

LUCA

I had not meant to interact with her. I just wanted to watch her without a screen, see her with my own eyes, and her eyes wide with surprise, her button nose covered with freckles that I missed on the screen but making her look so much younger than I thought.

I regretted telling her off for breaking the rules because as much as I hated to admit it, these past two days were dull without her random messages. It had been aggravating and yet, I let my fingers brush against the keyboard.

I wasn't sure why I told her to stop. I hadn't meant it, but she'd put me on the spot and—

"Apologize."

My head jerked up to find Dom leaning against

the doorframe of my office. No matter how unfair and cruel I was to him, he was always coming back. I was not sure I warranted such loyalty.

"What?"

He walked in, taking in my fingers resting on the keyboard. There wasn't much that Dom missed; it made him both a fantastic ally and a ruthless enemy.

"The girl." He jerked his head toward the garden, where I presumed she was. "Apologize to her."

"Why would I do that?" I scoffed.

He gave me a half-smile, stealing a sweet from the candy jar she'd brought me back. "Because you were an epic ass to her."

"I can be so much worse!"

Dom cocked his eyebrow, letting out a short laugh. "Is that really your argument?"

I shrugged silently.

"I know you can be worse; hell, I've felt the brunt of it, but she doesn't know that. And you called her bad seed, a liar, and a thief in the same breath. That's a lot to take in."

"You listened to the conversation?" I asked slowly, hardly believing he would do that. Dom knew how much I valued my privacy—just as much as he valued his.

He snorted. "You bet your ass I did! This house is mortally boring! That was the entertainment of the year so far!"

"You're welcome to leave if you want to. Nobody's asked you to be here."

He shook his head, taking another sweet from my jar. "No, but I'm where I'm needed, where I belong, by your side, brother, whether you see it or not," he added, taking another sweet.

I ground my teeth. "Next time you take one without asking, I'll cut your hand off."

"Apologize, Luca."

I sighed. "Fine."

"Fine?"

I nodded. "Uh-huh."

"But—you never give in!"

I leaned back on my seat. "I'll do it if—"

Dom growled, "I should have known."

"If you go to the famiglia meeting next week."

He took a step back. "The famiglia? Why? I thought you didn't want to get involved anymore."

I shook my head. "I don't but Benny called to invite me. I think it was his way to ensure I was not coming. And for that, I need you to go."

Dom ran his hand in his black hair and looked away. "I'm only a soldier, Luca. I don't belong in a meeting with the famiglia."

"You belong where I say you belong." I might have been a wreck, but I was Gianluca Montanari—Mafia Prince, and what I said was law no matter what Benny or the others wanted. Only Matteo Genovese could and he probably wouldn't care enough to.

Dom sighed. "Fine, I'll go." He jerked his head toward the computer. "Now apologize."

I sighed and turned toward my computer. "I was going to do that anyway."

Dom chuckled. "Yeah? I would have gone to the meeting without your apologies." He turned around and left the room.

Asshole.

I looked at the screen again. *Next time you put pineapple on a pizza you will be fired. This is a crime against nature.* I pressed send before I could think better of it.

The tag that she'd seen my message appeared on the screen, but she didn't reply right away. I reread my message and winced—I needed to work on my apologies.

Why should you? You want to be left alone to die, don't you? My father's voice resonated. It has been quite close to the words he'd said to me when I woke up from my five-week coma.

'*I wished you would have died along with them, so I'd never have to see your murderer face again,*' he spat as soon as I had regained consciousness.

I had not been sure why then; my memory had been clouded but once I had remembered...I shuddered. I had agreed with him wholeheartedly.

A ping brought me back to reality; she'd responded, bringing a little echo of elation I was not sure had any place left in my life.

Pineapple is just misunderstood. Have you tried it?

A little smile formed at the corner of my lips. How was it possible that she could make me smile? It has been so long since it happened to me.

I don't need to try it to know it doesn't belong.

Agree to disagree.

I scoffed. She had fire that one, I liked it.

I'll bring some books down for your brother later.

Why?

"Good question," I whispered to the screen.

Thank you. She added a few seconds later.

I looked out the window, at the decrepit gazebo before turning toward the computer again.

Would you like to take care of the garden?

For real? I'd love to!

I shook my head; it took so little with her. I couldn't imagine what it would have taken with Francesca to make her that excited. Diamonds...it would have taken diamonds.

I reached for my phone and called the company we had on retainer to ask them to come and do what the housekeeper was telling them to do.

I knew she was enjoying walking around the garden. Dom and the other security guys saw her there often. She was a flower girl, that one, that much was clear. It was also why I suspected she enjoyed the kitchen so much. It was my mother's décor—*my mother*... My heart squeezed at the painful reminder.

I stood up and went to the wet bar. I'd been sober

for long enough. It was time to numb the pain and the memories. After I helped myself to a triple dose of whisky, I looked up at the mirror covered by a white sheet. All the mirrors of the house had been either covered or taken down—well, except the one in the rooms I was not going in.

I'd tried to keep them for a while, an additional reminder of my sins and crimes. Every time I looked at my mangled face, it reminded me of the lives I'd taken.

Three scars marred my face. I traced the main one, going from my left temple to my chin—pulling down the side of my mouth in a perpetual pout. How fitting. The second went right through my left eye, cutting my eyebrows in two, and down to my jaw. These two scars met in the middle of my cheek in an angry red *X*. The doctor said it had been a miracle I had not lost my eye. A miracle, as if I deserved any. The piece of glass had damaged my cornea a bit, but it only reduced my vision in this eye, forcing me to now wear glasses.

The third one went through the front of my left ear down the side of my neck only half an inch from the carotid artery—another miracle they said. Nothing more than a curse to me.

I took a deep breath before taking a big sip of my drink. I sighed at the heat settling in my stomach. In a few more drinks the pain would be gone, and so would my regrets and everything surrounding it. I was eager for the numbness of alcohol, hating every morning when I was just lucid enough to feel it all again.

I topped up my drink and walked to the side room, the main library, picking out some books for the child before I was too drunk to pick something age-appropriate. Or maybe I shouldn't; maybe he should know how fucked up life was. You're born, you live in pain, and if you're lucky enough you die early.

I shook my head; the kid was in social care and had serial killers as parents. He already knew how fucked up life was.

I picked three books and I looked at the abused copy of *The Kite Runner* I'd taken back. I was not sure how this book made it anywhere near her floors. I'd read it so many times and hated that she could see that, that she'd have a view of my mind.

I sighed, putting it on the top of the pile before taking the back staircase and leaving the books in front of her bedroom door.

I took a deep breath; as impossible as it was I could smell her, a mix of peach and lavender—not two scents I would have put together, and yet it worked well together.

It was so different from Francesca's over-whelming expensive perfume and thousand times more attractive.

I shook my head; I really shouldn't go there. First,

because I didn't deserve reprieves and secondly, who would even want to be with a beast?

I went back to my office, grabbed my glass, and sat back behind my desk just in time to see a message appear.

Apology accepted.

What was I going to do with her?

7

LUCA

I was not sure how it exactly happened—well, yes, actually, I knew how it happened. What I didn't understand was how and why I'd allowed it to happen. The daily chats with the fiery woman taking care of my home.

She was quite decent at it actually, better than I'd expected. She applied and got hired out of desperation from both sides and yet she managed to surprise me. She followed the rules...mostly. She cooked well, kept the house tidy.

On Thursday she'd come back with the books she'd given her brother and another pizza without pineapple this time. She'd also brought me a book and some more sweets. It was such a childlike thing to do—who brought sweets to a grown-ass man?

That woman did and against all odds it made me smile, something still so unfamiliar to me, it felt weird when I did use muscles I'd not used for a while.

The book was called *The Recluse* and I couldn't help but laugh at that. She really had a different sense of humor.

Did you enjoy the book?

Nope, it'd hit way too close to home to be enjoyable. *Haven't read it.* Liar. *I'm not much into books.* That was not a complete lie. At least I hadn't been much of a reader before. Too busy killing people, fucking women, and getting everything I wanted, when I wanted. But since I decided to exile myself in the middle of nowhere, reading, drinking, and wallowing in self-hatred had been my only pastimes.

How old are you?

I let out a startled laugh. *That's a random question.*

Not really. You know everything about me and I know nothing about you.

I twisted my mouth to the side. I knew that nothing could ever happen between us, for so many reasons it would have taken me forever to give them all, but at the same time, I was not inclined to let her know how much older than her I was.

Next question.

heavy sigh Fine. Why have you read The Kite Runner *so many times? It is such a depressing book.*

Fuck, she had to go right for the guts.

I growled. *I'm 32.*

I'm going to be 21 next month, she replied as if I'd asked. I knew everything about Cassandra West, even that it seemed to be impossible for her to ask for help, for anything. I presume it was due to being raised by emotionally abusive parents—at least I thought it was only emotionally. My hand tightened into a fist on my desk, almost involuntarily.

That girl had no idea what she had done when she'd started chatting with me through the anonymity of the screens. Hell, *I* didn't even know what I'd started until I felt waves of protectiveness for this woman, barely out of adolescence.

I turned toward the gazebo. The silly woman had it in her head to repair it and she had been working on it a few hours every day, and I was going out in the dead of the night with a torch to fix what she'd attempted to do.

I was not even sure why I was doing it; it would have been better if she'd failed. At least she'd realize then that not everything is worth saving. Every night I was swearing to myself I was done helping her, and every night I was going back like a fool.

The gardener is coming back next week to plant some of the flowers I ordered. Would you like me to show you what I've got and where I thought about planting them?

I shook my head. She wanted to see me; that much was clear, but she couldn't, not now, not ever.

If only for the fact that knowing who I was and why I was here could put her life at risk.

Don't lie to yourself, Luca. You don't want to see the look of horror she'll have when she sees your face. A face that used to make panties wet, now made women recoil and avert their eyes.

I remembered that the first time I saw Francesca after the accident. She'd always been a shallow bitch but still. I retreated into myself and she used it as an excuse to break our engagement and I've been told that Savio and she had been more than friendly—not that I'd cared. Savio could keep the poisonous snake she was.

Do as you please; I'm sure it will be fine.

Are you sure? I won't be here forever. You'll have to live with it.

Ah yes, I've been forgetting these days that she was not a permanent feature. I shouldn't care, she was just a domestic. She'd barely been here two weeks, and yet I was looking forward to her random thoughts and pointless chatter. It was a nice distraction from my discussions with Dom or the tedious call with my uncle I had to suffer through every so often.

She didn't know who I was or what I'd done and that felt nice. Even if I didn't deserve that small reprieve I still took it every chance I got.

It doesn't matter; it'll be fine. I'd let them die once she was gone anyway.

Jude sent me a text this morning. He's loving the books you lent to him.

Good, he seems like one of a kind, your brother.

He's the best. I think everyone says that about their own though. Do you have siblings?

And I was done. Her questions cut way too deep and I was not drunk enough to deal with any thoughts of Arabella. Because she'd been the best little sister, the best human there was, and I'd killed her.

I didn't answer her. I never bothered telling her when I was done. I just stopped responding and she usually figured it out on her own, never holding any grudges though. How peculiar.

I stood up, grabbed the unopened bottle of whisky, and dragged my ass to my bedroom, ready to get drunk for the day.

I walked or rather dragged myself to my office with the mother of all hangovers. I never should have started drinking again after I vomited last night, and yet I did. Thinking about Arabella had twisted my guts. Logically, even in my foggy brain, I knew Cassie didn't know that. She hadn't done it to torture me, and yet I couldn't help being angry at her because of it.

I walked into my office to find Dom sitting at my desk. What the fuck.

"What do you think you're doing?" I barked at Dom and winced at the mariachi band in my brain.

He stood up slowly as if he'd not just earned himself a bullet through his skull. You couldn't just walk in the office of a capo thinking you could do what the hell you wanted. That was a death warrant.

Are you a capo though? More like a human wreck.

"I was waiting for you." He shrugged. "I came to your room and knocked four times. I assumed you were either in an alcohol-induced coma or dead. I figured waiting for you here was just as good." He jerked his thumb toward the computer. "I bought new shoes."

I narrowed my eyes. "You don't seem upset about my potential demise. Sorry to disappoint."

He sighed. "I won't waste my time or sorrow on something you're so hell-bent on doing. You want to die? I'm done trying to stop you."

I couldn't deny that despite everything, his words stung. He was finally giving up on me. "And don't touch my stuff again, understood? Use your fucking laptop to buy your shoes or watch your porn, for fuck's sake."

"The porn was a tip for you, brother. I think you need to debug the hard drive. It will help with your mood."

I walked around my desk and sat on my chair. I grimaced. The seat was still warm—I hated that. I glanced at the screen and sighed with relief. At least he didn't leave it open on that porn website like last time.

"When did you get back?" I asked, even less in the mood for chitchat than I'd been before.

"Early this morning, the party lasted longer than I'd anticipated."

"Oh, there was a party? How nice." I couldn't help but sneer.

He rolled his eyes but sat on the chair across my desk.

"Yeah, I *so* belonged there," he said with heavy sarcasm. "They were all looking at me like I was a bug, and I think your uncle had a stroke when I told him you sent me." He shook his head. "And then there was Savio glowering from the back of the room and sticking his tongue down Francesca's throat every chance he—" He stopped and looked away.

"Ah." Francesca, my old fiancée who had been so quick to let me go after the accident. Something that should have pained me but I'd been relieved to see her walk away and even if it should have annoyed me that my cousin snatched her as soon as she left me, I didn't seem to care, not even a little. "I'm not sure he deserved such a punishment in life."

Dom's lips quirked up in a half-smile. "She is a piece of work." He agreed.

"What else?"

"Enzo kept me company against the far wall. We

were the wallflowers of the evening. It was nice but I think I lost my bonnet on my way back."

I rolled my eyes. Dom's dry sense of humor was the strongest when he was irritated. "How is he?" My concern was genuine for once. Enzo was everything his father and brother were not. He was sensitive and kind—completely ostracized but he didn't seem to care so much. They saw him like an idiot because of his stutter, but I knew the boy was smarter than they gave him credit for.

"You know—always the same. He misses you."

I nodded. "He's a good kid. What was discussed? What warranted a full famiglia meeting?"

"Your uncle wants a vote to reverse some of your father's decisions."

I leaned forward, resting my arms on the desk; that managed to get through the fog of alcohol. "What do you mean?"

"The legit business. Your uncle is not so much into expending that. He wants to grow the other side of it."

I frowned but remained silent in an invitation for him to continue.

"He is preparing to increase the drug and weapon side of things by taking some of the Albanian territories."

"The Albanians? Aren't they protected by the Russians?"

Dom shrugged.

I sighed, running my hands over my face. There was a reason why my father had been named head of the famiglia despite Benny being older... Benny was a hot-headed idiot. "He's going to start a war." Fortunately, I didn't care enough to step in.

Dom shrugged again. "They are putting it through a vote. If the others agree with him, they'll get the war they deserve."

I scratched at my untidy mountain man beard, nodding.

He cleared his throat and I knew I was not going to like what was to come.

"Yes?"

"Matteo Genovese wants to see you." He announced as if it was a threat and to be fair it probably was. Matteo Genovese didn't just want to see you for no reason.

"Genovese can go fuck himself," I grumbled.

Dom snorted. "I'd like to hear you say that. Even the almighty Luca Montanari won't get away with that."

"Umph. What will he do? Kill me?" He could actually; he could do it in front of everyone and he would walk away unscathed.

Matteo Genovese, a king among men...literally. He was originally sent to the US eighteen years ago as a dignitary by the Italian families to monitor us, the US families. He was here to ensure we followed the basic rules of the original families, but he didn't meddle in the family feuds; he didn't care who lived or died. He was above the laws, above *our* laws. He was the Tin Man, a cruel king with eyes as pale blue as the ice around his heart, who killed with a certain triviality that made even the most violent made man uncomfortable.

Nobody angered or disrespected Genovese and got out with all of their teeth…or fingers, but I was past the point of caring. Most days I would welcome death as a blessing, a reprieve, and the torture he might do to me? It wouldn't have been a first and it would only be physical pain, nothing as horrendous as the mental pain I felt constantly.

I sighed. Death? How sweet would it be?

Dom cocked his head to the side. "Why don't you just put a bullet through your brain and be done with it." His words were harsh, but his flaring nostrils, set jaw, and the quiet desperation in his eyes showed he didn't mean it.

I traced my induction tattoo over my black T-shirt almost subconsciously and traced from memory the rosary that was wrapped around the dagger on my chest with the single word on top of it —'Omerta.' The rosary represented God—the irony of it was not amiss to me but somehow despite everything, a little part of me still believed there was a God up there, an avenging God on a mission to punish me every step of the way for sending home, much too early, two of his most extraordinary angels.

And I knew that, if there was even a minuscule chance I'd see them again, suicide would take that away for good.

I shook my head. "I won't call him."

Dom shook his head. "He said he tried to call you a few times. Luca, we both know Matteo doesn't call for a chat."

I was getting irritated now. Dom was acting like a parent; I felt chastised and it rubbed me the wrong way. "As I said," I said the words slowly, evenly. "Matteo Genovese can. Go. Fuck. Himself."

He'd been beyond cruel with me after the accident, something I should have expected based on his 'Cruel King' nickname and yet.

My father had petitioned to disown me—despite being his only heir. He'd rather lose control of the famiglia than allow me to lead, but Matteo refused for a reason that remains a mystery, and then three weeks later my father was killed in an attack at his favorite restaurant—killing him, the East Coast capo and their two consiglieri.

Once my father had been gone, much to my relief I had to admit, I requested for my title, capo of the Montanari famiglia, to be transferred permanently to my uncle. A formality really, nobody wanted me... Fuck, *I* didn't want me, but again fucking Genovese, the thorn in my side, refused, stating I was not in the right state of mind to pass my title permanently and that he would revisit the issue at a later time.

Maybe he was ready to let me go now... No, of course not. He was a fucking sadist.

"Thanks for the message."

Dom nodded, standing up, understanding that I was dismissing him. "You're not going to call him, are you?"

I snorted. "Of course not."

He sighed, looking heavenward. "You won't be able to avoid him forever."

I gave him a mocking grin. "Watch me try."

"The more you make him wait, the angrier he'll get," Dom continued.

"If I wanted life lessons, Domenico, I'll call someone, anyone...but you." I had already been in a foul mood when I'd woken up then all this stupid family drama and Matteo... Dom needed to leave me alone with all his concern and wise words. "You're not my consigliere. You're the son of—"

His face morphed from weariness to pure anger. "Don't fucking say it, Montanari." He pointed an accusing finger at me. "I get it, you're hurt, you hate yourself, but don't make me hate you too, and if you say it—there won't be any turning back."

I should have said it—truly, I should have. *You're the son of a serial rapist.* But I couldn't because despite everything, having him here made it suck less. His unwavering loyalty meant so much more to me than I was ready to admit to him and even to myself.

"Just go, Dom," I said somberly. "I'll deal with Matteo the way I see fit."

Dom nodded. "As you want. We both know how productive it is to avoid your problems. Never would have pegged you as a coward and yet, here we are."

He didn't even give me the time to process his words and he was gone, and my mood went from bad to absolutely horrendous in 0.3 seconds.

Fuck them all.

8

CASSIE

Have dinner with me tonight.

I read the message four times. We'd indeed been talking daily but that was a big step I hadn't expected.

I decided to cook something special and use the notebook I found in a kitchen cabinet. It was all written in Italian, not a language I spoke, but it seemed to be a family recipe book. There were food stains in it, some erasures and smudges for trials and errors. It was a work of love.

"Manzo Braciole, it is," I muttered, mentally thanking Google Translate for helping me.

It took me over three hours to prepare but the divine smell that filled the kitchen was worth the effort.

As the meal simmered, I went upstairs to dress for dinner.

Despite just being a dinner request, probably born of his loneliness, I couldn't help the butterflies in my stomach to finally talk to him in person.

We've been exchanging messages daily for the past ten days and it was lovely. He made me laugh and I enjoyed our talks—the anonymity of the screen somehow making it much easier for me, and I suspected it was the same for him. This was why I'd been so surprised by his invitation. I thought he'd never want to meet me—not in person at least—yet here we were.

I had a hard time reining in these butterflies causing havoc in my stomach as I put on my green polka-dot summer dress. It was still early spring and much too cool to wear this type of clothing, but it was the only decent thing I could wear.

No, it isn't Cassie; it is not a date.

But my racing heart and anticipation seemed to be thinking otherwise.

I grabbed my white cardigan and kept my face free of makeup except for a little pink gloss. I didn't want to go all out in case I was completely wrong.

Which you are, the voice of reason taunted.

I went back downstairs and set the table for two. Not too close to be too cozy but not too far either.

I put a candle on the table and rethought it about

five times, putting it back and removing it every time I was bringing something to the table.

I was just that nervous, overthinking every detail.

It was my first date. I growled at my own train of thoughts. How could this be a date? I didn't even know the man.

I put the food on the table as my heart started beating faster and faster at the thought of sharing a meal with him. I felt like I was going to have a panic attack just at the thought.

I pressed the red button before having a chance to rethink it and took a deep breath.

He invited you, Cassie; he wants you there.

"What are you doing here?" He barked coldly looking from me to the table set for two.

Or maybe he doesn't...

"I...what?" I frowned, taking a step back toward the door.

"You know the rules, Ms. West. There aren't many."

"Y-you asked me to dine with you."

"I did no such thing," he replied, staying in the confines of the darkness. "Is it why you dressed up?"

"I—" I wanted to die at that moment, hoping that the plush burgundy carpet would just open and swallow me whole—taking my embarrassment along with it. "Sir, I'm sorry, the message—" *Just shut up, Cassie, and walk away now.* "Sorry," I repeated, turning around and rushing away.

"Stop!" he commanded just as I reached for the knob.

I froze, keeping my hand on the door.

He sighed. "Since you did all of this—let's eat."

I felt the light dim behind me, and I turned around slowly as if I were facing a rabid animal, and part of me was certain I was.

He was sitting at one end of the table, his hood up, only faintly lit up by the fireplace.

His head was bowed down, stopping me from seeing his face. He looked even more imposing like that, his hands strong and wide—tightened into fists.

I took careful steps and sat at the other end of the table, trying to calm my heart at the rejection.

I opened my mouth to insist that I received a dinner invitation but closed it again. He seemed to be in such a bad mood already.

I took a bite, the meat melting in my mouth, the explosion of favor. This meal was amazing.

I heard his fork clang loudly on his plate.

I looked up and frowned.

"Who sent you?" he growled low, menacing.

I rested my cutlery softly on my plate. "Sorry?"

"I said, who. Sent. You?" he repeated louder, his voice so cold I shivered.

I let my eyes wander down to his hands balled into fists so tight his knuckles were bone-white.

"Sir, I—"

"Who?" he roared, swiping at the table, sending his plate flying and shattering against the wall.

I recoiled so hard I fell off my chair.

He stood up briskly, his chair tipping backward. He sprawled toward me slowly like a predator playing with its prey as I crawled on my hands and knees, keeping my teary eyes on him.

My heart beat so hard I could barely hear him over the deafening sounds in my ears. I didn't think I'd ever been more scared in my life.

"Is it Benny? To spy on me? Or no, let me guess Matteo to play a sick game? He knows me better than I thought. He figured what kind of girl could make me tick even if I didn't know it myself."

I was making him tick? I was not sure what he meant. I was now against the wall, recoiling on myself, letting out a sob.

"Did you think your fucking ploy would work? What were you going to do? Offer to suck on my dick to heal me?" His mocking tone felt like poison. "Do you have a magical mouth, girl? Have they tried it to make sure you suck good?"

"I have no ploy. Please, sir, you've got to believe me." I felt bile rise in my throat as he hovered over me, his face still in the darkness. Was I going to die?

"The dinner invitation, my mother's cooking?" He was speaking through gritted teeth, his body shivering with anger and indignation as mine was shaking with sheer terror.

He leaned closer, pulling back his hood with a jerk.

It was not the scars that made me recoil; it was the look on his face. A mix of anger and desperation I'd never witnessed before.

"Is that what you wanted to see?" he roared, leaning so close I could smell the alcohol on his breath. "The beast?"

"N-no, I...I—"

"Luca, stop!" a male voice commanded from behind him. "I asked her to come down to dinner; it was not a trick."

Luca straightened up and turned around slowly. I brought my knees up and rested my forehead on them, now sobbing even more freely both with fear and relief at the other man's interruption.

"What did you say?" Luca asked, his voice so eerily calm.

"Fuck, Luca! She didn't trick you. I did! I set up the dinner. She—"

I heard a door slam shut and then silence.

"Hey, Cassandra. Look at me." The voice was deep but gentle, soothing.

I looked up tentatively at the man crouching in front of me. His dark eyes were gentle, despite the harshness of his features, sharp cheekbones, predominant Roman nose.

I let my eyes trail down his suit and shrink back

when I noticed his shoulder holster and the black gun in it.

He glanced down and pulled his jacket closed. "Cassandra, I won't hurt you, I swear." He raised his hands in surrender.

I shook my head and sniffed. "I'm leaving." I sobbed before wiping under my eyes with the back of my hand. "I can't stay here; he's mean! He is a beast!" I shouted, hoping he could hear me.

"Cassandra…" he tried again, reaching for me tentatively, resting his warm hand on my knee.

I nudged it off. "N-no, I'm going. This is not what I signed up for. I didn't deserve this." I stood up clumsily, resting my back against the wall, my whole body still shaking with the aftermath of the terror that this Luca caused.

The man raised his hands in surrender. "Please, it's late. You don't have a car; you can't leave tonight. Just calm down and take a breath okay? If you still want to leave in the morning—"

"I want to leave!" I replied, scowling.

He nodded with a sigh. "Okay, then I'll drive you down to town myself in the morning, I promise."

I studied him more closely now. He was tall but leaner than Luca—at least I thought so from what I saw of him. They shared some similar features—dark eyes, dark hair, olive skin.

But where Luca had been a terrifying mountain man

87

with long hair, unkempt beard, and feral look, this man was well kept. He had a classic haircut, shorter at the side, a bit longer at the top, and a well-trimmed goatee.

"Who are you?" I asked, hating how feeble my voice sounded. After everything that happened, I'd stood tall. I didn't want to look weak now.

The man found you sobbing in the corner of a room, Cassie; there's no need to fake it now.

"Oh yes, I'm sorry." He gave me a sheepish smile. "I'm Domenico, but you can call me Dom. I'm Luca's head of security."

Ah, the guns on both sides of his chest made sense now but why did crazy mountain psycho need security?

I nodded silently.

"Why don't you come with me?"

I glanced at the broken plate on the floor, the tomato sauce staining the wall and floor, the color so similar to blood.

"I need to clean up." Why did I even bother? I was going to leave tomorrow and never turn back.

He took a couple of slow steps toward me. "No, you don't. Now you'll come with me and we'll have a drink and chat okay?"

I looked at him silently. "I swear you're safe with me, Cassandra. I won't hurt you."

It seems completely insane. I had just met the man and yet I believed him.

I nodded. "Call me Cassie."

"Cassie, what do you want to drink?"

"I- don't drink. I'm not yet twenty-one. I will be in a couple of weeks."

He smiled at that. "Following the rules?"

I shrugged noncommittally.

"Ah, I think it's okay to break the rules after the evening you had." He opened the door and gestured me out.

I followed him silently to the kitchen, my mind still reeling about what had happened tonight. The scarred man, Luca... He'd been just so angry and so fundamentally broken.

"Take a seat." He pointed to the small kitchen table. "I'll be right back."

I sat and took a couple of deep breaths. I liked that kitchen. It helped me feel better.

By the time Dom came back with two glasses, I was more or less back to normal.

"Chardonnay for you," he said with a smile on his thin lips, sliding the glass in front of me. "I think it's the best way to start."

I took a sip; it was fresh and nice. "I like it."

He nodded. "I figured."

He took a sip of his amber drink in the tumbler.

"Why have you done that?" I asked.

He sighed, leaning back on his chair. "I thought it would help him," he admitted.

"Help him?"

"Luca..." He shook his head. "He was not like that

before. He—" Dom winced. "He changed and he never talks to anyone except me and some mandatory contact, but with you—he enjoyed it and I thought… I'm sorry."

I looked down at my glass, tracing the ring with my finger. "I enjoyed our chats too. I liked him," I admitted, keeping my eyes down.

I looked up when he remained silent. He was looking away, his face taut.

"Who is he? Luca? Who needs a security detail like that?"

He shook his head before looking toward me again. "I can't tell you that." He seemed genuinely regretful about that. "It is not my secret to tell."

I shrugged. "It doesn't matter. I'll be gone in the morning." I tried my best not to sound defeated. I'd liked it here even if I'd been lonely sometimes. It paid well and I was left alone, but the terror I'd felt tonight? I could not get past that.

He nodded with a weary sigh. "I truly wish you wouldn't but I understand. I do." He reached in his jacket and got out a small white card with a number printed on it and nothing else. "It's my number. When you're ready to leave tomorrow, just text me and I'll meet you by the entrance to take you wherever you want."

I looked down at the card on the table. "Yeah…" I'd have to go back to Mrs. Broussard. I knew she would be happy to have me back; she had a big heart, but it was a step back and a responsibility she didn't need.

I let out a sigh as Dom finished his drink in one sip and stood up. "I've got to go to the security post by the gate for the change of security, but if you need anything, just call me, okay? Or come to my room—second floor, third door on the left. I should be back in an hour or so."

"I'm not allowed up there."

He gave me a small smile. "Who cares? You're leaving, remember?"

"Yeah… True." Did my voice sound as uncertain as it did to my ears?

"You know, it's not too late to change your mind. Luca, no matter what, he wouldn't have hurt you. He's changed but this—" He shook his head. "He just wouldn't. Have a good night, Cassie."

He left before giving me a chance to answer, and I stayed at that kitchen table a little while longer, finishing my glass of wine. I looked down at my now empty glass. I decided I liked wine and the gentle warmth that settled in my chest after drinking it.

I stood up and went to the utility room to retrieve the cleaning products. I knew that Dom said to leave it, but just the thought of the tomato sauce seeping through the old wooden flooring or permanently staining the expensive-looking gold and moss green flock wallpaper was bothering me probably more than it should.

I went to the room with an apprehension settling in my stomach. What if he was back there? I rested my hand on the handle and took a deep breath.

When I walked in I found the table still set the way it had been. The candle on the table... I rolled my eyes at my own stupidity. Did I think it was a date? Yes, you did—a date with the reclusive owner of the manor. Stupid girl.

I shook my head and stopped by the wall, the broken plate and food were gone. If it was not for the wet spot on the floor and the barely visible discoloration on the wallpaper, it was like nothing had happened.

I looked around. Even his chair was back up. If only I knew what I did to make him flip, maybe—

Don't, Cassie. Don't defend his behavior. Don't make the same mistakes you made before. Beasts will be beasts and monsters will stay monsters.

Jude. Jude was my goal and nothing else mattered.

9

LUCA

I woke up hangover-free for the first time in... Actually, I couldn't remember the last time it happened.

My anger yesterday had been so overwhelming and exhausting that I hadn't needed to numb the memories with alcohol.

I'd hated that I thought she'd lied to me for the meal. I'd put her on such a pedestal, I'd been disappointed, and then I'd taken a bite of the food and it felt like my mother had been in the kitchen, and I'd just flipped.

I felt the betrayal at that woman's trick, the pain of the memory of the last time my mother cooked that meal. I could almost hear Arabella's laugh, and for a few minutes, just for a few minutes, I hated

Cassie for making me like her, for exposing my pain so blatantly in front of her.

I acted out like a madman, terrifying her. Once Dom interrupted my trance, I'd left and checked the com system, and Dom had said the truth; he had been the one tricking her to have dinner with me.

I went back downstairs but hesitated. I'd been so angry, I'd shown her my face, and she'd gasped. This rejection had been like fuel on the fire of my rage; I somehow expected more from her.

Once I was calmer I went back to the salon, unsure what I would find and what I could say. I was thankful that Dom had stopped whatever I'd been about to do or say to her.

The room was empty. I looked at the corner where she'd cowered and a new wave of guilt washed over me… Like I needed any more guilt in my life.

I cleaned the mess I'd made as if it could also erase the mess I made with her tonight.

I waited a while in the room, hoping she would come and clean. Maybe I could apologize in some way, but she never came back, and I gave up after a while, not sure how I could even make it better.

After waking up more or less normal this morning, I grabbed a granola bar and a bottle of water from my room and took the back stairs to the home gym. I'd been too drunk to visit it for a while but today I wanted to use all this energy and anger against a punching bag instead of lashing out at the girl. I was quite surprised she didn't go packing last night.

I found Dom sitting on a bench, curling some weights.

I was angry at him for what he did. It was all his fault at the end of the day; he had no right to trick me the way he did.

I scowled at him silently, not sure where to start.

He stood up and put the weight back on the stand.

He rolled his eyes at my glare. "I'm going back up in a minute, have at it."

I pointed an accusing finger at him. "You had no right to do what you did!"

He nodded. "I agree. I didn't realize that—" He grabbed his T-shirt from the floor and put it on. "Never mind, I've got to get ready."

"No, finish what you're saying. And you're not working this morning."

"I'm not, but I have to drive Cassie back to town. She's leaving."

I should have been relieved and yet, the unfamiliar stabbing in the middle of my chest stated otherwise.

I frowned. "What do you mean 'leaving'?"

He let out a humorless laugh. "Did you think that poor girl was going to stay after the fear you caused her?"

The betrayal at him taking her away was so powerful even if unjustified. I wanted to hurt him right back. "Ah, and you know all about instigating fears in poor women, don't you?"

That was a cheap shot and I knew it. It was my knee-jerk reaction except that I was both the knee and the jerk.

He reached for his bottle of water on the floor and took a drink.

"Once upon a time you were a mafioso with ethics, with morals. This was why you were so respected and butting heads with your father every day and it is also why they all admired you, me included. But you see, the more I tried to convince her to stay, the more I was telling her how you used to be, the more I realize that you may never be that man again."

Ah, he too was giving up on me, just when I needed him to tell me to go to her. When I needed him to convince me I could get some forgiveness from her.

"What happened to you thinking she was good for me?" I sneered. "Wasn't it why you pulled that stupid stunt?"

Dom nodded. "It's true. I still think she is good for you, but I forgot a crucial part. "

I crossed my arms on my chest. "Which is?"

"You're not good for her."

I snorted. I knew that I was not good for anyone anymore. What did my father call me? Poison, yes that was it and yet, despite everything, I was determined to make her stay.

His phone vibrated in his shorts pocket. He grabbed it and sighed after reading the text. "She'll be ready to go in a few minutes. I need to shower."

"I'll go talk to her." I wasn't sure where that came from. I was barely good at talking to her through the computer... Why did I think...

Dom turned to go up the stairs, but I didn't miss the grin on his face just as he gave me his back.

"It was your plan all along!" I called after him, somehow impressed.

He kept on going up but stopped just as he reached the top. "You're the boss, you figure it out," he replied before disappearing down the corridor.

"Asshole," I grumbled but took the front stairs up to her room before I had a chance to overthink it and admit to myself that it was better for her, and in extension for me, that she left and never looked back.

I took a deep breath as I stood in front of her door, the apprehension in the pit of my stomach both new and unsettling.

I was—well, I used to be—Gianluca Montanari, fearless and adulated underboss. I'd never felt apprehension before, men like me never did because we always got what we wanted.

I'd never feared or got a refusal and yet that was exactly what I expected from the fierce young woman behind that door.

I pulled my hood up and knocked. I knew that

with my black oversized hoodie I looked more like death than anything else, and in retrospect, it was exactly what I was.

"Come in!"

I opened the door and stepped in.

"I'm sorry," She started looking down at her suitcase, a bright-green shirt in her hand. "I'll be done packing in a—" She stopped as she looked up and saw me standing there. "What are you doing here?" Her tone turned cold and wary.

I couldn't blame her for that either; I've been nothing but a heathen to her.

She shook her head when I didn't answer, throwing her shirt in her suitcase. "Don't worry, I'm on my way out. I'll go spy on someone else."

Yeah, I deserved that. "I'm sorry." The words felt foreign in my mouth—I'd never been the kind of man to apologize, for anything.

"What?" she asked but didn't stop her task of picking up the folded clothes from the small pile on her bed to put them in her suitcase.

"Could you just stop for a minute? Please." That too had not been a word I often used. I didn't ask, I ordered.

She slowly put back the shirt she was holding on the bed and eyed me warily, crossing her arms on her chest.

"I'm sorry," I repeated, my view of her slightly shadowed by my hood. "Yesterday wasn't the best of

98

days for me, and then I thought you were lying to me." I shook my head. "I don't deal well with lies and then you cooked—" I swallowed painfully around the ever-present ball of pain and guilt in my throat. "You cooked my mother's favorite meal—just the way she did it and—" I sighed.

"I've done nothing wrong," she said with a small voice. "You had no right to snap at me the way you did, scare me the way you did." She shook her head. "I- I don't feel safe here anymore. I can't help but wonder what will be the next thing I do that will make you snap and what could happen to me if Dom is not here to stop you." Her voice broke a little at her last word.

Fuck, I'd terrified that poor woman. I was also irrationally irritated that she saw Dom as her protector and me as the beast.

"I would never hurt you." And it was true. I had a moral code—I never hurt women.

No? What about your mother and sister? You didn't just hurt them; you killed them. My father's voice raised from his fucking grave to haunt me.

"How would I know that?"

"I tell you that." I sighed. I could see with her crossed arms and the stubborn jerk of her chin that I was losing the debate. Time for step two—negotiation. I knew what she wanted the most; I just had to give it to her.

"Listen, I need someone and you are the

least...*objectionable* so far." Objectionable, that was a way to put it. Enticing was more like it.

"Okay..." she trailed off.

"Stay until the summer and—" *And what, you idiot? You didn't think this through, did you?* I scanned her room, my eyes stopping on the picture frame on her nightstand of her and her little brother. "I'll help you get your brother back."

Her face brightened and I knew I had something. "Jude? How?"

"I know people—I have contacts." That was a way to put it. In truth? I used to own the city. "If you stay until then, I will make sure you have a job, a place to live, and a nice judge to sign the papers. I promise." I could do that so easily, at least I used to. Surely three months was not the end of the world to get everything she wanted.

"How do I know I can trust your words?"

That was a fair question; she didn't know me. She might have been desperate but she was not stupid, and that made me respect her a lot more than I already did.

"Because I never make promises I don't intend to keep. Because I believe that respecting a promise given is a question of honor and believe it or not, I'm all about honor."

She looked at me silently, her lips pursed. "Remove your hood."

I was taken aback by her request. "What?"

"Remove your hood," she repeated slowly. "I like to look at people when we're talking, especially when they're making commitments."

I balled my hands into fists. It was so bright in her room and with the way she looked at me yesterday. "I don't think it's a good idea."

"Why not?"

She was going to make me say it. "I saw your reaction yesterday. Why force yourself to look at the beast?" It was hard to admit that her flinching yesterday cut me. I knew I looked like a beast, but somehow her reaction managed to hurt me when I thought I was above it all.

She shook her head. "It was not your face that made me flinch; it was the murderous look in your eyes."

I had a hard time believing her; I'd heard Francesca talk behind my back. She was the worst gold digger there was and yet she'd said she could not marry me with the way I looked.

"Please." The gentleness in her voice surprised me because I didn't deserve it.

I stopped breathing altogether when I brought my hand up and lowered my hood slowly, revealing my face in the unforgiving morning sun.

I met her eyes, ready to see her flinch or tip her mouth down or even avert her eyes like many did— all the subtle signs of disgust that people often showed without meaning to.

Surprisingly there was none of those on her face as she looked at me, detailing my face with a scrutiny that made me self-conscious.

"You have nothing to hide," she said gently. "The only thing beastly about you is your attitude."

I let out the breath I was holding. As impossible as it seemed, she didn't look fazed or bothered by my scars. It was like she could see past them, see the Luca I used to be.

"What's your name?" she asked now but she looked more responsive; her arms were now relaxed by her side, the tension of her shoulders visibly gone. Was it really possible that she didn't mind me?

"You know my name, Luca," I replied gruffly. I'd shared more than I expected by bargaining with her and showing her my face. She was staff and yet here, in this room, she seemed to yield all the power.

She shook her head. "No, I mean your full name."

I knew that once I told her, she would rush on Google and find out my sins and then even if the scars hadn't disgusted her, the rest would, but I owed her that much and maybe it would be for the best too if I disgusted her and she kept away. I wasn't sure what it was about her, but she made me unsettled and I didn't like it.

"Gianluca Montanari," I replied with finality in my voice. I was done for now. "Let me know if you decide to stay." And I left her, closing the door softly behind me.

I waited in my office for an hour, staring at the HCS, wondering what could take her so long to decide.

I waited with some trepidation, relaxing when no car left in the next thirty minutes, but the more time passed, the more I was getting anxious and somehow irritated.

I'd made her an amazing offer! The kind of offer I never made. She was a fool to overthink it.

I took a deep breath, trying to keep the irritation at bay; snapping at her would clearly not be the right way to act.

Was she online now? Reading about all of my sins? Was it what was taking so long? She was bound to leave after all she'd read. I was a monster inside and out.

I stood up. I was done waiting like a lovesick puppy in front of a screen for a message that might never come.

I walked down the corridor to Arabella's room, and as every time as I stepped in, my dead heart squeezed in my chest.

The room had remained untouched. Everything was where it was supposed to be. I took in the bright floral wallpaper, floral bedspread, all the plush animals on her bed.

I sat at the foot of the bed and looked at the pink unicorn plush resting against her pillow. It had been a Christmas present and she loved it so much she was sleeping with it every night.

I grabbed the unicorn, resting it against my chest. I missed her so much.

I heard the floor creak in the corridor but it was much too subtle and light to be Dom. I knew it was her. I should have stopped her from coming in and yet, I didn't. I squeezed the unicorn against my chest.

"You're not allowed here," I said, keeping my back to her.

"I think we're past that," she replied gently.

I nodded. Yes, we were past that, we passed so many barriers I never intended her to cross. *Stupid, beautiful, brave girl.*

At least she didn't run away disgusted or terrified.

"So you're Mafia."

I almost laughed at that. Leave it to her to let that out so casually, like it was not a big deal.

"So you're the monsters' daughter," I replied with the same tone.

"I am."

"I am Mafia. At least I used to be," I replied, not ready to get into details.

She took a couple of steps into the room, but I kept my back to her, not ready to meet her eyes yet— not knowing what her face would reflect.

That woman was easy to read; everything she felt was right there in her face. It was so different from the women I used to be with, so different from Francesca.

"This was her room—Arabella."

"I'm sorry."

She didn't pretend she didn't know what I was talking about and I appreciated the honesty.

"Is this her?"

I glanced at her and the photo she was looking at. It was the last good real photo of Arabella, at Carter's wedding. She was standing beside the bride—Nazalie. She'd been so proud to have been the flower girl that day.

I nodded.

She grabbed the frame carefully and came to sit beside me on the bed.

"She was a very pretty little girl," she said, gently running her forefinger on my sister's smiling face.

"She was an angel." I put the unicorn back on the bed but I didn't turn toward her. I'd rather she only saw my good profile.

"Tell me about her."

Once again, I threw her a surprised glance. Most people tried to relate, telling you their own journey of grief, thinking it would help, but it didn't. How could it? Because voluntarily or not, they were switching the focus from you to them, but again that was not Cassandra.

"Bella was full of light and laughter. She could get a smile out of anybody and I mean genuinely anybody!" I shook my head with a low chuckle. "Even Genovese—the coldest, most ruthless man in our ranks. When Arabella went to him with her smile, he was melting."

"It looked like it." She smiled down at the photo. "Just looking at her smile in a photo is making me smile."

I raised my hand to rest it on top of her on the frame but thought better of it and rested it back on my knee. I had no place doing that. I had no right to touch her.

"She loved flowers, as you can see." I gestured around the room before pointing at the photo. "So here my friends Carter and Nazalie were getting married and Bella was their flower girl. It made her day."

"You managed to make friends despite your charming personality?"

She was teasing me, and fuck, did it warm my chest…and other places.

She looked up and winked at me and my dead heart jumped in my chest, her smile like a metaphoric defibrillator created just for me. She was dangerous, terrifying, enticing, mesmerizing…all in one.

She was the gates of a Heaven I was not allowed to seek, not allowed to reach. She was my fucking punishment.

Sinners like me didn't deserve women like her.

"You'd be surprised."

"Not that much actually," she replied evasively, and I couldn't help but wonder what kind of trash she found online.

"I killed her," I added, my voice breaking under the weight of this immutable truth. I saw their lifeless bodies flash before my eyes every time I tried to fall asleep. It was one of the reasons why I drank so much because it was best to be too drunk to think.

She rested the picture frame on the bed and rested her hand on top of mine. She was braver than me. "It was an accident."

I looked down at her hand on mine. It was so thin, so small and delicate—such a contrast with the lioness heart she had.

"I took their lives; I am responsible," I added stubbornly. I was drunk apparently. I didn't remember much from that night. I remembered the fight with my father, the champagne, and then nothing until I opened my eyes in a state of pain so intense I never thought I could feel worse and I'd been wrong. The pain I felt when I saw their lifeless mangled bodies slew me.

I involuntarily shivered and she squeezed my hand in comfort.

We sat like that for a few minutes, side by side, her hand on mine. I was getting uncomfortable in this position but I didn't dare move, much too scared that she would remove her hand and comforting touch.

"Why don't you help me build the garden?" she asked, removing her hand.

"Excuse me?" I turned toward her, surprised by the turn her thoughts had taken.

"I know you're already helping me fix the gazebo."

"How do you know?" I would not insult her with a lie.

She let out a small laugh. "Because I know how much I suck at it, but I'm trying my best, and then in the morning I come down and see it's good."

"Maybe it's the gazebo fairy?" I tried with a half-smile.

Teasing her felt so easy, as cliche as it sounded. I felt so much lighter with her.

"Is that what you want me to call you?" she teased right back. She shrugged. "I can if you want."

I shook my head, my smile widening.

"Help me build a nice garden full of flowers, an ode to Arabella. What do you say?"

I stood up and walked to the window to look out at the bare garden.

"I don't know."

"Why? Do you have better things to do?"

I shrugged. Spending too much time with her wouldn't be good for her or me. She managed to make me feel so much in such a little amount of time.

I couldn't get deeper with this girl. She was

forbidden for so many reasons, one of them being that she was perfect, pure, kind. She came from hell; she didn't deserve to go back in.

"So you're staying?" I asked, still turned toward the garden. It was easier for me to sound professional when I kept my back to her.

Her beautiful eyes, freckles, and sweet face had a tendency to make me forget how much I deserved my penance.

"I am," she replied carefully, probably noticing the change in my tone. "One more condition though."

I sighed. "This is not a negotiation."

"Of course it is."

"What do you want?" I replied a little more gruffly than I intended.

"I want you to help me at least twice in the garden, and if it's not your thing, I won't ask again."

"That's it?" I could maybe offer something else, maybe a dinner in the confines of the library.

"And a TV. I miss Netflix."

I had to laugh at that, it was so unexpected.

"Done," I replied before realizing I'd agreed to everything including the garden work.

"Very well. I'll see you later, Mr. Montanari."

"Call me Luca," I said, somehow mortified I did so. What the fuck?

I turned around, looking at her with wide eyes. She had to be a sorceress; there was no other way.

I eyed her through narrow eyes. I barely knew

this girl. She'd been here three weeks. Was I just that lonely that—

She smiled so brightly that I didn't have it in me to tell her I changed my mind.

"Very well, Luca. I'll see you soon." She swirled around and left before I had a chance to say anything stupid and ruin the progress we'd just made. Smart girl.

I shook my head. Cassandra West was a force to be reckoned with and part of me just wanted to surrender to her purity before I risked tainting her with my darkness.

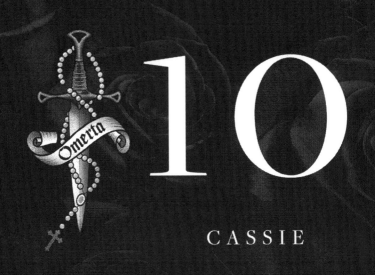

10

CASSIE

I stood by the bed of flowers, looking down at all the bulbs I needed to plant. I might have gone overboard with my order, but I had hoped for Luca's help but while he did good on his TV promise and I came back from my visit with my brother yesterday to a gigantic flat screen mounted on the wall across my bed with a Post-it on it with Netflix logins, he still had to make good on his promise of helping me with the garden.

I looked at my watch once more and sighed. Luca was twenty minutes late now. He was not coming, I could always ask Dom to help, but it didn't feel right somehow.

I knelt, reaching for the first bunch of red tulips

when I saw him exit the house by the back door, all dressed in black.

I leaned back on my knees, waiting for him to reach me. I couldn't deny that, despite everything, that man was a force of nature—well over six foot, wide, and exuding power. He was wearing black jeans, combat boots, and a black hoodie with the hood down.

My eyes trailed up to his face and the perpetual scowl he was sporting. He was tilting his head slightly to the side, and I suspected it was a subconscious way to hide the scarred side of his face.

Something I hoped he would stop doing once he knew me and how irrelevant his scars were to me.

He stopped in front of the flower bed, looking down at me, clearly annoyed with being here but he'd agreed.

I looked down, pressing my lips together to hide my smile at a grown man pouting.

"We need to start with the red and yellow tulips first." I pointed my trowel to the big case to my side. "I'll take care of this side; you can start here with the yellow." I pointed to my left. "Oh." I leaned back and grabbed a blue metal box. "I've put together a little box of what you'll need."

He grabbed the box and settled on the side I told him to. He had yet to say a word and he was clearly surly and annoyed at being here.

I was quite certain he hoped that his behavior

would weigh on me until I told him he could go. Ah, he was in for a treat. Being raised by my horrid parents had one advantage—other people's bad attitudes rarely weighed on me.

"You can look on how I'm doing it if you need, and then do the same and—"

"I know how to plant flowers. I've done it before," he replied gruffly, scowling even more fiercely at the box I'd just given him.

I shrugged. "Okay," I replied as amicably as I could.

I was at my second plant when he spoke again.

"How did you know I'd come?"

I looked up at him. He was staring at the men's gardening gloves I'd put in his box.

"Because you said you would," I replied, removing a strand of my hair from my forehead with my bent wrist.

"I know but after what happened to you..." He shrugged. "I suspected a little more doubt."

"What do you mean?" I asked but went back to work. It was easier for me to talk to him if I was doing something.

"Well, after the thing with your parents broke down, everybody turned their backs on you to the point that you ended up sleeping on the sofa at your old maid's one-bedroom apartment."

I was surprised and a little uncomfortable at the amount of information this man had on me but at the same time, I shouldn't have been surprised. He was Mafia after all.

"I didn't have many friends," I admitted, and by not many, I meant none. "With my parents' lives, I was a mother to Jude most of the time so with Jude, school, and everything, socialization took a back seat."

"Still, nobody offered you any help."

"Mrs. Broussard did; she offered me a home." I put a tulip in the ground. "And my cousin in Calgary offered me her home."

"You have a family?"

I knew what he didn't say. *Your record showed none.*

"I do. Well, India is my second-degree cousin. She is lovely and asked me to move in with her. It would have been easier to go somewhere where nobody knew me or hated me by association but—"

"But?"

I glanced at him but he was focused on his task too. I was grateful not to be under his scrutinizing dark stare that seemed to see to the depth of my soul.

"It would have been impossible to leave Jude behind. Social services told me it would take forever for India to get custody and even then she is very young, single, and in a foreign country so I said no. I don't mind the hate and the hardship as long as I'm here for Jude."

"He's lucky to have you."

Was that longing in his voice? I remember the

way he'd sat in his sister's room, holding that unicorn against his chest as if it were a lifeline. He'd lost a part of him when she'd died, and I couldn't even imagine his pain. The thought of losing Jude made me physically sick.

I felt his loss all the way down to my soul.

"I'm lucky to have him. He is unique, in more ways than one."

Luca nodded, reaching for a tulip, weirdly twisting his body to grip it as if he was in pain.

I was about to ask him about it when he continued.

"So he likes to read?"

"Jude? Yes, he loves it. It's more than that, to be honest. He is obsessed with words, always has been."

"Why's that?"

I shrugged. "Not sure, but it started so young. Believe it or not but he knew how to read before he was four." I let out a chuckle. "As you know my parents were not that keen on parenting and I was not available enough to read stories, so, you know, he did it himself. His psychologist calls it hyper-lexia. It sometimes happens to children on the spectrum."

Luca nodded and I was glad he didn't ask more about Jude being on the spectrum.

"Our parents considered him flawed; I consider him a gift."

Luca looked up at me, his eyebrows arched in

surprise. "You're wise beyond your years," he said thoughtfully.

I let out a startled laugh. "I'm not that young."

"But much too young," he replied, reaching awkwardly for another tulip bulb.

I didn't reply to his comment because I was quite certain he'd been talking to himself more than he'd been talking to me.

"What are you doing with your days? I never see you around."

He glanced at me silently before concentrating on his task again.

"Come on, you're asking me all of these questions. It seems only fair I get to ask you some too."

He shook his head, still not looking up. "You know if you don't want to answer my questions, you can just say it. Nobody's forcing you."

I couldn't help but be a little deflated at his dismissal. I hadn't meant it as a jab but merely as a joke.

I sighed, going back at my tulip bulbs.

"Drink and wallow in self-pity," he said after a while.

"Sorry?" I was not sure what he was saying.

He sighed. "You asked what I was doing all day. Drink and wallow in self-pity."

"Oh." I'd suspected that much. I just didn't expect him to admit it to me.

"You're surprised?" he asked, looking up.

"I'm surprised you told me the truth."

"I won't lie to you, Cassandra," he said with such certainty that it made me shiver, his deep voice resonating deep in my bones. "I'd rather not answer at all than lie."

I smiled at him brightly. "I like that. I'm the same. Lies are too difficult to keep up with, too much to remember. By telling the truth, I never fear of being inconsistent. Nothing is more immutable than the truth."

He looked at me in a way that made me uncomfortable as if he wasn't sure I was real. "Yes, I couldn't have said it any better."

He twisted again to reach for a bulb.

"Are you in pain?" I almost made it to nursing school graduation; maybe I could help him.

"What?"

I pointed to the case with the bulbs. "You're getting the bulbs funny, are you sore?"

"Ah, no. It's—" He scratched at his bearded jaw with his gloved hand, leaving a little soil in his beard. "I'm giving you my good profile. I shouldn't subject you to the abject vision of my mangled face."

"Oh."

He nodded. "If you want we can switch places; it might be easier for both of us."

No, I didn't want to switch places. I wanted him to show me his face freely, left side included. I didn't mind the scars—hell, I even found them attractive. I'd seen on Google how he'd looked before the accident, all preppy and powerful with an uncanny resemblance with that dark-haired vampire from *Buffy the Vampire Slayer*, but the scars didn't take anything away from his handsomeness—no matter what he believed, what anybody led him to believe.

"No, I don't think so. I like being here and I'm actually enjoying the view." I blushed at my words. I was not a forward woman; I never complimented men or flirted. Hell, I didn't even know how.

His eyebrows puckered in confusion. Probably trying to figure out if I was crazy or a liar. I was neither, his scars were striking but they didn't take away from his rugged, masculine beauty—at least not to me.

I slid closer to him and removed my gardening gloves. I brought my hand up and brushed the soil from his bearded cheek.

He tensed as if he was made of stone under my touch.

I brought my other hand up and brushed my fingertips across his scarred cheek softly, barely a touch, and despite his frozen state, I saw his pupils dilate. He liked that I touched him.

His small reaction made me bolder somehow and I traced the scars with my forefinger. I traced the one going down in an almost straight line from the side to his forehead, down the corner of his eyes, the corner of his mouth to his chin. It tipped the corner of his mouth in a small pout.

"The scars are not ugly," I whispered softly, worried that I'd break the spell and he would pull away—retreating in his shell of self-hatred. "You're handsome. I like both sides of you." I kept my eyes locked on his—showing him that my words were nothing but the truth. It was not pity talking; it was the attraction I felt for him despite knowing how wrong and hopeless it was to feel something for a man like him.

"You don't have to say that," he whispered but remained immobile, letting me trace all the scars.

"I know I don't. But I mean it, every word. Please don't hide your face from me."

I didn't realize he had moved until he gently brushed his fingers along the seam of my bottom lip. He had removed his gloves while I was engrossed with his face and he seemed as mesmerized as I was.

His face softened, and for once I saw how vulnerable this man was.

"You're making it so difficult," he whispered so low I wasn't sure it was made for me to hear.

"What?" I replied breathlessly as he brushed his fingers slowly back and forth against my bottom lip.

"Staying away from you."

"What if I don't want you to?"

"Then you are just as much of a fool as I am."

I opened my mouth to reply when Dom and another guard rounded the corner.

We jolted back as if we'd just been struck by lightning, the moment definitely gone.

Luca stood up much faster and gracefully than a man his size should have been able to.

"I think gardening is not for me," he started, brushing the soil on his jeans, avoiding my eyes. "I'll find you some assistance for the garden." He looked at Dom and the other man who was watching us with curious interest. "Can I assist you with something?" he barked at them.

Dom shook his head but his eyes were not on Luca anymore. They were on me. They were questioning, speculative... I looked down with discomfort.

"Then keep on going; I'm not paying you to stare."

I kept looking down as if the bulb in my hand was the most fascinating thing in the world.

I saw Luca's feet turn toward me and I looked up, meeting his eyes. His face was hard again, his eyes almost accusing—as if he was angry at me for seeing through the cracks in his walls. He could build me up and break me with just one look, one word... His power over me was both exciting and terrifying.

"This won't happen again."

"What won't? The gardening or—" Or what? What did we just share? It was an intimacy I'd yet to experience. It had been different, meaningful even if I couldn't put a name on it.

"Both, everything," he replied curtly before straightening his sleeves, then retreating back to the house.

———

Even if I didn't really expect him to talk to me for the rest of the day, I still felt disappointed at his silence.

In this case, I knew that his silence said a lot. He got scared—of what, I wasn't sure.

Working alone in the garden today had been difficult. I was sore and weary on top of my disappointment at Luca's reaction, so I retreated after dinner to enjoy some TV.

I took a hot shower to try to ease my muscles and settled on top of my bed with a gigantic bowl of popcorn.

I was about to start the show when I heard a gentle rap on my door.

My heart jumped in my chest at the thought of Luca coming to my room.

"Come in," I called, sitting straighter on the bed.

I couldn't help the little pinch of disappointment I felt at seeing Dom enter the room. I just hoped it didn't show on my face.

"Ah, sorry I'm not the one you want to see."

Okay, maybe it did. That wasn't good; I liked Dom. He was such a sweet, gentle person.

"No, I'm just surprised to see anyone." I pointed to my pastries-covered flannel pajamas. "I'm not really dressed for visitors."

He seemed to be blushing a little but I couldn't be sure under the dim light. "Yes, sorry, it's still early. I just thought—" He cleared his throat and jerked his thumb toward the door. "I'll just go. We can speak in the morning."

"No!" I jerked straighter on my bed, almost sending my popcorn to the floor. I was always so alone here, and I was craving a little company. I sat cross-legged on the middle of the bed and pointed to the peach-colored chair close to my bed. "Sit down, please. I like your company."

He walked in and smiled with relief. "Me too."

"So what can I help you with?" I asked after he sat down. He looked so...foreign in this room.

Here, everything was light and delicate and he was a big man, all dark with a black suit—the difference between him and the decor was striking.

He leaned back in his chair and smiled. Dom's smile was so carefree, so lovely. How was it that Luca and he were so different?

"It's actually more what I can help you with."

"Okay?"

"Luca asked me to help you with the garden."

"Oh." I couldn't help the powerful deflation that

filled me with his words. Somehow part of me hoped that Luca would come around and come to the gardens tomorrow. "You don't have to. I can manage. You have enough work, I'm sure."

He gave me a half-smile and a side-look that seemed to say 'I see right through your bullshit.' "I don't mind. I'm bored out of my skull here most of the time. As you can see we never have visitors and the security is like Fort Knox, so you know…" He shrugged. "Doing a bit of yard work will be a welcome distraction."

"Are you Mafia too?" I blurted out. I stopped wide-eyed; what the hell was wrong with me?

He let out a startled laugh. "Did you really just ask me that?"

"What?" I shook my head. "No…yes… Maybe?" I winced.

He chuckled with a shake of his head. "Yes, I am. Well—" He cocked his head to the side. "I guess you can say I'm on leave. I'm Luca's security."

I nodded silently. If Luca's out of it, so was he. It made sense.

"What are you watching?" he asked, jerking his head toward the screen that was paused on a basketball game.

I was grateful for the change of subject. I was worried I'd made things even more awkward.

"*One Tree Hill.*" I settled back on my bed, my back against the headboard.

"Any good?"

"I'm only on episode three so far… Lots of teenage drama brewing."

He nodded. "Ah, teenage drama…the best."

I chuckled, then extended the bowl of popcorn toward him in a silent invitation for him to stay and watch.

After an episode I saw him twist and wince in the chair; it was a small, narrow one. It was comfortable for my five-one frame, but certainly not for his six-four frame.

I slid to the side and patted the space beside me.

"It's more comfortable here."

He raised his eyebrows in surprise as I realized how this may have come across. God, I sounded like a sleazy man making his approach.

"No. I just mean it in a friendly way. It's just—" I felt my cheeks burn under the crushing weight of my discomfort. "I'm not good at this. I-" I shook my head. *Shut the fuck up, Cassie! You're a stupid girl who invited a grown-ass Mafia guy to be on your bed with you; what did you expect?*

I took a deep breath. "You don't want to date me, do you?"

"God, no!" He let out with a recoil like the thought itself was repulsive.

Well, it didn't matter that I felt the same; his extreme rejection stung.

"Okay then, so no harm done, right?"

He looked at me silently for a few seconds, as if he was trying to decipher something before nodding.

He removed his jacket, toed off his black dress shoes, and joined me on top of the bed before reaching for the popcorn bowl and resting it on his lap.

"You know, for what it's worth, even if I wanted to date you or sleep with you—heaven forbid."

Okay, jab number two. "Yeah?"

He shook his head. "My feelings or intentions shouldn't matter. This invitation, right here, doesn't give me any right on you. Do you understand?"

I looked up at his face, startled by the intensity of his words. He was looking down at me, his body tense, his brows slightly furrowed with determination, his dark eyes shining with a righteous fire that I didn't expect in this situation.

"Okay?"

"No matter what you might say or do—consciously or not, it never gives a man any right on you or your body. You need to remember that, always."

The intensity of his words made me shiver. Had he witnessed things? No, I didn't want to think about that. "I know."

He let out a breath. "Great. Now that's settled. Let's see what teenage drama we're dealing with."

I nodded, still a little unsettled by his serious speech and the force of his rejection.

"Are you gay?" I asked halfway through the episode. I gasped at my own remark as he choked on his popcorn. I just thought it and—I winced. I needed to get my mouth in check. They were not just anyone, and frankly that was not okay.

"Excuse me?" he asked, his voice raspy after the coughing fit he just had.

"Never mind." I waved my hand dismissively. "Let's watch the show."

"I am not gay," he replied a little while later.

"It wouldn't matter if you were," I replied honestly, still too embarrassed about my question to look up at him.

He paused the show and I braced for what was to come.

"I know. But I just wonder what made you say that you know...for science."

Even though I could hear the smile in his voice, I was still so uncomfortable. It seemed that I lost the little filter I had since moving here.

"It's just—" *Lord, take me now.* "Well, I know I'm not the most beautiful woman in the world or anything, but I'm the only woman around, and you seemed almost repulsed at the idea. I just thought—" I shrugged. "I don't know what I thought."

I gave him a side-look as he launched the show again.

He popped a few kernels of sweet and salty goodness in his mouth, his eyes trained on the TV but I knew I'd unsettled him.

He let out a sigh. "We all have scars, lovely girl," he said, turning toward me with a sad, almost wistful smile. "Some are out there, on your skin like an armor —a proof of your struggle. But some, the most vicious and destroying of all, are internal and they grow, fester, and…" He stopped suddenly and let out a shaky breath. "You're amazing, you are perfect, and I feel a strong attachment to you that is unfamiliar and unsettling. I feel like you're family and it's again all new to me. Be grateful that it is not romantic—be grateful that all I want from you is your friendship and your trust."

"Grateful?" I asked, my cheeks warming at the kindness of his words. It was not crazy though; I felt the same from the first day and I was glad to have a friend now. I'd been so alone for too long.

He nodded. "Yep, otherwise Luca would have killed me."

"Why?" My heart accelerated. Was it at all possible he felt something for me? "Oh, wait. Is it because he doesn't approve of fraternization between staff?"

Dom chuckled. "Yes, sure, let's say it's that."

I opened my mouth to ask more but shook my head. What was the point?

We'd just started to settle in to watch the show again when he spoke.

"Just—" he started.

"Just?"

He took a deep breath. "I saw you in the garden with Luca."

I was not sure I liked how the subject started. "Okay…"

"Just—" He shook his head. "Luca is an amazing person, or he used to be. I think he still is under all the pain and guilt and whatever else he feels." He patted my leg. "I saw him freak. I saw him retreat in his shell. Be patient with him, be forgiving. He is worth it."

I looked up at him in a sort of awe. He was a true friend; he saw it too. I was not crazy…the connection I had with Luca. I might have been young and inexperienced, but I knew it was something special. The way I got lost in his dark orbs, the way a mere touch made him shiver, that had to be special.

"I promise."

He nodded and that was the end of it.

We watched a couple more episodes or at least I thought so because I fell asleep, my head against Dom's shoulder, not feeling lonely for the first time since the FBI turned my life upside down.

11

LUCA

It had been three days since the incident in the garden when she had unsettled me. When she'd touched me, I didn't want to recoil from her touch— quite the contrary. I wanted to lean into her touch, seek her comfort, and I didn't deserve it.

Her touch has quieted my pain, my heartache. I wanted more, and I'd never wanted more—I'd never felt the need for anyone, especially not a woman, and yet her fingers on my skin... It felt like redemption and I craved her.

She'd shaken me to the core, and the only thing I could have done was run away and hide, hoping this weakness would disappear, but it didn't.

I fought it, fought her, until I couldn't anymore until I stood in this kitchen, watching her knead some dough with a yellow apron that used to be my mother's.

"It smells like orange and cinnamon."

She froze at the sound of my voice, and it grated me the wrong way. She was just getting so close to Dom these days. Two peas in a pod and that bothered me a lot more than I cared to admit.

She stopped kneading the dough and turned around slowly, wiping her hands on the apron, looking at me with wariness in her eyes. I couldn't blame her for that either—I've been the moodiest man ever every time I was with her.

I'd contemplated coming down with an oversized hoodie again, to hide my face from her and the world, but I wanted to test her, see her reaction before she got her guard up, and I also wanted to show her in my own way that I started to trust her with who I was.

I almost smiled when I saw the appreciation in her face at my tight black T-shirt and jeans. I was not usually vain—at least not anymore. But I've been working very hard on my physique during my self-imposed exile. She appreciated the view, weirdly enough it was as if she, unlike anyone else, could see beyond the scars and the pain to see the man I used to be.

"Yes, I'm making Sicilian cassatelle with ricotta. Dom said it's his favorite."

I felt the pinch of jealousy at the mention of Dom.

Was she into him? She was going to be disappointed. Dom and her? It was impossible.

"Baking his favorite. That's nice." I was glad at how neutral my voice sounded despite the turmoil of emotions at seeing her in the kitchen like that, wearing my mother's apron. I hope he choked on one.

I nodded, wondering if she could see the jealousy I felt in my face.

"Do you need anything?"

I sighed. She was being professional and I wanted her to be with me like she was with Dom. "No, not really." I sat on the stool in front of the breakfast bar, facing her. "Am I bothering you?"

"No! Of course not. It's your home. You go as you pleased."

Okay, not really the answer I hoped for. I would have much rather liked her to say she wanted my companionship but it was a start.

She turned around again, working on her cassatelle.

"Where did you get the recipe? It smells good."

"I- Ummm." She seemed reluctant to answer.

I let my eyes trail off the counter to find my mother's notebook on the side.

"It's okay. You can use my mother's recipes. Dom always loved her cooking." I took a deep breath. "You can use it for my meals too."

She threw me a narrowed look full of doubt over her shoulder, making me laugh.

"I swear I won't snap again…at least not for the food."

She let out a low chuckle but turned around with her tray of dough, setting it on the counter facing me.

"What's your favorite dessert?" she asked me, and right then I knew she'd forgiven me…again. How many times would she do that?

"Red velvet pecan brownies."

She glanced up from her task of filling the dough.

"What?"

She shrugged. "Nothing. It just seems awfully sweet."

"I'm a sweet man," I teased.

She snorted but her lips quirked up, and I felt like I'd won.

It was insane the power that little woman had over me without even trying. No matter how dark my thoughts were, how sullen I was, being beside her made me feel better. I teased, I smiled…I breathed. She terrified me.

I stayed a bit longer with her, settling in a sort of peace at just watching her cook and listening to her ramble. I'd noticed she tended to ramble when she was nervous and I was making her nervous. I just hoped it was in a good way, the best way. The way she made me nervous.

"You know, I think we can stop the whole process

around the meals. You know who I am." I tried to look calm as my heart sped up in my chest. "Maybe we can dine together at night."

She nodded and looked up, meeting my eyes with a bright smile that made me feel like a superhero. "I'd love that… But not tonight. I've got plans."

I deflated a bit and it annoyed me. I wanted to know what her plans were but I had no right to ask… It couldn't be that exciting though, could it? She was stuck here with me in the middle of nowhere. The guards have been ordered to stay away from her unless there was immediate danger.

"Sure." I nodded.

"Tomorrow?" She smiled again. Fuck, did I enjoy that smile. "I'll bring us pizza from town. What do you say?"

Ah, yes, I'd forgotten it was her weekly visit with her brother. "No pineapple?"

She chuckled. "No pineapple," she confirmed.

My elation was immediately tamped down when she added, "I'll ask Dom what kind of pizza he wants me to bring."

"Yeah, sure." *Dom will join us over my dead body, fiery girl. Dinner's you and me.* I stood up. "I've got to go. See you later?"

She nodded. "Yes, of course! I'll leave you some cassatelles in this box," she said, pointing at the rose-covered metal box on the counter. "You'll let me know what you think?"

"Absolutely I will but if I have to base on the smell so far? I'm sure it will be divine."

I was glad she didn't ask me what I was going to do because truth be told? I didn't have a clue. Dom was working with the new guards and I didn't feel like drinking so much anymore mainly due to the ray of sunshine who was taking care of my home.

I decided to use my time to be productive instead of self-destructive for once and looked into Cassie's situation and into her brother's. Maybe I could help... Maybe I could become the hero I wanted to be for her.

I was startled when I heard the ring of dinner. How long was I concentrating on what I was doing?

I looked down at my notepad and all the names I'd written down and had to call to help Cassie's situation.

I was a little disappointed when I found the library empty except for the amazing food waiting for me at the table.

I couldn't help but smile when I settled at the table and noticed the little pink metal box with the Post-it on top. 'I think they're delicious. Let me know what you think. ;)'

I was positive they were going to be delicious because she was a good cook and because she'd made them. Just that made it so much better already.

I ate quickly. I now had a reason to seek her despite her having plans this evening. I suspected these plans were either with Dom, which I was not very fond of or some Skype calls with her friend which I didn't really mind.

I brought my plate and box to the kitchen, but she was not there. I stood in the middle of the empty kitchen and realized that the warmth I'd felt there this afternoon was all her. Now it was just an empty room full of painful memories.

I took another cassatelle and walked upstairs. Her bedroom door was cracked open and I stopped as I heard her laugh; it was so carefree, so lovely. I smiled. I loved hearing her laugh. My smile froze on my face when I heard Dom laugh, my mood taking a dark turn almost immediately.

I'd never experienced jealousy before, not even when Francesca left me for Savio. I never cared enough to be jealous. It was unfamiliar and so unsettling, I hated it.

I knocked at the door, trying my best to rein my temper and my growing desire to punch Dom unconscious.

"Come in!"

I walked into the room, ready to tell him off for something…anything really to have him leave this room, but what I saw caught me off guard. I could only stand there, my mouth slightly agape like an idiot.

They were both in matching pink robes on her bed, surrounded by popcorn and other sweets. They both had pink headbands and some weird green mask on their faces like some kind of facial of some sort.

"Cosa c'è di sbagliato in te, stronzo?" I asked my head of security who looked more like an ugly oversized woman at that moment than the cold mafioso killer he was supposed to be.

Dom's lips quirked up. "We're having a girls' night."

"Ah." I nodded. "You finally grew a vagina? It was to be expected."

Cassie rolled her eyes and slapped Dom's arm playfully. I envied the kinship that had developed between them.

"Dom bought me a spa basket to cheer me up after the bad news I got from the social services." She smiled at him. "It was for two so I invited him to join."

I frowned. "What bad news?" I asked gruffly. I was getting more and more annoyed by the minute. Not only was she seeking him during her free time, but she was confiding in him too.

I'd never envied Dom before—I guessed there was a first for everything.

She waved her hand dismissively. "Don't worry about it; it's okay."

I want to worry about it, I thought but kept quiet. Dom was looking at me like I was a science experiment, analyzing every word, every move... I hated it.

"Do you want to join us?" she asked and it settled my annoyance to know that she didn't want to spend alone time with Dom.

Join you, alone? Yes, absolutely. Join you and Barbie Dom? I'll pass. I shook my head. "No, I just wanted to tell you the cassatelles were delicious."

She beamed, resting her hand on her heart. "Thank you! I'm so glad you liked them. Next time I'll make you the red velvet pecan brownies you like."

That warmed my chest more than I could say.

I smiled at her and that also felt strange. How long was it since I truly smiled?

I turned to Dom. "Also I'm glad I caught you. Sparring tomorrow? Eight?"

Dom's smile widened; he knew why I wanted to spar. *Well, good luck, asshole. You might think I'm an out-of-shape alcoholic, but I can fight dirty.*

"I'll see you girls later."

———

I made it to the training room only a few minutes before Dom came down with a shit-eating grin on his face.

He knew I was pissed off about last night and he enjoyed it.

I cracked my neck and stepped into the sparring ring, getting ready.

"Not even a little chitchat?" he asked, his grin turning taunting.

"I thought you've done enough chitchatting during your girls' night."

Dom shook his head. "We've not sparred in a very long time. I missed it." He removed his shirt, rolling his shoulders.

I glowered, looking down at the tattoo on his chest, matching mine... The dagger, the rosary, and the pledge binding us. Our branding, our allegiance to our blood, our legacy, our commitment. Our motto was Honor, Protect, Conquer—honor our vows, protect our blood, conquer our enemies.

"I think it's time for you to go for a visit to *The Rectory*, to relieve some pressure." The Rectory was a high-end very expensive sex club but also the only one in the state having professionals able to cope with Dom's sexual preferences.

"The Rectory?" He nodded. "Maybe but is it for my well-being or do you want me to leave you alone with her?" He chuckled. "You can just ask. I may grant you the wish."

"Cazzo." I hissed as my elbow came out in one movement, hitting him right in the eye socket.

"Fuck," he growled, taking a step back and bringing his hand up to his eye. "You're playing dirty, Montanari."

"And you're not?" I asked, taking a fighting stance, my hands up in fists, protecting my face from retaliation. "Hogging her, being the perfect and sweet gentleman." I threw a jab. He dodged to the left, finally taking a fighting stance too. I meant business and he knew it. "Does she know what you are?"

He sighed. "Who's to say I'm not that guy?"

He threw a punch and I stopped it with my forearm. I gritted my teeth as the pain of the blow reverberated up my arm, straight to my head. I was more out of shape than I'd anticipated.

"I don't want her like that, and she doesn't see *me* like that."

The way he emphasized the word 'me' made my heart leap in my chest like a stupid teenager. Did he mean that she saw me like that? Fuck me, I had issues.

"What's happening with her?" I asked as we circled each other, both of us reluctant to throw another punch.

"What do you mean? Her life went to shit; you need to be more specific."

Here he was, annoying me again. He knew exactly what I meant.

I feinted with a left hook and punched him with the right. "Stop being an asshole."

He chuckled, rubbing at his jaw. "You're so easy to rile up."

I was, and it was all because of her. I was always good at keeping everything close to my heart before, but she was like an open wound letting all the feelings out.

"Domenico…" I warned him.

He rolled his eyes. "It had to do with the FBI. They'd put her in the list of 'person of interests' for her parents' murders, thinking she knew more than she let on."

I stopped moving around. "This is stupid; this woman would not hurt a fly."

"Obviously! And the FBI knows that too, but the bureaucracy is taking its time and as long as she is not officially removed from the list by a judge, she can't take her little brother out. She has to be supervised at each visit because she's a flight risk, and it's taking a toll on her because it is never-ending."

I nodded. "Why didn't you tell me that? I could have helped."

"Why didn't you ask her how she was doing instead of pouting like a five-year-old? Is it because when she touched you it made you feel something in your heart and in your pants?"

"Cazzo!" I threw a punch which he dodged and punched me right in the kidney. "Fuck!" I growled, holding my flank, and I almost folded in two trying to get my breath back.

"We're done," Dom announced ominously, getting out of the ring and grabbing a bottle of water. "Next time you want to spar, remember I've been training every day while you've been soaking your organs in alcohol for the past few years, okay?"

I threw him a withering look, making him laugh.

He wiped his face with a towel and looked at me as I rubbed my flank which still burned like a bitch. His face morphed from teasing to serious. "Also, next time, instead of acting like a stupid alpha caveman, talk to me, man."

I frowned, unsure where he was going with that.

"Even if you don't think that way about me—you *are* my best friend. My brother in every way but in blood. I've been offered everything by almost everyone to leave your side and join theirs, but I've preferred to stay with your sorry, angry, and suicidal ass than look for something else."

He took a deep breath and I exited the ring, walking toward him, emotion cloaking at my throat, making it hard to swallow. This wasn't something we did in the famiglia, show our feelings. Feelings were a weakness; we fought our hardest not to have them, and if heaven forbid we caught feelings, we were fighting like beasts to hide them from the world.

"Cassie is one of a kind. I saw her bring life back to you, and I'll kill myself before trying to take that from you but if you don't move, another will because she's something, that woman. She is young, yes, clueless of our world, of our ways? Most definitely. But she is brave, strong, and loyal. She can handle it; she can handle *you*. She is a fucking unicorn, brother."

I was now standing in front of Dom and did something I never thought I'd ever do. I pulled him into a hug.

"Thank you for staying with me. You saved my life," I admitted quite reluctantly.

"*Ti voglio bene,*" he stated, hugging me back.

It took me aback having Dom admit that he loved me, and I loved him too—with the same brotherly love that he gave me, and despite everything I couldn't tell him.

So I told him the next best thing… "*Io ti proteggerò sempre.*" I'll always protect you. It was the only way I could reciprocate and with the way his hold tightened, I knew he understood.

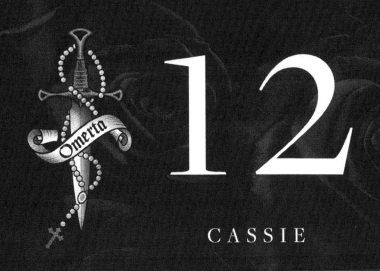

CASSIE

I was getting ready to leave to go see my brother when Luca appeared in the kitchen.

"Are you okay?" I asked, shouldering my handbag.

He cocked an eyebrow. "Good afternoon to you too."

I blushed, that was rude and I was happy to see him, once again getting that giddiness in the pit of my stomach. I liked that he didn't try to hide his face anymore; he was looking at me head-on.

"I'm sorry. I just didn't expect to see you. Is there anything I can help you with?"

He shook his head. "No, I know you're going to town and I was wondering if you can bring dinner?"

"I thought—" I stopped and shook my head. We had agreed for pizza yesterday but maybe it was his way to come and talk to me and I enjoyed seeing him, talking to him. Why did I question it? "Of course, I'll bring pizza."

He approached me and leaned against the kitchen island. I could see him from the corner of my eyes. I could feel his body heat, smell his subtle cologne. I closed my eyes and didn't even realize I leaned toward him, taking a deep breath.

"Are you okay?"

I jerked upright and blushed so brightly I felt like my face was on fire.

"Yes, sure. Fine."

"If you say so."

I nodded, avoiding his eyes as I could hear the smile in his voice. I hadn't fooled him; of course, I hadn't.

I cleared my throat. "Is Dom around?" I turned toward him and I didn't miss him tense, his lips purse. Was he jealous? No, that was ludicrous. I've seen the type of girls he was seeing before all of this —I was not even a blip on that man's radar.

"No, sorry to disappoint, he is in the city for the day."

Something he forgot to mention last night. "Ah." I waved my hand dismissively. "No, it's okay. It's just we're getting more flowers today, and I can't wait any longer if I want to make it to Jude's on time and—"

"I'll take care of them." He nodded.

"Are you sure?"

He rolled his eyes. I enjoyed that little playfulness in him even if it was rare.

"Okay then." I grabbed the cake I baked from the counter. "You can have them set by the atrium. The weather is supposed to hold for a few days." I jerked my head toward the general direction of the garden. "Just make sure it is only the pink flowers he is delivering today. We ordered some roses, some azalea, some begonias…" I sighed, I didn't need to bore him with all the details.

"No worries. I'm sure I can handle it." He buried his hands in his jeans' pockets. "Pink flowers were Arabella's favorites."

I finally looked at him with a small smile, the embarrassment from before gone. "I know it is. And purple." I pointed to the other side of the garden. "This garden is an ode to her."

He looked away and despite the beard, I could see his jaw budge. Did I offend him by doing that? I thought it would make him happy.

"Luca?" I put the cake back on the counter, moving from one foot to the other with discomfort. "I-I can change it, I'm sorry I thought—"

He looked at me, his face a turmoil of emotions. "Thank you."

I let out a breath. "What?"

He jerked his head toward my plan on the table. "This means more than you think. You are one of a kind, Cassandra West."

I waved my hand dismissively, my chest warming under the praise. It was not something I had been used to with the parents I had.

I picked up the cake again, attracting his attention to it.

"Happy birthday?" he read on it.

I let out a chuckle. "Yes, I know it's kind of sad to bake your own birthday cake but—" I shrugged.

He stilled. "It is your...birthday?"

"Yes. No."

He cocked his head to the side. "Okay..."

"No." I chuckled. "My birthday is on Sunday, but it's not a big deal, you know. My parents have never celebrated our birthdays. They never considered our birthing as being an achievement on our part."

"Lovely."

I snorted. "Indeed. Anyway, it's always him and me for birthdays and since I can only see him on Thursday afternoons, we're doing it today."

He nodded. "Fine, we'll do something on Sunday then. You, me, and...Dom."

My chest warmed at the attention. This man was supposed to be a scary beast and yet he was showing so much more attention than my parents ever showed me.

"Luca, no. You don't have to."

"I know I don't. I want to. Come on, we all need a little celebration. Sunday—it's a promise."

I smiled and gave him a nod. I remembered what

he said—he didn't make promises lightly and somehow I was excited for my birthday for the first time in a very long time.

"Oh, I left some new books for your brother on the console by the door. I'll see you tonight."

"Of course. Thank you again."

I watched him walk out of the room and I left my eyes trail down his butt. I may have been innocent but I was not a saint, and this man's ass in tight jeans was a work of art.

———

I frowned when I parked in front of the foster care home and found Jude and Amy waiting in front of the door.

Jude was wearing his jacket, grinning from ear to ear and bouncing on his feet with excitement.

"Is everything okay?" I asked, getting out of the car, my heart already speeding up.

"Cassie!" he shouted, running toward me and throwing himself at me, making me huff as all the air exited my lungs. "We can go out!"

I hugged him back and threw a questioning look toward Amy. I hoped he hadn't misunderstood; it would break both of our hearts.

She smiled at me and nodded. "Yes, you can take him out this afternoon. Just bring him back by five," she said, approaching us.

"How?" I shook my head. "You know what, never mind how. I get to take him out."

Jude let go of me and turned to Amy. "Thank you."

She winked at him before looking at me again.

"Does it mean that all this mess is behind us?" I meant the FBI interest in me, but I didn't want to worry Jude any more than he already was.

She shrugged. "Not completely. It's on its way but the bureaucracy is never-ending. But my boss said a Federal Judge Martin had cleared it with the district." She shrugged. "Unsure what happened here but just enjoy it—no more supervised visits."

I looked up to the sky and blinked back my tears as my heart swelled with gratitude for the broken, scarred man I was sure was the source of this small miracle.

"I'll bring him back at five." I looked at Jude. "So what do you want to do?"

He shrugged. "Anything, I don't care."

"Okay." I opened the back door of the car and waited for him to fasten his seat belt.

I sat in the driver's seat and met his eyes in the rearview mirror. "What do you say I take you to the bookstore and you can pick some books, and then we can go have a hot chocolate and a muffin from Starbucks?"

"Can we go to the comic book store instead? I love the books your boss is giving me."

"You do?" I asked, turning around on my seat and

looking at the small pile of books I'd set on the seat beside him.

He nodded, running his fingers on the burgundy leather cover of the book on top. "Yes, you will need to pick up the other ones when you drive me back."

I nodded and turned to start the car. I only had a few hours with him and I needed to make them count.

"You'll tell him thank you for me, won't you, Cassie?"

"Of course, I will. I tell him every week."

After Jude browsed for over thirty minutes and we bought three comic books, we settled at a table in the back of the local Starbucks and I was glad that I didn't get the lingering glares full of hate I had during our parents' trial.

I looked at my brother as he followed his ritual of breaking down his chocolate muffin into little pieces before eating them. Despite Amy's reassuring words, I couldn't help the wave of worry that settled in me every time I looked at him and how small he was for his age, how pale and delicate.

"How are you, munchkin, really?" I asked him as he took one of the little bits of the muffin from his plate.

He nodded. "I'm good, Cassie." He shrugged. "The center was not good at first. The boys were mean but I'm staying with the younger ones now, and the two mean ones are gone anyway." He gave me a small smile.

That was something that was true about emotionally abused and neglected children—they made do of everything, settling for much less than they deserved. But that would not happen to Jude; I would give him all he deserved.

"I will get you out soon."

"Yes, I know. Amy said you have a good job. When do you think we can go home?"

"We can't go home, Jude. The house..." I stopped, not sure how I could tell him that all we had left from our lives were the four cardboard boxes that were now stored at Mrs. Broussard's apartment. How could I tell him that everything, and I meant everything including his bike, had been seized and had been sold to pay for the victims' compensation?

"I don't mean the house; I mean home with you." He shrugged. "Wherever it is, it's home with you, Cassie."

I took a deep breath, trying to rein in my tears at his words. My brother was much wiser than his age and his love for me, the same as my love for him, was really what kept me going.

"By the summer it should be good. My boss is helping me to get you back." I believed Luca, I truly did because despite everything I knew about him, I could see he was a man of honor, and the kind of loyalty Dom had for him was not something you could buy. He had earned that.

"I like your boss."

I had to chuckle at that. I could almost imagine a meeting between Luca and Jude; that would be one for the history books. "You don't know my boss."

"That's not true."

I tensed for a minute, not sure I liked the idea of Luca going to see my brother behind my back. "Okay?"

"The books he gives me, he picks very well." He nodded at himself like he was having some internal debate. "I like him," he repeated.

I leaned back on my chair. "He is a good man." And he was, even if he couldn't see it himself. What he did for me? Allowing me to see Jude all by myself —it was priceless.

I could almost picture it, Jude moving in the house with me. It was a silly vision, of course. It was just a job I had there; I was not building a life, and yet I couldn't stop thinking about how much Jude would love the house, especially the library.

"He wrote to me."

"He what?"

"Luca, he left me a note in the first book and I replied."

"And you hid that from me?" I was more surprised than angry. Jude's Asperger's made it so hard for him to hide things.

"He is answering my questions," he replied. "Something you're not really doing."

Ouch that hurt and yet it was fair. "I'm just trying to protect you."

"I know, but he doesn't have to and I like talking to him."

I was dying to read their letters, but I wouldn't do it. Jude had a very hard time creating relationships and if he managed to do that through letters? Who was I to stop it? I would not betray him and if Luca helped him in any way, I just had to accept it.

"You can read his letters if you want," he said, taking me by surprise while I drove him back to the Home.

"It's okay, Jude. You have the right to have a friendship with Luca."

"I know, but it's okay if you want to. I'll go get the books in my room."

I waited a grand total of eight seconds after he went in before reaching for the pile of books on the back seat.

The letter was folded in half just in the cover of the first one.

Kiddo,

I'm glad you decided to keep on writing and I'm proud of you for sticking up for yourself. Being small is not an issue, it's an advantage. Let people underestimate you, it will serve you, believe me.

I know you are questioning everything but sometimes

there is just no way to explain. I can't tell you why your parents did what they did. What made them that way or if they will ever feel guilty, but know something I am certain of. What they are is not what makes you. What they did doesn't define you.

Look at your sister, so fierce, strong, and courageous. Your parents are not half the woman she is. Read this book and see that it is not where you come from that defines you but rather who you want to be.

I'd like to tell you that things get easier when you grow up, that you can spot the villain just by his black cape and the good guy with his sheriff star, but this is not life and I'm sorry kiddo. I truly am.

You can be a villain with good intentions and honor and you can be a good man who slips at the first hardship.

I traced the words with my thumb. 'A villain with good intentions,' that was what Luca was, I was sure of it. He had a good heart no matter how much he was trying to fight it. How was I supposed to resist him? Stop myself from pinning for him?

I looked up to see Jude and Amy approaching the car with a bag. I put the letter back in the book.

"Here are the books," Jude chimed, extending me the bag.

I exchanged the books from one bag to the other. "Thank you. I- Oh! I forgot I baked a birthday cake and—" I looked up at Amy. "Maybe you can take it in and share it?" I looked down at Jude and winked. "It's red velvet."

Amy nodded eagerly. "We'll never say no to cake."

"Perfect." I leaned down to kiss Jude's head. "I'll call you Saturday. Love you."

"Love you too!"

I waited for them to go back in the building before going to collect the pizza.

By the time I reached the property, it was raining buckets, and I was worried about the bulbs that were delivered today.

I rested the pizza on the kitchen table and rushed outside just to see Luca, soaked to the bone, running inside the greenhouse with the bulbs.

I felt guilty. "No, it's okay, leave it!" I shouted. "I'll come and do it."

Luca motioned me to stay behind as he finished.

I rushed into the laundry room and waited for him by the door with a big towel.

When Luca came back he was shivering. He grabbed the towel and tried to dry himself off.

"It won't work like that. You better go change your clothes."

He nodded. "Yes, I'll be right back."

"Thank you," I said before he exited the kitchen.

He waved his hand dismissively. "It was nothing; it took me five minutes."

I shook my head. "Yes, thanks for that but also for my brother. I know it's you." I walked toward him. "You don't know what it means to me."

He looked down at me, his eyes indescribable. "I'm glad I could help."

I was not sure what came over me, maybe it was just how hot he looked all wet, his clothes stuck to his skin, showing his impressive muscles.

I reached up, stood on my tiptoes, and grabbed his face, pulling him down to me, locking my lips with his on a chaste kiss.

He froze as my lips touched his and he didn't move until I broke the kiss.

"Thank you," I said again, blushing under the craziness of my actions.

He cleared his throat, took a step back, and then a second as if he were escaping a wild animal.

I looked at him, both mortified by my actions and hurt by the rejection, before spinning around and running upstairs to the security of my bedroom.

God, what got into me?

13

CASSIE

I took a deep breath and looked at myself in the mirror once more, trying to settle my stomach.

A birthday dinner between friends. That's all it was and yet, I couldn't calm my nerves.

I had ordered a new dress for the occasion and did my hair and makeup even better than I'd done for prom.

I wasn't sure what was going to happen but it would be the first time I saw him after the kiss on Thursday night. It had been chaste and sprung by gratitude—at least that was what I kept telling myself.

Then why did you use so much effort? a little voice taunted me.

He had not said anything. He had messaged me a

couple of times on Friday to tell me he was ordering dinner for the birthday and also to be down by eight p.m., but after then, complete radio silence.

I shook my head and rushed downstairs before I could change my mind.

The small library had a 'Happy 21st' banner above the fireplace. There was also some food and a small cake on the table as well as a bottle of champagne and a couple of gifts wrapped in silver at the back of the table.

Dom was leaning against the fireplace in light-blue jeans and a cream V-neck cardigan that I had to admit looked amazing against his olive skin.

"Hi?" I sighed, why did it sound like a question? I was just taken aback by Luca's absence. Maybe he was still in setup mode. I was a little early.

"Birthday girl!" Dom beamed before coming toward me and hugging me. "How does it feel to be able to drink?" he asked once he let me go.

I shrugged.

"I got you the best stuff there is. We'll do it responsibly," he added with a cheeky grin.

I looked around once more as if Luca would just appear in a dark corner.

"Where's Luca?"

"Ah, yes. He got held up." He scratched the back of his neck, visibly uncomfortable. "He told me to apologize and to wish you a happy birthday."

Saying I was offended and hurt was an understatement. I'd never taken Luca Montanari for an avoider and he gave me his word.

I shook my head as anger filled my chest as hot as coal. He didn't even bother sending me a note himself.

"No." I swirled around and exited the room.

Dom caught my wrist just as I was about to go upstairs.

"Where are you going?"

"I'm going to see him." I nudged my wrist but Dom kept it loosely in his grip. "I want him to tell me face-to-face why he is not keeping his word, why he made me a promise he won't keep, and why is such a stupid little kiss such a—"

"He *kissed* you?" Dom asked, his eyes wide with surprise.

I blushed with embarrassment. I didn't mean to admit that and somehow I thought Luca would have told him why he was avoiding the party—to avoid the confrontation with the stupid little girl with the embarrassing infatuation for the big bad wolf.

"No, *I* kissed him." I shook my head. "Not really the point there."

"I don't think that you going up there is a good idea." He jerked his head toward the top of the stairs. "I'll go talk to him."

"No, you won't. I'll go one way or another. Unless you're planning on restraining me," I replied, looking at his hand still circling my wrist.

He looked down and let go of my arm immediately. "No, of course not! I would never touch you in a way that makes you uncomfortable."

He said that with much more heat and conviction than the situation warranted but it was all I needed.

"Fine then. I'll go see him and he can send me away if he wants!" I spun on my heel and went upstairs, glad that Dom only had my back and couldn't see how worried I was at confronting Luca.

Would he treat me kindly? Or would he go back at being the beast he had been at the beginning? I was the one who got rejected after that kiss; I was the one who was supposed to hide and heal the slashes it caused at my barely existing confidence, not the other way around.

I walked into his office to find it empty.

I turned around and looked around the long corridor. "Which one is his room?"

Dom sighed. "I think it's a terrible idea."

I nodded. "Your concern is duly noted and when things explode in my face, you'll be free to give me a big fat 'I told you so.'"

He shook his head. "This is not what I want. I love having you here. I just don't want—"

"Which room, Dom?" I snapped. Lord, did I change in the past few weeks. If you had told me just a couple of months ago that I would demand things from a Mafia guy packing two guns, I would have said you'd lost your mind, yet here we were.

He looked heavenward and said something in Italian I didn't understand before pointing to a door on the left.

I nodded and followed the direction, tightening my shaky hands into fists.

I took a deep breath before knocking sharply on the door. When no answer came, I knocked louder.

"Luca. Mr. Montanari?" I wasn't sure I was allowed to call him Luca anymore. "I need to talk to you."

I waited for a few seconds and growled.

"Fine!" I opened the door and the first thing that struck me, other than the darkness, was the smell. The smell of illness—not the pungent smell of vomit, but the smell of sweat, fever...

I turned on the lights. "What the—"

I rushed to the bed to find Luca, shivering and looking ashen, his dark hair stuck with sweat on his forehead.

I brought my hand to his forehead and hissed. "He is burning up!" I looked up at Dom, now leaning against the closed door, a concerned look on his face.

"Did you know he was like that?"

Dom pursed his lips and nodded once.

I shook my head. "Unbelievable." I pulled back the covers and Luca moaned.

His chest was striking and crossed with three angry red scars as if he had been mauled by a bear, but I didn't even have a chance to linger as I noticed

161

the wet spots around his body, probably caused by his heavy sweating.

"We need to call a doctor." I took his wrist and looked at my watch. "His heart is much too fast, Dom! How long has he been sick?"

"A couple of days," he replied quite reluctantly.

It explained his silence but at the same time, it made me so angry to know he'd let his state get so bad.

"We need a doctor; call one now!" I ordered.

"No doctor…" Luca whispered.

Dom walked closer. "He doesn't want a doctor, for many reasons, and we can't negotiate on that. Call a doctor now and the whole family will know he is weak. This will cause more problems than you can imagine."

I knew that when he said family he meant Mafia. "Stupid Mafia," I grumbled.

Dom gave me a mirthless smile. "You have no idea. Can- Can you do something?"

My heart started to pump faster in my chest. I was only a student nurse, I was not all-knowing but what other choice did I have? I had to save him.

"I can try." I shook my head. "Can anyone get me meds? A thermometer? Anything at all?"

"I can get anything you want."

"Even meds on prescription?" I asked doubtfully. "You know I'm not allowed to presc—"

"Anything, Cassie. Just tell me."

"Okay, take notes." I pointed at the notepad and pen on Luca's night table. "A thermometer, a stethoscope, co-amoxiclav for IV, paracetamol, aspirin, some 0.45%, and some 0.9% sodium chloride and a drip of some sorts, an oximeter, oxygen…just in case. Just that for now and come back as soon as you've given the list to someone, okay?"

He rushed out and I could concentrate on Luca again.

I tried to sit him up a little on the pillows but he was dead weight and much too heavy. "Why are you so stubborn? You need a doctor. I'm just a nurse."

Dom came back breathlessly. "Luciano's going. I said it was for you, that you were sick. He'll be back in thirty."

I waved my hand dismissively. "We need to get the fever down immediately."

"Okay, what do you need?"

"I need to put him in a cold bath; he will hate it but it's the only way…" I looked at his face, his pale skin, his labored breath. "To be fair he is so out of it, I doubt he'll even realize. Can you carry him to the bathroom?"

He nodded, pushing up his sleeves before taking off his holster and putting it at the end of the bed. "Just get started on the bath." He pointed at the bathroom. "We'll be right over."

I rushed into the enormous white marble bathroom and started to fill the jacuzzi size bathtub he had in a corner of the room.

"You know, I think Mrs. Broussard's entire apartment could fit in this bathroom," I said as Dom dragged a barely conscious Luca into the bathroom.

"Fuck," Dom growled, adjusting his hold around Luca's waist. "He's heavier than he looks."

I rolled my eyes. "The guy is six two. What did you expect?"

"I'm six four," Dom replied with a wink.

"Congratulations, you win." I cleared my throat. "I...um... I need to get him out of his soaked pajamas."

"Okay." He pulled Luca's arm tighter around his neck. "I got him."

I took a deep breath, crouching down. *He's just a patient, Cassie. You've done this a hundred times; it's nothing more. Except that I didn't have feelings for my patients. I didn't kiss my patients. I didn't get my stomach in knots when I thought of them.*

I pulled his pants down, doing my best to avoid looking at his cock, which proved to be impossible, and even soft it was big.

I stood up quickly, hoping my cheeks were not as red as I thought they were. "Help me get him into the water."

As we lowered him down in the water, he started to jerk and moan.

He opened his eyes and looked at me. "*Tesorina*," he croaked before closing his eyes again.

"What is that?"

Dom shook his head. "I don't know."

"Just stay with him for a few, please. Make sure he doesn't drown."

"Where are you going?" Dom asked as he settled his arm behind Luca's back to hold him up.

"I'm going to open the window to freshen the air and change his bed. I'll be right back."

I opened the window and the whiff of fresh air made me realize how bad that room smelled. Why did he let it get that bad? Couldn't he show any weakness? He was just sick or was it something else? Something much more terrifying. Did he actually want to die? I didn't want to think it was the case but he had been quite anchored on a path to self-destruction when I moved in. I thought he was better; I thought I was helping but maybe it was what I wanted to see.

I shook my head as I moved Dom's guns carefully before stripping the bed.

Was that what my life was now? Being around guns? Fixing sick Mafia bosses? I shook my head. It was not just any Mafia boss. It was Luca, and despite everything, I saw his light shining through the cracks and I wanted to see more. I changed his bed and rummaged through his chest drawers for a pair of pajama bottoms. We didn't need him to overheat.

"Okay, I think we're good now," I told Dom, rushing into the bathroom a little breathless.

"Hey, just take a second. You don't have to be so rushed."

"Actually I do, he let it get really bad. He could die. I just…" I looked at Luca and despite still being out of it he looked less flushed. "He needs to be okay."

Dom nodded silently.

"Okay." I pressed the button to empty the tub. "Just hold him up. I need to dry him." I was pleased with how mechanically I could do it, and now that the initial shock was over at seeing his naked body in all his glory, I could finally concentrate on getting him dried off.

Once we were done and we'd settled him back in bed, I let out a small breath of relief as I touched his forehead. It was still hot but not as insane as before.

"The fever is down for now but we need to act fast. Could you go check if we have everything we need?"

Dom made two trips to bring everything back upstairs, and I realized that doing all that didn't even make him breathless. It was insane how fit that man was.

I asked Dom to help Luca up and despite my basic training with a stethoscope, I could say straightaway that he had a severe chest infection. The wheezing and crackling were unmistakable.

"Okay, as I suspected, it's a bad chest infection. I

even suspect pneumonia." I shook my head. He had been so reckless with his health. Idiotic, self-destructive man.

Dom just leaned against the wall, his face grim. He was genuinely worried about Luca, and once again I noticed that their relationship must have been much more than just bodyguard and boss. They had been friends once upon a time.

"He'll be okay. I'm going to fix him." I said that with much more certainty than I felt. I hadn't even finished my nursing training and while I took care of many patients at the hospital, I'd never done it on my own and certainly not unsupervised. Yet here I was making stupid promises I wasn't sure I could keep.

"If anyone can do it, it's you."

No, it's a properly trained ER doctor in an actual hospital, I thought bitterly as I set the oximeter on Luca's finger before setting up the IV with the saline then injecting the antibiotic directly into the bag.

I looked at the oximeter reading. His oxygen was in the low 90s. Definitely a source of concern. I took his temperature and it was still 102... Lord, how high must it have been before?

"You know I'm not an expert, right?" I told Dom after I was done setting Luca up. I covered him up with a thin sheet. I had to be careful not to overheat him.

He jerked his head toward the drip. "You seem like one to me."

I let out a weary laugh as I sat on the chair by Luca's bed. "I'm—I was just a nursing student. If he is not better in the next twenty-four hours, we will call a doctor, okay?"

He ran a hand over his face. "He won't like it."

I shrugged. "I'd rather he be mad at me than dead, so I'll take it. You can go and rest now. I'll keep watch tonight."

Dom looked at me with his dark eyes in a way that seemed to see deep into my soul. "You kissed him, huh?"

I rolled my eyes, mentally cursing myself for opening my big fat mouth. "It meant nothing."

"Sure it didn't. You want to know why I trust you with him over any other doctor or nurse? Because it's not fear or duty driving you to make him better. You care about him deeply."

I opened my mouth to deny it but he raised his hand.

"Don't bother, Cassie. You're so easy to read and I rather you be honest, okay? Now is not the time to play games."

"He is Mafia," I replied.

Dom nodded. "So am I."

"Yes I know but—" *But what, silly girl?*

"But you're not falling in love with me and it's the fundamental difference."

I shook my head. "He's so much older than me, and broken and self-destructive and—" I stopped.

"And?"

"I'm just me." It was a rather lame answer but I hoped it conveyed what I felt. I was just an ordinary girl, inexperienced, barely out of adolescence. A girl who thought knew a lot but was more naïve of our world than I ever thought. A girl… Just not enough for someone like him.

Dom cocked his head to the side. "You're saying that as if it's a bad thing."

I shrugged.

He sighed. "Can I bring you anything?"

"Yes, please. Could you make me a thermos of coffee and bring me the cookie box I have on the kitchen counter?"

"Sure, be right up."

Once Dom brought me everything, I grabbed a book from Luca's bedside and settled on the seat again, setting my alarm to ring every hour.

It took three days before I actually started to worry a little less. The fever had broken completely, and he seemed a little more alert and awake even if he mostly spoke in Italian.

On the fourth day, he was awake a little longer and I managed to feed him a little broth and some toast; however, he didn't make a lot of sense and continued to speak in Italian a lot.

"Mia piccola guaritrice, non lasciarmi innamorare di te. Spezzerebbe i nostri cuori. Ci farebbe male a entrambi," he had mumbled after he had finished his food.

"Sure, okay."

He smiled and nodded his head as if I had given him the right answer before he fell back asleep.

"He sleeps a lot."

I startled, turning my head briskly. "How long have you been standing there?" I asked Dom who was leaning on the doorframe.

"Not long. I didn't want to interrupt."

I chuckled. "There's nothing to interrupt; he is talking Italian nonsense."

"Nonsense, yeah." He looked at his watch and frowned. "Aren't you supposed to go see your brother?"

I shook my head. "I called Amy, the social worker. I can't leave Luca yet. I mean he is stable but I'd rather stay here. I'll have a video call with Jude with my laptop."

"That's kind of you, but you don't have to do that. You've gone above and beyond for him already. How long have you left his room in the past few days? For showers and quick naps. You need a break."

I nodded. I would not deny it; my face reflected my lack of sleep. "He is really getting better. I promise if he keeps like that, I'll step out tomorrow."

"You saved his life," Dom insisted. "Without you —" He shook his head, his Adam's apple bobbing as he swallowed through his emotions.

Once again I could see that their relationship was much more than boss and bodyguard. Luca was his family. I saw the love in his eyes; it was a little like I looked at Jude.

"I'm sure that in the end you would have gone against his orders." I rearranged the covers on Luca. "But yeah, you're right. He is too stubborn for his own good."

Dom rolled his eyes. "Pot meet kettle."

I looked up at him, crossing my eyes and sticking my tongue to the side.

"Hot."

I chuckled. "I know."

He sighed. "Listen. I must go to town for a while. We need more of the antibiotics and I've forgotten to order the food this week. Do you need anything?"

I shrugged. "Well, if you pass by the candy store…" I trailed off. I was so lucky I had a good metabolism because with all the sweets I ate, I should be five times my size.

"That's a given." He looked toward Luca once more. "Okay, I'll be back soon."

I went to the bathroom and wet a cloth. "You know you're lucky to have people who love you and care for you so deeply," I whispered as I gently ran the cloth on his face.

I went downstairs, made myself a sandwich, and brought up some food for him too, then settled on the seat by his bed.

I called Amy's phone.

"Hi." I smiled seeing my brother's face on the

screen. "I'm sorry for missing our weekly meeting, munchkin. I really am."

He waved his hand in a dismissive gesture. "It's okay, Cassie. I have lots of school work. I didn't finish the books you brought last week. How is Luca? Amy said he was sick."

I nodded. "Yes, but he is getting better now. He scared me." I was not sure why I admitted that to my kid brother but somehow I had to tell someone.

I had been so scared that night. I had been glad that my training had taken over, but I'd been so scared of him dying and the reason behind it was just as terrifying. I cared deeply for Gianluca Montanari, broken Mafia boss in exile… I didn't predict anything good and certainly not a happy ending for me.

"You're the best, Cassie. You always fixed me up." His grin widened.

I cocked my head to the side as a wave of tenderness submerged me. I'd been Jude's mother in so many ways, cleaning his wounds when he fell or taking care of him when he got a cold.

"You're right. I'm a superhero."

"Superheroine! You're my Wonder Woman."

I laughed. "Wow, Wonder Woman? That's one hell of a compliment." I pointed at my red hair. "I thought I'd be more of a Black Widow or a Mystique"

"No, they both have a dark side but you don't. You're all good like Diana."

"I love you, little brother."

We kept on talking for a few minutes, about his schoolwork and the books that Luca had given him. Jude was now addicted to Arsene Lupin, the gentleman thief...a thief with morals and a code.

Yes, leave it to Luca to share that with my brother.

I promised my brother to take him for the biggest ice cream in history next week to make up for it, but he didn't seem that upset either way. He had his books; he was happy.

"I'm sorry for scaring you," I heard a voice say as soon as I closed my laptop.

I jumped off my chair, almost crashing it on the floor "Jesus!"

"Not quite, I almost met him though."

"Not funny," I grumbled as my heart started to settle down.

"Not even a little?"

I glared, shaking my head.

"Fine." He sat up on the bed, wincing.

I went to the bed. "Lean forward," I said, wrapping my arms around his torso and pulling him forward toward me so I could adjust his pillows to make him sit more comfortably.

It was awkward this time though as he was conscious and I had my chin resting against his shoulder. I felt him turn his head a little and I felt a faint brush against my hair. Did he just kiss my hair? No, that was stupid.

I shook my head, helping him against the pillow before adjusting the cover around his waist.

"How are you feeling?"

"Like I've been run over by a truck."

I pursed my lips. "Yeah, well, I hope it will teach you a lesson and you won't do something that stupid again."

"I didn't think it would be so bad."

"Yeah, well… You scared me, Luca, really."

"I'm sorry, the last thing I want to do is scare you. I never want you to be scared of me."

"I'm not scared *of* you but *for* you? It seems to be my default mode."

He smiled as his stomach grumbled.

"I have a little food for you. Try to have that, okay?" I settled the tray on him with a peanut butter and jelly sandwich and a bottle of apple juice.

He looked up at me with an arched eyebrow. "I'm now a five-year-old boy?"

I rolled my eyes. "You need the sugar. Just eat up and take your antibiotics," I added, giving him two tablets. "You'll have to take them for at least another week."

"Yes, boss."

I sighed, sitting back on the chair while he ate, and I let my eyes wander on his naked chest, and in particular the tattoo he had there.

I was interrupted in my inspection when his fingers brushed against it.

174

I looked up and met his eyes before looking away, quite embarrassed at being caught red-handed.

"This is the famiglia tattoo," he said, still tracing it with his fingers. "We all have it—or a variation of it. It all depends on which family you are part of. This one is the East Coast family tattoo." He sighed, letting his hand fall back on the bed. "I got mine when I was fourteen. It was when I took my final allegiance test. Normally you take it between sixteen and eighteen, but what can I say—I always was precocious." He said it as a joke but the bitterness in his voice was unmistakable. "Sad that these stupid scars didn't take it away. It would have been the one good thing."

"Are you even supposed to tell me all that?" I asked gently, leaning forward on my chair to give him my full attention. I wanted to know, of course, but not if it would create issues for him.

He shrugged. "I don't really care. You saved my life, took care of me, washed my dick... You earned my trust."

I blushed crimson at the mention of his dick. "Dom was there when I bathed you! It was nothing untoward!"

He let out a little chuckle. "Hey, I'm just joking, but all that to say... You're in my trust circle now. All you want to know you can ask."

I nodded. "Okay, thanks."

"I need to use the bathroom."

"Oh! Yes, of course, let me help you."

"I'll take over."

I let out a sigh of relief as Dom walked into the room.

"You sure?" I asked.

"Yes, the idiot is now awake and you've barely slept or eaten for the past four days. Go eat something and go to bed... I may have left you a little present on the kitchen table."

I beamed. Nobody ever really bought me presents before—not without something else in mind.

I looked at Luca who winked at me "Yes, you go. Dom loves seeing my dick; it's more a favor to him than anything really."

Dom snorted but approached the bed.

"You do look tired, Cassie," Luca added, finally serious, concern etched between his eyebrows. "I'll see you later."

"Yes, I'll see you later." I turned toward Dom. "Take care of him."

"Always," he replied just before I exited the room.

I wanted to go check my present but suddenly the adrenaline and anxiety of the past few days vanished to only leave a powerful feeling of weariness, and I barely made it to my bedroom before sinking into oblivion.

14

LUCA

It took another four days before really being back to myself...well, a beat-up and sore version of myself but at least I was functioning.

I had almost died, I knew that, and I also knew that there was no turning back anymore as far as Cassie West was concerned.

She more than saved my life and despite everything stacking up against me, I realized she truly cared about my broken self... What a miracle for me but what a curse for her.

I had wanted to keep her at bay, to stop her from penetrating my walls, but I'd never stood a chance. There was too much goodness, too much light in her, for it not to weaken the darkness surrounding me.

She had been a beacon of hope with all the kind

words, all the gentle touches, and all the quiet strength I witnessed during the few moments of lucidity during my sickness. It had meant everything.

After a shower, that tired me a lot more than it ought to, I walked through the house, looking for Dom.

He had been weird since everything happened, tiptoeing around me...acting like I needed to be handled with care—I hated that.

I found him in the game room playing pool by himself.

"Is this what I'm paying you for?"

He rolled his eyes but leaned on the pool table, getting two balls in with one shot.

"I'm actually not on work time yet," he replied, rounding the table, assessing his next move. "I'm glad to see you're back to your charming self."

"I want to spar."

Dom looked up, surprised. "Spar? With whom?"

I raised my eyebrows in surprise at the question. "Is that a trick question?"

"Well, it must be Cassie because it fucking ain't me."

There was a type of sparring I was longing to do with Cassie which involved a lot fewer clothes and a lot more pleasure than my usual sparring session with Dom.

"Why the fuck not?"

Dom laughed. "No offense, Luca, but I enjoy at

least a little challenge. Come back when you can actually be up for more than a few minutes without leaning against a wall like a geriatric patient."

I jerked straighter; I didn't even realize I had been leaning against the wall.

"I need to blow off some steam," I admitted. "Being stuck in a room and a bed for a week really got to me."

"Oh, yeah, I'm sure you minded the nurse." Dom grabbed a pool cue and threw it my way. "Play with me."

My lips quirked up in a half-smile. "No, that was a perk."

He nodded, looking somehow troubled as he arranged the pool balls.

"What is it?"

He shook his head. "Nothing."

"Dom…" I let out on a sigh.

"You talked a lot when you were feverish."

"Did I?" I asked as cold sweat formed at the back of my neck.

He nodded. "Mostly in Italian but—"

That was a relief. I didn't need Cassie to realize how fucked up I was.

"You talked to your mom and your sister."

I took a deep breath and looked down at the table, adjusting myself to break, doing anything I could to avoid Dom's eyes. I had seen them when I was in the worst of my condition when I suspect my life was only hanging by a thread. I'd seen them both in a beautiful garden, and they had told me that it was not my fault, that I had done nothing wrong and I needed to move on and be happy. That they wanted me to be happy and loved, and seeing me like that was breaking their hearts.

"Yeah…" I croaked before clearing my throat under the weight of emotion at the memory of this illusion that had looked all too real… *Maybe it had been real.* "I need a drink."

"Cassie said no. The antibiotics you're taking are too strong. You'll have to wait a few more days. Don't make me call her."

I frowned; nobody told me no; nobody ordered me anything. "Cassandra West is not the boss of me."

Dom snorted. "Sure she's not!" He turned toward me with a mocking sneer. "*Mia piccola guaritrice, accarezzami il cazzo per favore.*" He taunted with a high-pitched voice.

"I never asked her to stroke my dick!"

Dom laughed again. "No, but we both know you wanted to."

I shook my head. I remembered calling her 'my little healer' though—I had done that.

"She won't break your heart, Luca."

I took a shot and sent my ball in. "No, she won't. I have nothing left to break."

Dom gave me a knowing smile. "We both know that's not true. I *saw* that it's not true."

I welcomed the quick knock at the door. Anything was better than a heart-to-heart with Dom.

"Yes?"

Cassie opened the door and her face lit up when she looked at me. I loved how she reacted to me because every time her green eyes were set on me, my heart jumped in my chest.

"You look well," she said with her usual bright smile.

I nodded, smiling back. "Thanks to you."

She waved her hand dismissively, turning an adorable shade of pink at the compliment.

"Is there anything I can do for you?" I asked as she kept looking at me silently.

She blinked quickly. "What? Oh yeah."

It pleased me to see how she responded to me. She was genuinely attracted to me, despite everything... It was a true wonder.

"Your friend Matteo is here for you."

I let out a scoff, turning toward Dom. That was a good one!

When I noticed Dom tense and pale a little, I realized it was not a joke they'd planned; it was the truth.

"Have you met him?" I asked, trying to keep my voice as cool as possible. Cassie meeting Genovese was probably one of my worst nightmares.

She nodded, apparently oblivious to the lead weight that had formed in both mine and Dom's stomachs.

"Yes, lovely man. He's in the kitchen."

I nodded. Matteo Genovese had invaded my space —not something I appreciated. "Perfect, great, I'll go see him. Why don't you go with Dom?" Go anywhere as far as possible from Matteo Genovese and stay locked away until he left the property.

"Yeah," Dom continued. "You deprived me of TV goodness while you took care of this one. I want to know who took that pregnancy test. My money's on Brooke."

She looked from me to Dom a few times, clearly not buying it.

"Cassie...please," I continued.

She let out a sigh of surrender. "Fine." She turned to Dom. "And it's totally Hayley who's preggo."

I waited for them to go upstairs before taking a deep breath and walking into the kitchen to confront my doom. Matteo never left the city and him driving over an hour to come here? It didn't mean anything good.

I found him sitting at the kitchen island with a glass of milk and a red velvet pecan brownie—*my* pecan brownie—like he belonged despite looking like a freaking kingpin.

"She said it was your favorite," he said to me, not looking up from the plate.

I studied him, dressed in his designer suit, his dark hair styled to perfection. To be fair, for as long as I've known Matteo Genovese, I'd never seen anything other than the picture of perfection.

He turned his head slowly toward me, his cold, emotionless eyes studying me as he finished his bite.

His eyes had always been unsettling and after years of not seeing them, it took some getting used to again. Most of us had dark-brown eyes, but his were the lightest blue I'd ever seen. There was even a story going around in our circles saying that his eyes were just reflecting the color of the ice that replaced his heart...the cruel king.

"Gianluca. You're alive."

I remained silent, not really sure where he was going with this opening.

He sighed, wiping his hands on the paper towel Cassie had given him. The perfect hostess. "I'm frankly a little disappointed. I hoped you'd be dead or dying because I don't see any other reason for you not taking my calls and not responding to the message your puppy carried back home. The only other reason would be sheer stupidity and I expected a little more from you."

"I've been busy."

"Fucking the help?" He cocked his head to the side as if he was pondering the idea. "I could almost forgive you if it was the case."

"Do. Not. Touch. Her," I growled, my nostrils flaring. "She has nothing to do with anything."

His lips curved up in a malicious smile; I'd shown

him what he'd wanted to see.

He stood up. "We need to talk."

I nodded, turning around and walking away in a silent invitation to follow me to the office.

"Want a drink?" I asked as I helped myself to a glass of scotch. Never mind Cassie's instructions, it was mandatory for the conversation that was going to happen.

He shook his head and took a seat without invitation. I had offered him a drink by politeness—Matteo rarely drank in public.

"So…" He threw a bored look at his surroundings. "You…the broken Mafia prince, hiding in his mansion in the middle of nowhere." He gestured at my long hair and beard. "Becoming a savage…"

I snorted. "Is that what they call me? Broken Prince?"

"I think it is quite fitting actually. You're a petulant child who just ran away from his responsibility because he got hurt."

I gritted my teeth so hard I was surprised they didn't shatter. How could he understand? That man was a psychopath.

"I wanted to give up my place; my father agreed."

"And I refused," he added as if it was okay that he decided for me. He had the power to, and it still didn't make it right.

"But you said you would leave me be."

He nodded. "I did but I believe I've been more

than patient. Now you are ordering flowers, sending your consigliere to famiglia meetings."

"Dom is not my cons—"

"Did you think that asking favors from the federal court would not come back to me? Please, Gianluca, you're not that stupid."

"I was collecting a debt."

"So you were," He twisted the signet ring he wore on his right ring finger. The ring was engraved with the Trinacria symbol, a rare ring, one that was given to you as a symbol of your authority. Matteo Genovese was the only one allowed to wear this in the US; he was our boss—our commander, judge, and executioner. He had been sent here when he was only fifteen to rule over us all. He was our capo dei capi and he ruled over us with an iron fist.

One that was both feared and revered... The problem with me, the thing that aggravated him more than anything, was that I had nothing left to lose anymore, no real pressure point.

I looked up to the closed door to my office. At least I used to. For two years that man had lost his power over me, but he had it back and he clearly knew it.

He reached inside his jacket pocket and I tensed. He could still decide I was not worth the trouble and shoot me in the head.

He retrieved a long black velvet box. "Since I was coming, I picked this up from Lucia Jewelry. It's a lovely custom-made piece...diamond...platinum... $14k, was it? What a thoughtful gesture for someone you don't particularly care about."

I narrowed my eyes into slits, that fucker had known everything before even stepping a foot in this house. "Who do you own?"

He laughed. "All of them." He shook his head. "Did you think I would have just let you walk away and grieve in your corner without direct eyes on you? Well..." He shook his head. "I should say all but your consigliere... That one is annoyingly faithful."

"He is not my consigliere and I'm not the capo—"

Matteo slammed his hand on the desk. "Enough!" he bellowed.

I stopped, startled. Matteo was the calm angry type. I'd seen the man slit a traitor's throat and wipe the knife on the guy's shirt with the same bored look on his face as when he was attending church.

"I could make your life very, *very* difficult, Gianluca. Do. Not. Test. Me," he snapped coldly, and if I knew anything about Matteo, it was that he never made empty threats. "But I could also make it so much easier."

I leaned back on my seat. "Easier?"

"You know what I did for you when you were fourteen—what I got you."

I stiffened; that was a secret I didn't want out. "That is long gone, Matteo, and I've repaid you tenfold."

He nodded. "Yes, you did, but I still didn't have to agree to it. It was risky then. I was brand new but I took your side."

"Not for free," I reminded him. "What's your point with this?"

"You know you can't marry whoever you want, right? As the capo you must marry within the cinque famiglie, but I'll help you marry her."

My heart jumped at the idea of having Cassie. "No, she deserves better. I want to keep her out of this."

"Do you?" He looked down at the gift box on my desk. "It's too late, you know that, right? She knows too much—there's no out for her. You made sure of that."

"She doesn't know anything."

"Is that true, Gianluca?" He ran his forefinger back and forth on his bottom lip. "You know how I deal with liars." He grimaced. "It would chagrin me to have to torture her just to make sure, but if it's what you want."

"Don't hurt her. Everything she knows was my right to share."

"I won't hurt her…if you don't make me do it." He laughed. "I mean I could hurt her just see you bleed but I like her."

Lord have mercy on her—being liked by Matteo Genovese almost sounded like a curse. *Just like your feelings for her are one*, the stupid little sadistic voice in my head taunted.

"When you come to your senses and bang her, give her a ring and have her finish her nurse training. We need more healers in the famiglia."

I shook my head.

"They're making the simpleton's life a misery."

"Enzo is not a simpleton. Why do you even care?"

He scoffed. "I don't, but you do."

"What is it you want?"

"You have to take your place and I don't give a fuck about your little internal turmoil. You are the capo, and you will take it from that crazy bastard who thinks he is intelligent."

I shrugged. "Take him out."

He rolled his eyes. "That's unsophisticated and I can't—until his idiocy causes the actual war that is already looming, my hands are tied. Benny is too much, too flashy, too full of himself." He pulled out a white envelope from his pocket. "The fat bastard is organizing a masquerade ball for his sixtieth birthday next Friday... A masquerade like a sixteen-year-old girl with a taste for theatrics."

I had to admit I am surprised that neither Benny nor Savio informed me of their stupid party. They have been trying so well to pretend they cared, to pretend they wanted me within the famiglia instead of six feet under... So him not even sending me an invitation did ring all sorts of alarm bells.

Matteo slid the envelope toward me. "It's a fake name. Go with your girl. Send your puppy. I really don't care. You need to see what he is doing and you need to stop it. I've been more than patient with you, Gianluca. I've given you more leeway than I've ever given anyone. Don't make me regret betting on you." He stood up, straightening his tie and cuffs. "You better go or send someone, and I expect you to take your place back very soon, Gianluca. I've never been known for my patience or leniency."

That was the understatement of the year.

"Don't make me come back here; you won't like it if I do...and she won't either."

I tightened my hands into fists on my desk, trying to rein in my rage. Standing up to Matteo was a way to have hellfire rain on me—on her—and it was not something I had wanted.

I gave him a sharp nod.

"Oh and one more thing before I go... Next time I call, you better answer or call me back straightaway because I swear you won't like the outcome."

"Sure thing."

"I'm glad we understand each other. I really don't feel like getting my hands dirty."

That was a blatant lie; Matteo lived for chaos and pain. His name was more than fitting. Matteo meant gift of Gods and he truly thought he was our god, our king...our fucking *psychotic* king.

189

"Tell the girl thanks for the brownie. I'm glad to have her in the famiglia."

I remained silent as he left me in the office. I'd screwed up in epic proportions.

I had wanted to protect Cassie, keep her just at the frontier between the normal world and mine. I wanted her close but I cared enough to not want to curse her along with me, and despite all my best efforts, despite all my attempts not to fall, I took her down with me.

I brushed my hand along the box of the custom-made necklace I had ordered for her. I should have known better but I wanted her to have something special for her birthday, something meaningful that would express what I felt for her without her actually knowing what it truly meant.

I should have taken into account that Matteo was as smart as he was cunning. Now she was on his radar and there wasn't much I could do.

Give him what he wants against her freedom. He wants you back on top. He'll give it to you. It's not like he really cares. She's just a means to an end, my voice of reason claimed, and there was that stupid little voice coming from my mangled heart. *Maybe she doesn't want to be free; maybe she wants to stay here—with you.*

I leaned back on my seat, closing my eyes wearily.

How am I going to save you, Cassie West, and more importantly, do you even want to be saved?

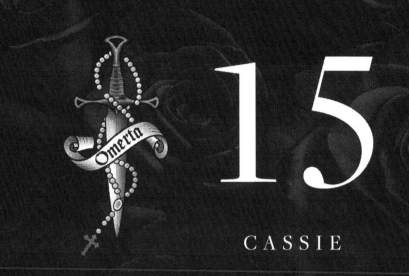

15

CASSIE

I stabbed the trowel a little bit harder than necessary in the soil. I was still a little annoyed with what had happened yesterday even if I had no real reason to be.

Luca had told me he trusted me, that I was now in his circle of trust, and he sent me to my room like a child as soon as one of his colleagues showed up.

I shook my head, putting the bulb in the ground. I knew I was new to the whole Mafia thing but still.

That man had been lovely. Well, it was true that I almost died of a heart attack when I'd turned around to find him there, standing in the kitchen.

Matteo, he said his name was, and he had been a work of art. I didn't think I had ever seen a man so beautiful in my life. His face had been perfect, flaw-less...with a straight nose, well-defined jaws, and lips that would make girls weep, and eyes so light blue that they almost looked unreal against his tanned skin and black hair.

And his accent, sweet Lord, have mercy! How come Mafia guys were even that hot? Weren't they supposed to all be short, fat, and bald?

I sighed at the thought of Luca and the kiss I'd given him.

"Why so gloom?"

I turned to see Dom standing beside me, his arms crossed on his chest.

"Do you really want to annoy me? I've got a trowel, you know."

He raised his hands in surrender. "Scary…"

I nodded. "Yes." I leaned back on my heels to have a better look at him. "What can I help you with?"

"I'm taking you out."

"Taking me out? Like…" I ran my thumb along my neck in a cut-throat way.

He rolled his eyes and shook his head. "Only you, I swear…" He sighed. "No, I'm taking you to a masquerade ball, in the city."

I stood up, adjusting the cap on my head. "Masquerade? Why? When?"

"Yes, you know…a ball with masks."

It was my turn to roll my eyes. "I know what a masquerade is, Dom. It just seems so…random."

He shrugged. "Why not though? It's fun and you've been cooped up in this house for months and what about before? Did you ever do anything fun like that? I'm sure you didn't go to parties when you went to high school."

He did have a point. It sounded like fun and I had never been to an actual party before except to the one organized by my killer parents where I had to play the role of their perfect daughter.

"I have nothing to wear for it." I'd have to spend more of my savings and I was not too overly keen on that. "When is it?"

"Next Friday and don't worry about having anything to wear, I have you covered, Boo."

"Boo?" I asked, arching an eyebrow.

He cocked his head to the side. "I was trying something new… No?"

I shook my head with a startled laugh. "No, definitely not."

"So, the masquerade? Yes?"

I really wanted to go but I didn't want Luca to think I had a romantic relationship with Dom. It was stupid to even feel concern because Luca hadn't shown me interest, at least not in a romantic way but…

"Is Luca okay with that?"

Dom smiled brightly as if I'd just asked the most interesting question he'd ever heard. He nodded. "Yes, he said as long as I don't touch what doesn't belong to me, it's fine. If not, I'll lose my hand."

"What belongs to whom?"

Dom chuckled. "Speaking of Luca, he asked if you could go see him in his office."

My heart jumped in my chest but I tried to contain my excitement at the thought of him seeking me out. It could be for work, of course, but I was thrilled, no matter what.

I nodded. "Okay, I'll go now."

"Don't run too fast! I wouldn't want you to slip and fall," he shouted after me.

I kept on walking but flashed him my middle finger and I walked into the house followed by his raucous laugh... *Prick!*

I took a deep breath when I reached the second floor and knocked on Luca's door.

"Come in."

I opened the door and my stomach twisted when he met my eyes and smiled. I had noticed that it was a nice, soft smile, one he was only giving me.

I couldn't help but smile back, somehow uncaring that I'd been annoyed with him not even five minutes ago.

"You wanted to see me?"

He pointed to the chair across his desk. "Yes, I wanted to discuss what happened yesterday."

I nodded and took a seat.

"Matteo Genovese is—" He looked away and scratched at his beard. "He is dangerous, very dangerous."

He hadn't looked like it. "He was very good-looking."

Luca snorted. "He is the type of man to bleed you when he wakes up and has breakfast beside your dead body. I kept you away to protect you—not because I don't trust you because I do, more than I ever trusted a woman before. I just—" He sighed. "I just want you to know I didn't want to hurt you."

"I was not hurt." *Liar.*

He opened his drawer and retrieved a long black rectangular box. "I got you that for your birthday but obviously things didn't go the way I expected, but here you go. Happy belated birthday."

I didn't know what was in the box but I had to blink back tears at the intensity of emotions a gift from Luca ignited in me.

"It's not much," he added quickly, sliding the box toward me.

I let out a shaky breath, grabbing the box and opening it slowly. Inside I found a silver necklace made of geometrical forms, pentagons and lines, linked together with flowers made of crystal. It was absolutely beautiful and unique.

"I love it..." I whispered, brushing it with my fingers. I looked up. "Thank you so much."

He looked at me with something so similar to fondness that my heart leaped in my chest again.

"So, ummm, Dom invited me to a masquerade. Is it okay?"

He frowned. "Why wouldn't it be?"

My stomach dipped at the sadness caused by his rejection. What did I expect? I was just a silly naïve girl. He cared for me but just the way Dom did and it was probably also why he had been distant since I'd kissed him.

He didn't want to have to openly reject the sweet idiot.

I gave him a resigned nod. I was done hoping for more. He was powerful, older, educated, and most of all deeply broken. He needed so much more than me.

I stood up. "Thanks again for the necklace."

"I'm not worried about Dom because he doesn't touch what doesn't belong to him."

I stopped, my hand on the handle and turned my head to look at him.

"And who do I belong to?" I asked, my heart starting to gallop like a mustang in my chest.

He leaned back in his seat, resting his hand on his lips, looking at me with his piercing dark eyes as if he could see right through me.

"Have a good day, Cassie."

Despite him dodging the answer, I couldn't help but smile when I stepped out of his office, clinching the box against my chest. He may not have claimed me with his words but his eyes did and it was enough for now.

When I came back to the house on Thursday after my weekly outing with Jude, I found a black box from a famous designer in front of my bedroom door as well as a shopping bag containing various smaller boxes.

I took the boxes in my room and found the most beautiful dress ever. It was a floor-length, one shoulder, emerald-green evening dress. The top was embroidered with thin golden flowers, flowing down in a relaxed A-line from the waist with a slit so high I expected it to be indecent once I wore the dress.

The first box in the bag contained golden and green shoes exactly my size, the second had a gold shawl, and the last box contained a golden venetian mask ornated with light emerald lines creating a beautiful intricated design.

Dom had outdone himself. Everything was so beautiful and well coordinated. I trailed my fingers on the dress and decided to try it on right away.

I discarded my clothes and stepped into the dress. Once I closed the side zipper, I swirled around to face the mirror and was taken aback by how stunning the dress looked on me, the perfect contrast of colors between my milky skin and red hair. I ran my hands on the trimmed waist and flaring on the skirt. It fit me so perfectly.

I couldn't help but blush a little at Dom's awareness of my body... I took my phone out to snap a pic but my phone pinged with a text from Dom.

Can you come to my room?

I frowned. I knew where his room was but I'd never been there. *Sure, I'll be there in five.*

I removed the dress carefully and put it in the wardrobe before going to see Dom.

"Come in," he said after I knocked.

"Are you...okay?" I asked. It was a stupid question really. Dom was in bed at six p.m., his neck covered in a light rash. He was clearly not okay.

He sighed, shaking his head. "No, well, I'm okay now but you know I'm allergic to seafood, right?"

I nodded mutedly, studying him, my nurse training taking over.

"I ordered Chinese and I may not have been careful. My allergies flared and if it wasn't for Luca getting my EpiPen." He shook his head.

I rushed to his side and looked at his rash. "It must have been a really bad one." I confirmed, as I moved the bed cover a little lower and noticed the rash ran down his chest too.

He sighed. "I've got...trouble for a few days after severe allergies."

I nodded. "Yes, it's pretty common." Most severe allergic reactions and the EpiPen reaction had the tendency to cause an upset stomach. I understood what he was not saying.

I shrugged. "It's okay, Dom; there will be other parties." I was glad that my voice didn't carry the disappointment I felt. I had been looking forward to going somewhere for once and looking like a princess.

He shook his head. "Absolutely not, Luca is going to take you."

I couldn't help the thrill that filled me before deflating as reality came crashing because one, it would not be fair to force hermit Luca to do something that trivial, and two, it would be quite heartless to use Dom as a replaceable piece.

"No, it's okay—"

"It seems only fair; he's the one who organized everything," he added, interrupting me.

I arched my eyebrows in surprise. "Luca did?" It was not something I had expected.

He nodded. "Yep, he thought you needed a little distraction from everything happening in your life, from all your responsibilities. He picked the dress...everything."

"Luca? Gianluca Montanari did that?"

Dom chuckled but it sounded tired. I had almost forgotten how this bad allergic reaction could have affected him. "Surprising, isn't it? He must really like you."

I flushed with pleasure. "I, no, he's just being nice."

Dom looked at me with a knowing smile on his face. "Sure, yeah...that must be it. Mafia bosses are generally known for their nice and caring nature."

I rolled my eyes. "I'm not sure leaving you is smart."

"No offense, Cassie, but I'm a thirty-two-year-old man. I'm pretty sure I can handle myself fine."

I crossed my arms on my chest. "Like you did when Luca was sick?"

"Hey!" He rested his hand on his chest in mock offense. "First, that one is on him, not on me. And second…" He twisted his mouth to the side. "Okay, I don't have a second but it's only an evening. You'll be back before I know it."

I sighed. "Yes, but Luca…"

"What about Luca?"

"Are you sure he's okay to step in? I really don't want him to do something he is not keen on doing. He's been staying in for over two years now. I'm not sure…" *I am not sure I'm worth the effort*, I added to myself but I knew it would piss Dom off if I said that. He was my own personal cheerleader.

"Between you and me?"

I nodded.

"I don't think he realizes it himself but he is probably thanking the heavens right now to have the opportunity."

I let out a short laugh. "I hope it is true… I—" I took a deep breath. "I like him."

"Oh, you do? Wow… That's brand-new information."

I rolled my eyes; the sarcasm was strong with that one. "No, I mean I like *like* him." Yep, I was a seventh grader again.

Dom looked at me silently, like I was dim. "Did you think you were smooth about it?"

Suddenly panic settled into me. "Do you think he knows?" If he did, I swear I'd never be able to look at him in the eyes again.

Dom snorted. "He should, normally he would, but he is so stuck in his self-hatred I don't think he realizes that people can see beyond that." He took a deep breath and settled a little more comfortably on his pile of pillows. "Run along now. I need my beauty sleep."

"Okay, but you call me if you need anything, please."

"Scout's honor!" He promised, raising his hand in a *Star Trek* salutation.

"This is not how it's done. That's a Vulcan salute."

He shrugged. "It is in Italy."

I narrowed my eyes suspiciously. "No, it's not; I'm not that clueless."

"Ah!" He winked at me. "It was worth the try."

I shook my head. "See you on Saturday."

"Have fun and for what it's worth, I think Luca *likes* you too… Maybe you should pass him a note in class and ask him if he does," Dom added as I reached the door.

I couldn't help the hundreds of butterflies flying around in my stomach at the thought but turned around to glare at Dom. "Luca's right, you really are an asshole."

I left the room followed by Dom's raucous laugh and yet despite how worried I was about him, I couldn't stop the jittering feeling about Luca liking me and spending the evening with him at the ball, dancing with him...

Yep, tomorrow couldn't come fast enough.

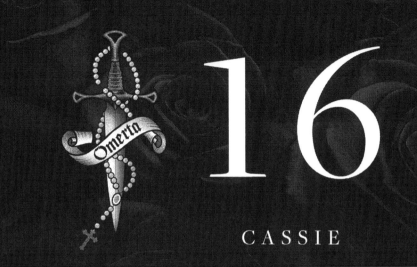

16

CASSIE

We had to leave at six and the more time passed, the more nervous I got. I'd prepared my overnight bag early in the morning and I watched about three hours of YouTube tutorials on doing my makeup and hair, but when I looked at myself in the mirror now, I was happy to say it had not been for nothing.

I gave myself a sophisticated look. I made my eyes smoky, making them even greener, and added a bright-red lipstick, putting the accent on my pouty mouth and creating a contrast on my porcelain skin.

I pulled my hair up into an asymmetrical French twist, letting just a few strands of soft curls out to soften the whole look.

I smiled at my reflection, bringing my hand up

and brushing the necklace Luca had given me for my birthday.

I was beautiful today. I looked like a confident woman—someone almost beautiful enough to have attracted Gianluca Montanari's attention even before his life went to hell... Even before he considered himself broken.

A knock at my door brought me back to reality.

"Coming." I took a deep breath, grabbed my overnight bag, and opened the door.

I couldn't contain the gasp that escaped me at the version of Luca standing in front of me. I'd seen photos of him before the accident, but they didn't render him justice.

He had cut his long black mane, not in a too short, conservative way but just long enough to curl on the collar of his tuxedo shirt. He'd also shaved his beard, making his scars more striking but also revealing his sharp jawline and strong chin.

He was a force to be reckoned with and when he looked at me like that, as if he wanted to eat me alive...I didn't stand a chance.

"You're stunning," I whispered in a daze, taking in his powerful presence in his perfectly tailored tuxedo.

His mouth curled up in a soft smile. "You stole my line."

I flushed brightly, not realizing I had said these words out loud.

"Cassie, *sei più bella di mille stelle.*"

I didn't even know what he'd said and yet, it was doing things to my lady parts—that also was a new feeling but quite recurring around him.

I cocked my head to the side as he extended his hand to grab my bag.

"You are more beautiful than a thousand stars," he translated.

"Oh, thank you." I blushed again, looking down at my feet. "It's the dress."

He shook his head, extending his elbow like a gentleman for me to take. "No, the dress doesn't matter; any dress would look beautiful on you. You shine like the brightest of all stars."

I smiled back, not really knowing what to say anymore. I took his arm and went down the stairs silently, enjoying his strong presence and his woodsy scent.

We stepped into the most luxurious limousine I had ever seen, not even in movies.

"Trevor will leave us at the ball and get our bags to our rooms," he said as he sat across from me in the car.

"Okay." I nodded. "Where are we staying?"

"The Grand Hotel. We have rooms side by side… Is that okay?"

"Sure, yeah." Then why did you feel a little disappointed at the idea of two rooms? I look at the black box beside him on his seat. "What is that?"

"My mask. Do you want—"

"The mask!" I gasped, touching my bare face. I'd left it on my bed along with the shawl. "Stop the car!"

Luca tapped on the closed partition window and the car stopped just as his phone started ringing.

He got it out of his pocket and I saw the name Matteo flash on the screen.

I looked out the window; we'd only just exited the iron gates.

He rejected the call. "Okay, we'll turn around," he said just as the phone started to ring again.

"No, just stay here and speak to him." I jerked my head toward the phone. "I'll have the guard drop me with the golf cart and wait for me. I'll be back in ten minutes."

He sighed, looking down at his phone. "Okay, be quick." He picked up. "*Pronto.*"

I got out of the car and gestured to the security guard.

"I'm sorry. I forgot something in the house; could you take me back?"

"Of course, miss."

I removed my shoes as we reached the house. "I'll be back in a minute." I put my shoes on the seat and ran up the stairs to my room.

I grabbed the shawl and mask and I was about to go down the stairs when I heard a creak upstairs.

I frowned and went up to the second floor as quietly as I could as apprehension and fear mixed together. I should have called security, not gone upstairs by myself, but I was worried for Dom.

I found Dom in Luca's office going through his stuff, seemingly really well, and the disappointment I felt at his betrayal of Luca was overwhelming.

"Were you even sick?" I asked, my voice shaking with the sadness I felt.

He froze, a folder in his hand, looking at me like a deer in the headlights.

"What are you doing here? I saw you leave."

I raised an eyebrow. "What am I doing here?" I gestured to the office. "You are betraying Luca."

He raised his hands in surrender. "No, Cassie, I swear, I'm doing that to help Luca. I would never betray him."

"I have to tell him." I turned around, ready to leave.

"No, don't, please, I beg you." The urgency of his tone made me turn toward him again. "Cassie, you know me; you know I care—for you, for *him*."

"Dom, I can't betray him."

He shook his head. "Please, just until tomorrow. When you come back I'll tell you everything, and if you still want to tell him, I won't stop you."

"You promise?"

He nodded. "I promise, Cassie."

I sighed, looking at the clock on the wall. I had already passed the ten-minute mark. "I won't say anything… Don't make me regret it."

"You won't."

I shook my head. "Tomorrow?"

"Yes, tomorrow."

"Fine."

"Also you look absolutely stunning!" he shouted after me as I went down the stairs.

When I made it to the car breathless, I could see that Luca was not in as good of a mood as he had been before the call.

As soon as I sat back in the car, Luca knocked on the partition and the car drove off again.

"Sorry it took me longer than it should have," I offered as he scowled out the window.

He turned toward me and let out a sigh. "No, Cassie, it has nothing to do with you." He let out a small smile which looked strained but he tried. "It's just Matteo being Matteo." He waved his hand dismissively.

"Okay... So, tell me about this masquerade?" I tried to make conversation and convince myself I was doing the right thing by hiding Dom's secret.

He rolled his eyes. "It's an ostentatious over-the-top look-at-me birthday party."

"Oh." I didn't expect him to be so blasé about it. "You know if you don't want to go—"

He shook his head. "No, I do, if only to see you in this dress but—" He sighed, leaning back in his seat. "I let go of this side of my life over two years ago and I'm not so eager to go back. But..." He raised his hand, knowing I would offer to turn back. "It had to be done, today or tomorrow... My time was up." He was so cryptic, I wanted to push, ask him why his time was up but it was not my place.

"I've rarely been to the city, you know." I smiled, remembering my last trip there. "I took Jude there just a couple of weeks before our lives went down in flames. It was the best day ever. He is crazy about musicals but our parents didn't think it fit the idea of a boy and you know." I waved my hand dismissively. "It was too much trouble than we were worth. So I organized a surprise day for this birthday. We took the train to the city and we went to an afternoon performance of *The Wizard of Oz*. I then took him to the Donuts Palace where I'm sure he ate his body weight in donuts and he slept off his sugar coma on the trip back." I smiled brightly at the memory of his little snoozy head lolling on my shoulder.

"You've never visited the city?"

I shook my head. "Not really, no."

He rubbed his chin as he was doing every time he was thinking. "I'll show it to you one day."

I nodded and looked away as my cheeks reddened with pleasure at the idea of him taking me on a trip.

We stayed in comfortable silence for a while and I perked up as I saw the lights of the city on the horizon.

"Almost there," Luca confirmed but his voice

carried a wariness I didn't fully understand but could empathize with.

"You have not shown me your mask yet." I pointed at the box, trying to get him out of his own head.

He smiled, seeing right through me but played along. "Ah, yes, I think it's very fitting." He got it out of the box and put it in front of his face.

The mask was terrifying and I had to do my best to keep my face smooth. The mask was in the shape of a skull and designed to be a stand-out statement piece for a masquerade ball. The face of the mask was painted in white and gold leaves, and crystals were giving it a distressed effect to achieve a look of antiquity. The only things I could see were his dark eyes, his sensual mouth, and strong chin.

"It's a *demone*," he said, removing it.

"It is terrifying," I agreed.

"Just like me."

I shrugged. "Maybe to others but not to me."

He shook his head. "No, not to you...never to you."

I wanted to ask what he meant by that but the car stopped and I realized we were in front of a majestic house. There were a few people dressed in evening attire going up the stairs.

Luca sighed, tightening his mask around his face. "Okay, time to put your mask on. Just a few rules."

I frowned as I put on my mask. "Rules?" I

thought we were here to have fun; rules didn't predict anything fun…or anything safe. "Is it…dangerous?"

I could not see his face anymore but he pursed his lips as his shoulders tensed. "No, you are safe with me, always."

The certainty in his voice made me relax and even without these words, I'd felt it with him after our rocky start. Luca Montanari made me feel safe.

"I feel safe with you," I admitted. I was not sure if it was the masks or what, but it was easier to say things when we were hiding like that.

His eyes heated up as he studied me. "Stay beside me all evening, okay?"

I nodded.

"If anyone asks you to dance, you refuse," he added seriously.

"But I'd love to dance."

"And that's why I'm here."

Somehow I couldn't picture him as the dancing type, my broken, angry man… I kept forgetting he had a life before all this and based on the little things I found online, it was quite a busy one.

"Sure, I will stay with you."

Luca got out of the car and extended his hand to help me out. As soon as I stepped out, he grabbed my hand and intertwined our fingers, sending a flash of electricity up my arm and down my spine.

Was this a normal thing? I never felt anything like

that with any man before. I suspected it was just a Luca thing.

We walked up the few stairs to the house and just stepping into the hall felt like stepping into another world. It felt like stepping in some kind of palazzo with the high ceilings, white marble, and gold undertone. Everything was overly luxurious.

Luca stopped us in front of a security desk and extended his card.

"Mr. Benetti, welcome to the party."

I threw Luca a side-look as he bowed his head. What was up with the fake name?

He turned around and we walked into a huge ballroom that looked more like some kind of carnival than anything else.

The party was already in full swing; Luca had made us late on purpose. There were women dressed as birds in high golden cages, jesters on the side, and a man dressed as a king sitting on a golden throne at the end of the room.

"This is…"

"Ostentatious? Vulgar? Ridiculous? Narcissistic?"

I chuckled. "I was about to say unbelievable."

"Yeah…that too." His hand tightened on mine and I looked up before following his eyes to a group of three men sporting some weird cross-neck tattoos.

"Do you want to dance?"

I nodded once as he took me to the dance floor and made me swirl.

I gasped, grabbing his big shoulders as we swayed to the rhythm of the music. I didn't expect him to dance so well, being so big and wide, and yet, he was Luca Montanari... I suspected there wasn't much the man couldn't do if he put his mind to it.

The more we danced, the closer he held me, I could feel his heartbeat against my chest.

"I like you, Luca Montanari," I whispered despite myself and his pace faltered ever so slightly, the only sign that he heard me.

When the song ended he grabbed my hand again. "Do you want to see something cool?"

I nodded.

"Come with me." We stopped at the buffet first for a drink and he exchanged a few words in Italian with a man in a jester mask. Once he turned toward me and bowed his head, I recognized the icy blue eyes of Matteo Genovese.

"Is everything okay?" I asked Luca as he pulled me to a darker corner.

"I'm not certain," he admitted truthfully before twisting a light fixture on the wall and a little panel just beside me slid open.

"How—"

"Come, quick," he whispered, pulling me in and sliding the panel shut again.

We were in the dark for a few seconds before he got his phone out and turned on the flashlight.

He grabbed my hand again and pulled me up a set of stairs. "How do you know about this?"

"This used to be my home; I know all its secrets."

I missed a step with my surprise but Luca held me up.

"God, thanks! I could have hurt myself."

"I'll always protect you."

I opened my mouth but closed it again. This promise was so ominous and the effect it had on my mind and body were...unsettling at best.

"I thought Hartfield was your home?"

"It is," he confirmed, opening a door and gesturing for me to go first.

It took me to a small alcove-like balcony on the first floor, half hidden by the decoration, giving me a full view of the ballroom.

"This is amazing!"

Luca pressed behind me, resting his hands beside mine on the railing, trapping me in his arms, his warm chest against my back.

I shivered but didn't dare move. His faint cologne, his body heat, his strong presence—it was all so intoxicating.

"How come you don't live here?"

"I never liked this house. I used to live in a condo downtown. This is not home. My mother and Arabella were not fans either. Hartfield was home for them."

I leaned back against him, letting my head dip

back a little, resting it against his shoulder. "I love Hartfield."

Luca leaned down a little, brushing his lips against my neck. "I can't stop thinking about it." I shivered at his warm breath on my neck, his strong body against my back...the intimacy of the moment.

"What?" I asked breathlessly.

"The kiss...the one you shouldn't have given me and is now branded in my chest." His lips brushed my jawline. "You ran away before I had a chance to recover."

"What if I had waited?"

He brought his hand up and turned my head to the side. As soon as I met his eyes he leaned down and kissed me. It was hard, bruising. He nipped at my bottom lip, demanding access to my mouth, and I was only too happy to surrender.

As soon as I granted him access, his tongue slid in my mouth, caressing, tasting, dominating. I could feel my arousal expanding and if that man could do that with just one kiss, I could only imagine what it would be like to have him pleasuring me in my bed and suddenly I wanted nothing more than this man, this pure brute force, to be my first.

I shivered and moaned in his mouth.

Luca growled, starting to kiss down my neck as his hand trailed up the slit on my dress, touching my bare thigh until he reached the hem of my underwear. He brushed his thumb back and forth against the fabric as he lightly bit my neck.

I raised my arm, reaching behind me and wrapping my arm behind his neck as I parted my legs slightly, inviting him to touch me like we both wanted to.

"Cassie…" His tone was a warning but I didn't care. I was drunk on him and I wanted more even if we had no future, no chance—even if tomorrow didn't come, I wanted him. I had the right to be selfish for once.

I tilted back my hip a little, pressing on his hardening cock.

He growled again as his fingers slid under the hem of my underwear to brush against my heated core, the statement on how aroused he made me, how much I wanted him.

I spread my legs a little more, not caring if it made me needy and wanton—I just wanted his fingers on me, in me, releasing the overwhelming pressure that had settled in my lower belly.

"You're soaked," he whispered against my ear before nipping my earlobe hard enough to send a little zing of pain which strangely enough only increased my pleasure as he brushed his fingers against my slit.

"Always for you," I admitted and it was the truth. I'd touched myself thinking of him more times than not.

He pressed his thumb against my clit as he slid his middle finger inside of me. I gasped and squeezed around his finger.

He hissed, pressing his now fully erect cock against my back. "You're so tight…"

"Luca…" I whispered in a lustful breath.

I closed my eyes, leaning more heavily against him as he thrust a second finger inside me, making me feel so full. He pressed his palm against my clit as he pumped his fingers inside of me faster, harder. I felt myself coming as I never came before and when my orgasm hit, it felt like falling off a cliff. I forgot the people dancing and talking just below me; I forgot the responsibilities, the impossibility of my relationship with Luca—I even forgot my name.

Luca locked his lips on mine and kissed me deeply, muffling the scream caused by my earth-shattering orgasm.

I felt like my legs were made of Jell-O and I was grateful that Luca had one arm wrapped tightly around my waist, keeping me up.

I opened my eyes just in time to see him bring his two fingers to his mouth, sucking them clean.

His eyes darkened even more as he slid his fingers out of his mouth. "You taste good enough to eat," he whispered appreciatively before licking his bottom lip.

"Why don't you then?" I couldn't believe how brazen I sounded and yet I wanted him.

"Cassie, if we go now." He shook his head. "There won't be any turning back."

"I don't want any turning back."

He kissed me again, much more softly than before. "Let's go then."

He took my hand and took me back downstairs and I followed him in a post-orgasmic daze.

Luca stopped just as we excited the secret panel, pulling me behind him.

"I told you to go and check the kitchen; are you that stupid, little brother?" I heard a man spat.

I peeked over his shoulder to see a big man in a jester mask hover menacingly over a smaller, painfully thin man.

"No S-s-s-avio, I j-j-just—"

"I don't have seven hours to waste on a fucking reply. Do what you're asked, *stupido*."

"*Basta!*" Luca barked.

The two men turned at once. The smaller one smiled, the big one glared.

"Gianluca, I didn't know you'd be there."

"How would you, Saviolino? My invitation must have been lost in the mail," he added with a strong voice, standing even taller.

"Enjoying the party?"

"It was… informative to say the least."

"Who are you hiding?"

"None of your concern. Now go, Savio, check on the kitchen."

"What?" He scoffed. "I'm not doing that."

"Remember who you are talking to, Savio." The threat in Luca's voice was not even barely veiled.

The Savio guy who I legit disliked left grumbling and I slid beside Luca, smiling at the smaller man.

"You sh-shouldn't have d-done that."

"Why? Your brother is a cazzo."

"I c-can defend myself," he added, irritated.

"I know," Luca replied. "But I love giving your brother a taste of his own medicine." He pulled me beside him. "This is my friend, Cassie."

Friend? Right, that's a way to put it.

Luca looked down at me. "This is my favorite cousin, Enzo."

"Nice to meet you, Enzo."

"You too, C-Cassie."

Luca squeezed my hand. "We have to go but text me okay? Don't let them bully you."

"Y-You left t-t-two years ago." He shook his head. "I c-can deal."

Luca sighed as he watched his cousin leave, blending in with the crowd.

"Do you want to stay?" I asked, secretly hoping he would refuse.

He shook his head. "I've seen all I had to see and I have other plans."

He pulled me through the crowd and outside of the house to the limousine.

As soon as he ordered the driver to go, he

removed his mask and mine before pulling me toward him.

"Where were we?" he asked, his eyes locked on my lips.

I felt brave again and kissed him as he circled my waist and deepened our kiss. That man was kissing me as if I were what he needed to breathe, as if I were his oasis in the middle of the desert, and I never wanted him to stop.

When the car stopped in front of the hotel, he sighed, readjusting his cock in his pants.

He grabbed my hand, went to the VIP counter, then grabbed our two rooms cards before he pulled me toward the elevator.

I followed him mechanically, apprehension now battling with my lust. I was going to lose my virginity tonight to a Mafia boss twelve years older than me... I would have never thought it would happen like that but I wouldn't change anything.

He used a key card to enter a room. I noticed my purple bag on the chair but didn't even have a chance to do or say anything as he leaned down and swept me off my feet, carrying me bridal style to the bed.

"You're mine now," he said in a low voice, putting me in the middle of the bed.

"Yes, I am."

He growled, letting his eyes trail down my body. "Good girl."

I got even wetter at his words and pushed my legs together, trying to create the friction I was craving.

He smirked seeing that and I enjoyed this cocky side of him.

He took my shoes off and pulled down the side zipper of my dress before pulling it down.

"Raise your hips," he ordered and I did as he asked and he removed my dress, discarding it on the floor.

The dress has not been adapted for a bra and I was now lying in bed in nothing but my thong, my breathing erratic and my body on fire under his heated gaze.

"You are stunning, Cassandra," he said, discarding his jacket, shoes, and bow tie but always keeping his eyes on my body. "You're a siren, one I'll happily follow to my death." He removed his shirt and crawled over me on the bed.

He leaned down and licked one of my nipples.

I hissed, arching my back.

"You like that, don't you?" he asked, licking my other nipple before taking it in his mouth and sucking on it.

It was all new to me and I feared I'd die of too much pleasure. Was it possible?

His hot, wet mouth was heaven. "Luca. Oh, Luca."

"We're just getting started, *anima mia*."

He kept on kissing down my stomach and didn't stop as he reached my silk-covered pussy.

I raised my hips instinctively for him to kiss my core again.

He let out a breathless laugh, visibly as drunk with desire as I was. "Eager for my mouth, aren't you?"

I nodded, my hips raising on their own accord.

He hooked his forefingers on each side of my panties. "Don't worry, I'm going to eat your sweet pussy real good."

I should have been embarrassed by his dirty words and yet I seemed to get wetter if at all possible.

Once my thong was gone, I spread my legs; there was no shame anymore, no self-consciousness. I needed his mouth on me.

He spread me wider, resting my legs on each side of his broad shoulders, and pressed his hot tongue on my pussy, licking the slit slowly.

I gasped, grabbing the bedspread in tight fists as he started to give openmouthed kisses to my pussy. "Fuck, Cassie, you taste so good. How did your ex-boyfriend get their head out of between your thighs?"

"I've not, they never—"

"You've never been eaten before, anima mia?"

I shook my head.

"What a shame, they don't know what they missed," he added before disappearing between my legs with renewed ardor. He used his tongue, his lips, his fingers, and all I could do was hold tight and try not to pass out from a pleasure so intense.

I came, screaming his name. If I died now, I'd die a happy woman.

Luca kissed my inner thighs tenderly before standing up, his lips glistening with my arousal, his hair in disarray by my legs and fingers.

He kept his eyes on me as he undid his belt and his zipper, getting his hard cock out.

My eyes widened and he gave me a prideful male smile. He enjoyed my reaction at the size of his cock.

"This is what you're doing to me. I'm hard for you...all the time."

He crawled on top of me and kissed me deeply. I could taste myself on his tongue and it was deliciously wicked.

"I can't wait to fuck you," he whispered against my lips as he rubbed his dick up and down my slit, lubricating it.

I had to tell him; he was really big and I'd never done it before. He had to know it was my first time.

"I've never done this before," I whispered before kissing his neck.

He bit the ball of my shoulder. "Have sex with your much older Mafia boss?"

"No, sex...at all."

He froze, his dick pressing gently against my entrance. "Are you saying..." He frowned as if I made no sense.

"I'm a virgin."

"Dio mio!" Within a second his body was gone and

he was trying to tug his hard cock back in his pants. "You should have said!" he barked accusingly.

"What? Luca. What?" My brain was still slowed by the pleasure fog of the orgasms he had given me. "Luca, it's okay. I want you to be my first." I sat up, reaching for him.

He shook his head and took a step back. "I don't want that! No, I can't do that." He turned around and left the room without a look back.

I looked around, completely at loss, and my heart shattered in a million pieces under the force of his rejection, and then for the first time since everything went to shit in my life, I let myself cry.

17

CASSIE

I woke up at five a.m., parched and with a killer headache. I was not surprised though. I had cried for hours last night, literally crying myself to sleep, and probably stopped crying when I had no tears left.

The rejection had cut me deep and I was mortified to have to face Luca today.

I shook my head. No, I couldn't do it. I'd need a few days before seeing him again.

I stood up and grabbed a bottle of water from the mini-fridge, drinking it in one go before jumping in a hot shower and putting on an oversized red jumper dress and black leggings, feeling a little more like myself despite the deep cut his rejection had caused.

I packed my bag and folded his jacket carefully,

leaving it and his shoes in front of his bedroom door before taking the elevator down.

I was grateful the hotel was close enough to the station and I was on a train back to Riverstown before seven a.m.

I texted Dom to come to pick me up; we needed to talk anyway, and a car ride seemed to be the best way.

I was actually surprised to find him there; I had expected him to dodge me.

"Why didn't you come back with Luca?" he asked as he started the car.

I glared at him.

"Does he know you're here? What happened? Did he screw up?"

"I think you have some explaining to do," I said, ignoring his question.

He sighed. "Yes, I do… I'm not even sure where to start."

"Did you even get an allergic reaction?" I asked. If the rash had been faked, it was impressive.

"Technically, yes."

"Technically?"

"I did get an allergic reaction, but it was not completely an accident."

I twisted in my seat, looking at him with horror. "You poisoned yourself?" I asked, hardly believing my own words. "Who does that?"

He sighed. "It sounds way worse than it is really."

"Does it?"

"It's still super early. What do you say we stop for a coffee and a muffin on our way back, and I'll explain everything then?"

My stomach grumbled, begging for food. "Fine! A coffee and muffin to go, and you and I park somewhere and chat in the car, deal?"

We stopped at the drive-through and ordered a vanilla latte and a Nutella brownie for me and a black coffee and a banana whole grain muffin for him. *Urgh, gross!*

We drove a little and took a side road and parked in the very quiet parking lot of the mountain trail. It was a rainy day, not something the usual hikers would particularly enjoy.

"So, what about your suicide attempt?"

Dom rolled his eyes. "It was not a suicide attempt. I knew exactly what I was doing. It's not the first time I had an allergic reaction on purpose."

"Why would some—" I stopped, waving my hand dismissively. "You know what? So not the point right now. Why did you do it this time?"

He took a sip of coffee. "Two reasons. One, Luca is clearly smitten with you and I knew it was killing him to send you off to the ball with me so I thought if I gave him a little push, maybe he would stop being a chickenshit and act on it…which based on your early return and the couple of texts I got from him, backfired."

"Clearly," I replied, still mortified at the memory of how he rejected me just seconds before making love to me. "What's the second reason?"

"I think someone wants Luca to die."

I froze. Of all the things I expected to hear, that was not one of them. As if on cue, Dom's phone rang and Luca's name flashed on the screen.

"I have to take that." He put it on speakerphone. "Hello."

"Do you know where she is?" Luca asked, his voice laced with worry.

I would have almost felt bad for leaving like that if my mortification from last night was not so fresh.

"With me, in the car back to the manor... You're on speaker," he added quickly.

"Cassie?"

My heart squeezed in my chest at his warm, deep voice calling my name.

"Yes?"

"What happened?"

I looked at the phone with a frown; was he crazy? Didn't he remember the humiliation from last night?

"I woke up early and didn't want to waste a day. I decided to go back to work."

Luca remained silent for so long I almost thought he hung up.

"I see," he finally replied.

You do?

"Fine, I'm on my way back; we'll discuss more when I get home."

No, we won't. "That won't be necessary."

"I think it is."

"And I assure you, sir, it isn't."

He sighed wearily. "Cassandra..." He said in a warning tone.

"Sir..." I replied with the same tone.

"I'll see you when I get there." And it sounded much more like a threat than a promise.

The line went dead.

"That was nice, and not awkward at all." Dom sighed, putting the phone back in his pocket.

"You think someone wants Luca dead?"

Dom nodded sharply. "I don't have proof yet and this is why I needed Luca away. I wanted to look in his papers and all because..." He leaned back in his seat, closing his eyes. "Luca never drank much in public settings, and especially when he was in a car with his family. He did fight with his father that night. Gianna and Arabella were not supposed to be in a car with him, but I know him better than that. It just doesn't add up. And he had been drowning in his pain and self-pity for so long, spending every day drunk. He didn't have the right frame of mind to think it all true. But his father was killed in a shoot-out in a place where he should not have even been!" Dom threw his hands up in exasperation. "It is so obvious and nobody is saying anything, and then Luca gave everything to

Benny and Savio and they act all…" He turned toward me. "I think it's an inside job and I will prove it."

I nodded. I didn't like the vibes I got from that Savio douchecanoe last night anyway.

"Benny always had a megalomania to the highest level. Neither are the brightest—definitely more brawn than brains but…" He slapped the steering wheel in frustration. "You brought Luca back to life; he is more responsive, drinks a lot less. He is looking into famiglia stuff again. If I'm right and Benny and Savio are behind it, they'll be back for him and I want proof so I can take them down before they take him down."

I couldn't help the happy pinch I felt knowing that I may have been part of Luca's recovery despite what happened last night. "Can you just, you know." I wiggled my fingers at him.

"What does—" He mimicked my gesture. "Mean?"

"You know…make them disappear."

"Oh, I see…" He nodded. "Like feet in concrete in the bottom of the ocean? Or more like in the foundations of a building in construction or even the good old buried deep in the middle of the woods type scenario?" His lips quirked up at the corner.

The bastard was mocking me! I crossed my arms on my chest and glared at him. "Forget it!"

"No, no, it's interesting." He smiled earnestly now. "What reference are we working with? *The Sopranos?*

The Godfather? Don't tell me *McMafia*; that's just insulting."

I flipped him the bird, making him laugh.

"No, I wish." He let out a sigh. "But there are rules that we all need to abide by. I can't just take one of my famiglia out without proof and even then I'll need to get approval from the council who basically is Matteo Genovese."

I winced.

"Exactly. Luca is Genovese's favorite but still..." He cocked his head to the side. "And I'm far from being one of his favorites. He sees me as an irritating puppy at best."

"So what are we going to do?"

"We?" he asked, arching his eyebrows in incredulity, a small smile tugging at the side of his face.

"Yes, *we*. I'm not letting you go in alone, and I won't risk Luca's life if I can help it."

Dom grabbed my hand and squeezed it. "He wouldn't want you to get in harm's way."

"And I know you will keep me safe."

He nodded. "Yes, of course I will."

"What do you need?"

"I don't know what he did to anger you, but I need you to forgive him. I can't have him go back at being a sullen drunk."

"I'm not angry at him. It's..." I blushed with

R.G. ANGEL

discomfort. "He didn't do anything wrong...not really. I'm just— I'll talk to him."

"Perfect, let's go."

"But did you find anything last night?" I asked as he turned the car around.

"A little, but not as much as I thought." His voice was tight with frustration. "Luca seems to want to forget everything, but I found some of the scene photos and there are no brake marks on the road..." He shrugged. "I don't know but don't you think you would try to slow down if you lost control of your car? And there's— I went to the city and sneaked into the hospital; there's weird stuff in his file—page numbers are not how they should be...colors are different... Different handwriting for the same doctor..."

I frowned. "All little things but enough to make you question everything."

Dom threw me a quick side-look full of relief. "Exactly! I'm so glad we're on the same page."

"We'll figure it out. Have you tried to speak to the doctor or the policeman in charge?"

He sighed. "I did... The doctor died in a house fire a couple of months after the accident, and the cop was shot seven times in the chest in a house break-in a week after."

"I see... Could be a coincidence," I said, not even believing it myself. "But...it looked a lot like tying up loose ends to me."

"Yes."

"Why don't you tell him? He's going to be mad when he finds out."

Dom shrugged. "He might but he's been so down in the pit of despair… He won't believe he is not to blame, at least not now."

"Okay, we'll figure out something."

When we reached the house, Luca was waiting for us, his arms crossed on his chest as he glowered at the car.

Dom rolled his eyes. "Boy, dad's fucking mad."

"Why?"

Dom let out a low chuckle. "You are so clueless it's endearing."

As soon as the car stopped, Luca opened my door. "Cassie."

I frowned at the cold edge in his voice. "Luca," I replied, getting out of the car.

Luca looked up at Dom. "I thought you both walked home. It took you…" He looked down at his watch. "Over an hour to come back."

Dom shrugged. "We stopped in the woods for a quick fuck but this one took a long time to come."

I looked at Dom, my mouth open with shock as I could hear a low growl coming from Luca.

Did men actually do that? I looked up at Luca… He looked ready to kill Dom. It made no sense though since he left me all hot and wanting in the bed last night.

Dom laughed. "Works every time. I'll see you later." He threw me a last look before going up the stairs, whistling.

"Cassie," Luca started, his voice much softer now, so soft it almost felt like a caress on my skin.

I nodded. "We need to talk, I know. Where to?"

Luca seemed taken aback by my acceptance, and to be honest, if it had not been for my chat with Dom, I would have gone into hiding to lick my wounds.

"The library?" he suggested, gesturing me up the stairs.

I nodded and followed him silently there.

"Cassie, about last night, I'm sorry," he started as soon as he closed the door behind us.

I swirled around. He looked so delicious in his tight black T-shirt stretching over his wide chest and thick arms, his hands buried in the pockets of his light-blue jeans.

I wanted to ask if he was sorry for leaving me dejected and wanting on the bed or if he was sorry for touching me. Either way, it would sting.

"Don't apologize." I waved my hand dismissively, trying to sound detached despite the shame and rejection still squeezing my heart painfully.

Luca frowned.

"There's nothing to be sorry for. You've done nothing wrong." I meant that...mostly. "We all have the right to change our minds. You didn't have all the cards in hand. You didn't know about my...virgin status." I felt the heat of the blush from rising to my cheeks—being a redhead with such pale skin didn't help me sound stoic.

His frown deepened as he crossed his arms on his chest. Was he getting angry?

"A lot of men are not into inexperienced women. I get it, honestly." *Or at least I'm trying very hard to.*

"Okay, let me get that straight. You think I ran away because you are a virgin and it made me want you less?"

I shrugged.

"Cassie, it made me want you *more*."

I arched an eyebrow with disbelief. "You ran away pretty fast." I shook my head. "It doesn't matter anyway. No blood, no foul. We're okay."

He stood there studying me as if his dark eyes could see straight into my soul, and my body shivered at the intensity of it.

"I became darkness to protect the light, Cassie. I'm all darkness and you didn't deserve to be tainted —not by me. That part of you doesn't belong to me."

"It was mine to give, Luca. I get to decide who I want to give that part of me to." I took a deep breath.

"You don't know what you're saying. You hate your parents for the people they killed. How many people did they hurt? Five? Ten?"

I pursed my lips in irritation; I knew he was no angel... "What's your point?"

"I've killed at least five times that number with my own hands!" He showed me his hands in emphasis. "And have ordered many more. My hands are covered with a river of blood."

"Were they bad people?"

"What?" He arched his eyebrows, my question taking him aback.

"Were they bad people?"

He seemed to think about it. "Yes, but It's not really the point here, is it?"

"Actually it is. My parents killed old defenseless people out of greed. My parents are monsters. You killed killers and liars and people with blood on their hands."

He shook his head. "Don't make me the hero in this story, Cassandra."

I laughed at that. "You're not a hero—I'm not delusional. I might not *know* this life but I know enough. You are a villain," I agreed. "But a villain can always be the hero in someone's story... Just like the hero can be the villain in someone's story. It's all about perspectives."

He let out a weary sigh. "Cassie..."

"It's fine, I get it, I promise. I'm not mad. There's nothing about last night that you need to atone for but—"

"But what?" he encouraged. "Ask anything."

"I would very much like if we could just go back to before yesterday, pretend as if nothing happened,"

I asked gently. "I'm too embarrassed and I'd like to forget, please."

He looked away for a second as if he didn't want me to see how it made him feel.

He finally looked back at me, his face his usual placid mask. "Yes, I think it's wise. Friends?"

I nodded. "Of course." I forced a smile. "I'll see you later, okay?"

He nodded, moving from his spot in front of the door. "Yeah, later."

18

LUCA

It had been four days since the party at my old home and despite everything, only the end of the night unsettled me.

I'd not looked forward to going there, seeing the house my parents used to live in, the place I was driving my family back to when I'd killed them.

But Dom had his allergy and I knew I could not turn back. I'd committed to Matteo and I knew that Cassie had been looking forward to an evening out, and somehow just the thought of disappointing her unsettled me much more than it ought to.

She'd made the experience so much better than it could have been. She didn't know but she had been my anchor on that night. I hated how my uncle had transformed the house. I'd hated seeing him sitting like a fucking king looking down at his subjects. I'd hated seeing the men with the eagle tattoos on their necks. The fucking Bajrak of the Albanian Mafia invited at a famiglia party when we'd finally managed to settle on a rocky truce with the Russians.

I'd felt on the verge of exploding the whole evening, my uncle so much more of a fool than I'd originally thought, but then I felt her tiny hand in mine, everything just stopped...hurting. I hadn't planned what I did to her in the secrecy of the alcove but that woman breathed such life and fire into me I hadn't been able to stop myself. I had to touch her, possess her.

No matter what I promised her, I couldn't forget how she tasted, how soft her skin was, how her moans had resonated all the way down to my soul.

I've been fucking my hand every night since then, but this desire still burned so deep inside of me.

She might have said it was all forgotten and forgiven, but she'd put a sort of barrier between us; the easy relationship had fizzled. She was more guarded and I hated that.

I couldn't blame her though; what I'd done was bad, really bad. Well, at least it would be the way she saw it...as rejection.

If only she knew that walking away from her, so beautiful and so receptive to my touch, had been the hardest thing I ever had to do.

But when she admitted she was a virgin, the

chivalrous part of me had reared its ugly head. I had no right to take something that couldn't belong to me.

I was dying to be her first, her last, her only. But I needed to be deserving of this part of her, this little piece of her history that would only belong to me, but I wasn't. I was a sinner with blood covering my hands.

She didn't know Matteo locked us with the famiglia, but I knew I could grant her her freedom. I could see how desperate Matteo was for me to take my place.

I'd do it for her. I'd step up and take my throne in hell if he promised to leave her alone and not curse her to a life with us. I'd do it.

"Your cousin Savio is here."

I looked up, startled to find her standing in front of my office.

I grimaced. "Is he?"

She chuckled. "Yes, he is waiting in front of the gate. I needed to find you, but I didn't know where you were." She smiled sheepishly.

I leaned back in my chair, a smile tugging at my lips. That woman managed to make me happy even when I didn't think it was possible anymore. "I was hiding very well too. I bet you never would have expected to find me here, in my office," I teased, playing along.

"Nope."

"And how long did it take you to find me?"

"Twenty minutes so far."

I let out a startled laugh. "That's my girl," I said, sobering up almost immediately.

She gave me a soft look and gentle smile. She didn't miss what I called her and she liked it. If only she knew how much I loved calling her mine.

"I'll let you deal with him. I'll be in my room watching my show. No offense but I'm not a fan of him."

"Who is? I think he is the only one who is a fan of himself."

I helped myself to a glass of scotch before ringing the guard and asking him to escort Savio up to my office.

I'd need a drink to face the narcissistic asshole.

He knocked at my door.

"Come in."

He stepped in and anything I was about to say died in my throat. He hadn't come alone; he'd brought Francesca with him...

Francesca Morena...my ex-fiancée and his current squeeze. She didn't belong here for so many reasons. The first one was because she was an opportunistic, money-driven bitch...a perfect Mafia wife but not to be trusted in business settings.

"Francesca, at what do I owe the displeasure?" I took a sip, not offering a seat or a drink. They were not welcome and I couldn't care less about decorum.

She walked closer to my desk, swaying her hips with every step. She went for the sexy secretary look —a black pencil skirt, a red see-through blouse with matching lipstick, her long dark hair in a high sleek ponytail.

It used to do things to me—my dick responding to her beauty. My darkness feeding on hers but not anymore.

"*Mi sei mancato*, Gianni, *tesoro*," she breathed with her sexy voice, leaning forward on my desk, trying to show me her ample cleavage... What a waste of her time.

"You missed me?" I asked, arching an eyebrow. "Too bad I can't say the same."

She let out a throaty laugh, resting her perfectly manicured hand on her chest. "Gianni, come on."

I gritted my teeth. "I'm Luca or Gianluca. Not Gianni." I looked up at Savio. "Can you put a leash on your girlfriend?"

Savio popped his gum. His hair parted to the side and was almost shining with all the product in it. With his shirt half open, the thick gold chain and his gold *corno portafortuna*, the chili pepper-like pendant resting on his chest hair... He looked like a walking cliché of cheesy Italian culture. This pendant was usually worn as a sign of virility...a protector of your sperm. Fuck, I couldn't think of any half-sane woman who would even wish of his jersey-shore-reject's sperm.

"She's not mine; she does as she pleases," he replied, his eyes tracking down to her ass. "We just had a little fun."

Like I would ever stick my dick in any hole he'd been in... I'd rather cut it off.

"I see..." I nodded. "What do you want?"

He finally caved in and sat down heavily on the seat across my desk, Francesca still leaning seductively against the side of my desk... If she thought there was even a chance in hell I'd touch her again, she had another thing coming.

"So you decided to get out of your hermithood." He started popping his gum again.

"What is it to you? I can do as I please."

He shrugged, running his hand in his over-gelled hair. *Okay, Travolta, dial down the '70s.* "I like to know what's happening in my town."

I let out a startled laugh. "*Your* town?"

He frowned like he couldn't see where he went wrong.

"I'm the capo, Savio. You seem to forget that."

"No, you're not; you relinquished your title."

"Not officially. I'll take it back when I please."

"*If* you please..." he insisted.

"No, *when* I please. And it may be sooner rather than later."

"Have you informed my father?"

I cocked my head to the side. "Why would I? I'm

just taking back something that I loaned him for a while."

"I wish you luck getting it back."

"I don't need luck, Savio. I've got all the power."

"Is it because of the redheaded vixen?" he asked, licking his bottom lip in a way that made my stomach turn. Savio was not known for taking no for an answer as far as women were concerned. For him 'no' was merely a suggestion.

"What redhead?"

"Your maid?" he continued, leaning forward on his seat. "Dad said she's just a kid…but she's the one you took to the ball, isn't she?"

He had no idea if it had been her or not. Enzo had not ratted me out. He was a good kid.

"What if she is?"

"I wouldn't have pegged you for a man who wanted little girls," Francesca piped in sultrily. "I thought you were a man of taste," she added, resting her hand on her hip.

"I have no attraction for her." I looked Francesca dead in the eyes. "Or anyone."

Savio licked his lips again and I knew what that bastard was thinking. If he knew how I felt for Cassie, he'd do everything in his power to take her. If she was on his radar, the poor girl was fucked and I'd have to kill him with my bare hands—consequences be damned.

Savio was three years younger than me but always

had some stupid inferiority complex about me. He didn't just want to be like me—he wanted *to be* me, and it always included what I had or what I coveted.

And Cassandra West was the ultimate prize. For me, she was everything.

"So I can ask her out? She is a little flat but she's so short and tiny." He bit his bottom lip. "I bet her pussy is the tightest I'll ever try."

It took all my willpower not to jump over my desk and stab him in the neck with my letter opener.

"With as small as your dick is?" I grimaced. "I'm not sure anything could feel tight."

Francesca let out a small chuckle under a breath. We both knew it was the truth. What Savio didn't have in his pants, he made up in ego.

Savio glowered.

I sighed, waving my hand toward the door. "Be my guest, ask her out, but check with Dom first. I think those two have a thing going on."

"You'll pick him over him?"

"Are you actually asking me that? Of course, I would, every time."

"Cazzo," he muttered. "You're telling me the little girl is having a thing with Dom? Domenico Romano?"

I gave him a curt nod.

"Uh…" Savio nodded. "Well, she is definitely more appealing now. If the girl can deal with Dom's kinks? Mmm, mmm, mmm. I want a piece of that ass."

I shrugged again. "Ask him." I was impressed by how placid my voice sounded. "If he is game, do what you like."

Francesca threw him a victorious look. "I told you it was just stupid; Luca could never go as low as settling for that insignificant girl."

Savio stood up. "I'll go see my man, Dom," he said.

His man? He was in for a fucking wake-up call. Dom hated Savio even more than I did.

"And maybe the three of us can go party later on? I noticed a strip club by the interstate. Maybe we can have some fun," he continued, rubbing his hands together with excitement.

I couldn't help but grimace at the thought. I'd passed this place; it looked like an STD with walls. No, thank you.

Francesca ran her hand up my arm and gently raked her nails against the side of my neck.

"I don't think Luca will be able to come. He's going to be very busy with me tonight."

I turned toward her. "How about no? Francesca, let me make it clear to you. There's about zero percent chance of me ever touching you again. You were a goal, a body I had to make do with to satisfy my father, but as you said yourself when I was at the hospital. I'm a beast now and I can do what the hell I want and you, sweetheart, are not on the list."

"Come on, Luca. I knew you before Hell when you were the king—before the darkness."

"Yes, you did, and you left. And I have to admit I'm so grateful for that."

She shook her head. "It's because of the girl, isn't it?"

"I already said—"

She rolled her eyes. "Oh, the hell with what you said." She took a step back. "I know you, Luca, and I'm not as stupid as your cousin. I see the way you look when you talk about her. She may be Dom's but you want her."

I turned to see that Savio was gone and two things hit me then. One, even if I wanted to free her, Cassie was now on everyone's radar because I was as smooth as an elephant in a china store, and secondly, I was way, *way* past caring for her. This woman cared for me despite the darkness; she followed me there and took my hand, and it would cost me too much to say goodbye.

I exited the office and followed Savio's voice to the first floor. I'd tell him to fuck right off, that the girl was not his to touch.

My heart stopped when I found him leaning on Cassie's doorframe, talking to her inside.

That man was going to die.

I stomped downstairs, ready for murder. How dare he invade my girl's privacy. I knew her well enough; she would have never opened the door to him like that.

"Fuck me sideways; you were right."

That stopped me dead in my tracks.

"I usually am, why this time?"

He pointed to the bedroom and when I looked in I saw Cassie and Dom on her bed, both propped against the headboard, his arms around her shoulders, her head leaning against him.

I knew it was platonic between them and yet I couldn't help the pang of envy I felt. I envied how easily it was for him to bond with her despite all of his traumas and scars and how easily she trusted him despite how terrifying he was.

"Dom's off this afternoon." I turned to Savio— pointedly ignoring Francesca. "He can do what he pleases."

"Or who he pleases," Dom added with emphasis, pulling Cassie closer to him. I knew he was just playing along, telling Savio to piss off, and yet part of me still wanted to kill him for claiming what was mine—even if it was all pretend.

Also, she is not yours, my conscience reminded me. *Not yet, but soon.*

Something was off with Cassie. I could see it in the way she was avoiding my eyes. I wasn't sure what it was, but I felt it and I desperately wanted a moment alone with her to talk.

"I wanted to see if you wanted to go for a drink."

Dom threw me a side-look and I gave him a small nod, something Savio missed but not Francesca. No, she didn't, because she knew. She knew everything.

Dom nodded. "Sure. I know a great bar; let's go." He kissed Cassie once more on the forehead and got up.

"There are hot girls at the bar, right?"

I rolled my eyes as Dom chuckled. "The hottest, bro, except for you, babe," he added to Cassie's attention.

I sighed, pointing at Francesca. "Take her away, please."

"Luca…" she started with her annoying whine.

I shook my head. "Nope, not hearing it. I want you gone." I looked steadily at Savio. "You better take her with you and make sure she never comes back. Understood?"

Savio snapped his fingers to Francesca before pointing at the stairs.

She glared at him but started down the stairs.

"You're not coming?" Savio asked as he and Dom reached the top of the stairs.

"I'll meet you there. I need to speak with Cassandra for a minute."

"But—"

"He'll meet us there," Dom barked, cutting him off. "Let's go before I change my mind."

I waited for them to disappear down the stairs before closing the door and turning toward Cassie.

She was standing straight, on the other side of the bed, her arms crossed on her chest, clearly defensive and I had no idea why. Was it because of Francesca? Was she jealous?

"You know she means nothing—Francesca and I—"

"I wanted to discuss the deal we made."

I took a step back with surprise and rested my back against the door. *What deal?* "Okay?"

"You said if I stayed until the summer you would help me leave and get my brother back."

I nodded. "I did…" I trailed off warily.

"I need to know if it's the beginning or end of summer… The beginning would be best."

I was completely thrown off guard, the beginning of the summer was only a month from now. Just the thought of her leaving caused a grieving pain. "No."

"No?"

I shook my head. "What happened, Cassie, tell me."

She shook her head. "When is it?"

I sighed. "I thought—" I stopped. You thought what, Luca? That she'd stay with you forever, knowing who you are and what you did? She was raised by monsters who neglected her her whole life and she went through all that, made all the sacrifices to save her brother just to bind her life with a beast?

It made sense and the realization hurt more than it should have. She wanted me, she liked me but nowhere near what I felt for her.

"Do you really want to leave?" I asked her, not able to conceal the tinge of despair in my voice.

"I—" She stopped and shook her head.

Something had happened; that much was sure, but it was not relevant now. We were reaching the end of the road for what it was. Dom, Matteo, and now Francesca knew how deeply this girl appealed to me. It seemed that the only person who didn't know it was her. It was only a matter of time before anyone else found out what she meant to me and if I really wanted to offer her a choice, it was now or never.

Soon she'd be bonded to me whether she wanted it or not.

I sighed. "Fine, you can go." It was the right thing to do, so why was it hurting so bad?

"What?" She arched her eyebrows in surprise. "We made a deal, I—"

"And I'm honoring that deal." I nodded. "My lawyer in town has been working on this deal. You can leave today. If you decide to leave, I would rather you did so today. Take the car. I'll give the lawyer a call and text you the number. You call him and pick your options; he will also help you apply for your brother's custody. He is already working on it, to be honest."

"Why make me leave today?"

I shrugged. "Why not? It won't hurt me less tomorrow to see you leave."

She frowned. "Hurt you?"

I stayed silent; how could this woman be so blind?

"I heard you talk to them in your office. I came up to make sure you were okay..." She looked away. "You told them that you didn't care—that I didn't matter."

That was it. How was it so easy for this girl to believe the lies but she couldn't believe the truth I showed her.

"Truth is, Cassie, I was fighting your place in this world with all I had. I was trying to make a choice for you, a choice I had no right in making." I gave her a small smile. "I wanted to be selfless, spare you this life that, no matter how much I will want to shield you from, will taint you. But pretending, keeping you at arm's length, not taking what you were so generously offering, made me miserable and I think it made you a little miserable too."

"Luca..." she whispered, taking a tentative step forward.

I raised my hand to stop her in her tracks. We could not play this game any longer. This back and forth was dangerous for her and me.

I had to set this ultimatum now, even if I didn't want to.

"So you can go now, get everything I promised you. You'll keep on going on with your life and sometimes think of me or not... Get that lovely, quiet, white picket fence life you deserve." I stopped to take a deep breath. I could picture it, this lovely hallmark life for her. She deserved nothing less but the pain it woke in me constricted my lungs in a steel vise.

"Or you can stay here, with me, but not as my housekeeper or whatever but as mine." Just saying the words eased the pain. "But you need to know that, if you choose me, there's no turning back, Cassie. Once you're in, there's no out. I'll get your brother back; he'll move in with us, and we'll build our lives. I must go back to my role. I'll be the capo again, and if by some kind of miracle you decide to stay, you'll walk in the darkness with me, holding my hand and keeping the path lit up with your goodness. You'll be the little voice of reason in my ear when the darkness engulfs me; you'll be...*you*."

"Why?" she asked, wrapping her arms around herself as if she needed the comfort.

"Why what?"

"Why should I stay?"

I gave her a tired little smile. "You know why. Of course, you do. And the thing is in this life we don't know how much future we have left. I witnessed that front row by taking the future of two people I loved more than life. What's gone is gone and in my line of work nothing is guaranteed, the future even less and I crave to have you in it. Is it fair? Absolutely not. Do you deserve better? Undoubtedly. But, Cassie, anima mia, there's only you."

"What does it mean? Anima mia?" she asked, her voice a soft whisper.

I sighed, opening the door. "I'll tell you. If you decide to stay I will. But think long and hard because no matter how much I want to keep you, I'm done lying. This life is no fairy tale and I'm not a Prince Charming and it will be a commitment you won't be able to just walk away from."

"Where are you going?"

I let out a humorless chuckle. "I'm going to go get really, really drunk with Dom and the wannabe Tony Manero and when I'll come home, either you'll be here or you won't, but either way, Cassandra West, I'll never regret meeting you. Because you showed me that even a sinner like me could love, that despite everything I was not dead inside, that my heart could still feel, and just for that it had been all worth it."

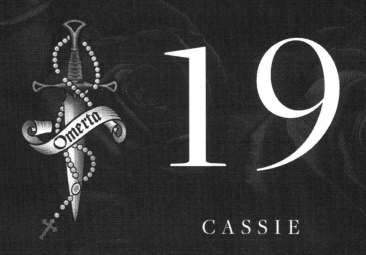

19

CASSIE

I was lying in my bed, watching the moving shadows of the moon play on my ceiling. I reached up and traced the necklace Luca bought me.

He gave me a way out, everything I wanted. He promised he would get Jude back and I knew his words were binding but he also asked me to stay, and when he looked at me, letting his guard down, I knew I was lost, and even if I had not been ready to admit it to myself yet, letting myself love a man like him was terrifying.

I wanted to leave him and this life behind. He'd been right, I had wanted a quiet life and I knew I'd never have that being with the capo of the Mafia. I was not an expert and Dom had been right, my Mafia references had been limited to *The Godfather* trilogy and a couple of seasons of *The Sopranos*, but I was not an idiot. I knew it was a lot of blood, violence, and death.

I'd even dialed the number of the lawyer as soon as Luca texted it to me, but no matter how much I'd wanted to press send, I couldn't because of the idea of walking away and never seeing him again; never feeling how I felt terrified me a lot more than being part of this world I knew nothing of because there was something I knew. I knew I'd be with Luca and I knew he would keep me safe and would be there for me and Jude, and this was enough to make the choice that I felt was right for me.

The commotion from downstairs interrupted my thoughts. Without thinking I slipped out of the bed and ran downstairs but stopped midway down the stairs.

Luca was there with Dom and Savio, Dom somehow trying to keep him up.

The three men turned toward me and the surprise in Luca's face morphed into something that made my stomach flip as his dark eyes tracked up my body.

I realized at that moment that I hadn't bothered putting on the robe, and my tank top and booty shorts I slept in didn't leave much to the imagination.

I was about to excuse myself and run back into the room, hoping to die of mortification before seeing these men again, when I noticed blood dripping from Luca's right eyebrow and the bloodstains on his left side. I rushed down, my embarrassment suddenly forgotten.

"You're hurt–" I whispered, standing in front of him.

"It's not my blood," he replied darkly.

I nodded, gripping his hand, leading him into the kitchen.

"Sit." I pointed to a chair before retrieving the first aid kit from under the sink. "Take off your shirt."

Luca didn't fight me and just sat down.

"Do I even want to know what happened?" I asked when he gave me his shirt.

"You don't have to do that," he called after me as I walked into the laundry room. "It's only a shirt."

"It's not just a shirt; it's your favorite shirt. Just give me a minute." I soaked it in water and baking soda and when I walked back in, I saw that his eyes were slightly glazed over and he seemed less in control.

"Are you–is he drunk?" I asked the guys that were standing by the kitchen door. Dom looked protective, Savio speculative.

"No, I'm not but I was getting there." He sighed as I pulled a chair to sit across from him.

I threw Dom a questioning look.

Dom rolled his eyes. "Our man has a temper, and a guy rubbed him the wrong way."

"I see." I looked at Luca and shook my head. "You went all caveman."

He hissed as I gently pressed the cotton ball soaked with disinfectant just above his brow.

"Why did you stay?" he whispered as I cleaned the cut.

I kept on working silently. I didn't want to share my feelings in front of witnesses.

He caught my wrist, keeping his eyes locked with mine. "You stayed," he continued as if he could hardly believe it. "After everything I told you, after the commitment it imposes, after giving you an out... You stayed." I didn't miss the longing in his voice and eyes.

I walked in between his open legs and looked down at his scarred chest. I was too scared to look at him.

I traced one of his scars on his chest with my forefinger. "For you, Luca Montanari, a thousand times over," I whispered. It was a quote from his favorite book and I knew he would understand. I would go through every trial for him.

His hand tightened around my wrist. "Get out!" he barked.

I looked up, startled, and I saw he was glaring at Dom and Savio standing behind us.

"I live here," Dom started.

"No, tonight you don't," he replied, glaring at them. "I don't care where you go, but I want you gone." He pulled me closer, sliding his hand under my top and resting a possessive hand on my stomach.

"Tonight, I'm claiming what's mine," he said, looking at me with so much heat in his eyes my heart started to hammer in my chest.

Savio started to say something, but Dom told him something in Italian, and I finally heard the door close and the room was finally silent, except for the loud grandfather clock in the hall and my ragged breathing.

Luca kept looking up at me in silence, brushing his thumb back and forth against my stomach.

"I didn't dare hope you'd stay," he admitted breathlessly, as affected as me by the heat of the moment, the air between us crackling with our desire.

"I couldn't leave you." I brought a hand up and ran it through his hair. "*Ti amo, mia bella bestia*," I said, hoping I was not butchering his language.

His face lit up, and he pulled me closer until I was straddling him on his seat, my core pressed against his growing erection.

"Hearing you speaking Italian…" He trailed off, pulling me forward, kissing my neck. "I love you, my heart, my soul." He brushed his fingers against the necklace he had bought me. "When I gave it to you, I said it was just because I found it pretty, but it is serotonin because serotonin is the source of your happiness and well-being. You're my serotonin, Cassie; you make me happier than I thought I could be. More than I deserve."

I grabbed his face and kissed him, but it didn't take him long to grab the back of my neck and take control of the kiss. He nipped at my bottom lip, just hard enough to make me gasp, and he invaded my mouth with his tongue, tasting me like he was a parched man finding an oasis in the middle of the desert. His lips were demanding, firm, passionate, the kiss so ardent my entire body felt on fire under the sensual pleasures that just a kiss from him enticed in me.

I moaned in his mouth, rocking my hips against his hard cock. The taste of bourbon on his tongue, his rugged musky scent, his strong hands pressing my core even more tightly against him made me dizzy with an overwhelming lust for my Mafia prince.

Luca broke the kiss and looked into my eyes as we both took a series of ragged breaths. I was glad I was sitting on him because the passion of his kiss had turned me into mush and I wasn't sure my legs could have supported me.

He kept his eyes locked on mine as he reached up for the thin straps of my tank top and pulled them down until the pink piece of fabric was bunched at my waist. My nipples were hard and demanding attention under the heat of his eyes. I've been bare like that to him before and once again despite my inexperience and the bright light in the kitchen I didn't feel self-conscious—not with him. He was looking at me as if I were a treasure, a dream he had just made and the force of his desire was so transparent in the way his hands tightened almost painfully on my hips, in the way his tongue dipped out of his mouth to lick his bottom lip as if he could already imagine my erected nipple in his mouth. His brown eyes looked black now, revealing his ravenous sexual desire for me.

I looked down as he moved his hands from my hips and trailed them up slowly. One over my side, the other dragged gently over my smooth, flat stomach, the vision itself was unbearably erotic, his strong, large hands going up my slim frame. His darker skin, a striking difference to the alabaster, unblemished skin of my stomach.

He stopped when both hands were cupping my breasts and he squeezed gently.

I hissed, rocking my hips against him again. I was completely soaked now and I had no doubt he could feel my arousal through his pants but I was far too gone in my delirious need for his touch to care.

He brushed his fingertips over my nipples before squeezing my breast a little more forcefully.

I let out a loud, lustful moan as I closed my eyes, arching my back, offering him my breast, silently inviting him to do something…anything. I wasn't sure what I wanted, what I needed, but I knew it was him…of all it—him, him, him.

He sucked one of my nipples into his mouth and I

let out a cry of relief at feeling his hot mouth and tongue on my body.

"I love you." I let out on a breath.

He growled, letting go of my nipple before licking them with the flat of his tongue in quick succession.

"I love you too, more than life," he said, his voice almost sounding pained.

In an instant, I was lifted from his lap and he was carrying me up the stairs.

I looked up at him; his jaws were tight, his eyebrows etched in concentration. He looked like a man on a mission.

I brushed my hand on his jawline. "I want you."

He looked down at me, his frown deepening. "Not as much as I want you. I'm trying my best to contain the beast for now but…" He let out another growl.

I realized we were in his room when he laid me down in the middle of the bed and stood up, tracking his eyes all over my body.

"I still can't believe you're mine," he whispered mostly to himself before reaching for his belt.

I looked at him, mesmerized by his movement as he kicked off his shoes and removed his pants and underwear, releasing his hard cock pointing angrily toward his stomach.

I was not an expert but even if his dick was not the giant size that would send you running in the other direction, it was long and thick, and I couldn't stop the little wave of anxiety to penetrate my lust at the idea of his big cock entering my petite, virginal body.

Luca's hard features softened. "It's going to be fine, tesora."

That man could read me like an open book. "I'll be gentle," he added before grabbing my booty shorts and bringing them down, leaving me panting and wanting on his bed.

"I trust you."

He crawled on the bed and knelt by my hips, parting my legs and looking at my wet pussy.

Once again I was surprised by my lack of embarrassment at being so brazenly opened to him, showing him the most intimate part of my body and what his mere touch and kiss had caused.

He licked his lips with desire as he caressed my lower belly with his hand before cupping my pussy possessively.

I raised my hips instinctively as I let out a strangled moan. "You're—you're driving me insane." I wanted the ache to stop, the pressure in my lower belly. I wanted to come. "Luca, please."

He started to caress me slowly, rubbing my slit up and down with the tip of his fingers. I grabbed at his bed cover, spreading my legs as far as they could go, not caring about anything other than his touch.

His fingers spread my nether lips open as he pressed his thumb against my clit. He stroked my pussy with expert fingers.

"Is that what you want?" he asked, sliding a finger deep in me.

"You, I want you…all of you."

He thrust his finger into me slowly before adding a second one, stretching me deliciously. He increased his pace while rubbing my clit a bit more forcefully.

"So tight, so wet… All mine."

His possessive statement took me over the edge and I orgasmed just as forcefully as I did when he made me come with his tongue after the ball.

I had barely come down from the high he caused as he lay beside me to take my lips in a passionate, forceful kiss.

"Say you're mine," he ordered against my lips before kissing me again.

"Yes, yours, always," I replied when he broke the kiss, allowing us both to catch our breath.

The heat of his powerful body over mine, the strength of his touch, his low animalistic growls at the back of his throat made me feel like I was on fire. I wrapped my arms around his shoulders, pulling him closer. I wanted more of his weight on me; I wanted him in me.

I ran my tongue on his lips, down his throat, tasting him, exploring him. I was so lost in him.

I thrust my hips up in a desperate move, and he seemed to finally be ready to grant me my wish as he used his hand to spread my legs wider as he moved, settling between my legs, and a fresh rush of wetness seeped from me as I felt his cock brush against my folds.

He wrapped his hand around his cock and brushed the tip up and down my slit, while murmuring words in Italian that I couldn't understand but still ignited the burning passion in me.

He stopped for a second, locking eyes with me before pushing the tip in. I gasped at the intrusion.

He kissed my lips. "It will hurt, tesora. I'll go slowly. Don't move, I barely have control." His voice was reflecting the primal hunger I could see in his eyes.

"It's okay. I want all of you."

He gave me a sensuous, dominant kiss that took my breath away as he pushed in slowly, inch after inch.

I tensed up as I felt a bit of pain and he stopped immediately, nudging against the soft barrier of my virginity.

He looked at me, his face a mask of complete lust-driven need to be fully in me.

I nodded and he thrust forward, getting the last few inches of him inside me at once.

The bite of pain was immediate and my body tensed, my mouth opening in a silent cry.

I blinked back the tears as he remained immobile in me, waiting for my body to relax.

"I'm sorry, tesora," he whispered, kissing my eyelids. "It will be better with time I promise."

I opened my eyes and ran my hands up and down his back, the pain and burning replaced by an uncomfortable fullness that I didn't mind knowing it was him inside of me.

"It's already pretty good now," I said sincerely. "I love having you in me."

"All seven inches of me?" he asked with a masculine smirk that was all his.

"All seven inches of you." I kissed the side of his neck. "You can move now. I'm okay."

Luca started to move with short, shallow thrusts, allowing me to get used to the intrusion. He kissed my neck and trailed his hand up until he reached my breast and plucked my erected nipple between his fingers.

I gripped his shoulder and bit his neck. He growled, deepening his thrusts. I brought my legs up, resting my heels at the top of his ass.

"Harder," I let out with a gasp.

He accelerated his pace and thrust harder, deeper and all that mattered were my moans, mixed with his grunt of pleasure, the rhythmic sound of his flesh against mine, the bedframe hitting the wall with each powerful thrust. He was possessing me, dominating me, making me his entirely and I never wanted it to end.

"I'm close," he grunted reluctantly. "Touch yourself, I want you to milk my cock when I come."

HIs dirty words aroused me even more and he hissed as I squeezed my walls against his cock.

I brought my hand to my clit as his thrusts turned erratic and one rub was enough to make me orgasm and he came, shouting my name.

When he was done he fell heavily on top of me and despite the discomfort his weight may have caused me, I didn't want him to move.

I wrapped my arms and legs around him and kissed his neck. "I love you, Luca."

He sighed with contentment. "I don't think I'll ever get used to you saying those words, Cassie. I hardly believe someone like you could love someone like me." He kissed the top of my head before disengaging himself from me and I felt the loss of him.

"Stay," I whispered, trying to pull him back on top of me.

He let out a small, tired laugh. "We have all night; we have all our lives, amore. I'll be right back."

I watched him go into his bathroom and come back with a wet cloth.

I looked down between my legs to see his fluid and mine seeping out of my body as well as a little bit of blood on my inner thigh

I blushed, closing my legs; that was much too intimate. I'd go shower real quick.

Luca rolled his eyes as he knelt on the bed. "Cassie," he said with a warning tone as he parted my legs with his hands. "You are mine, Cassandra. Mine to care for, mine to protect, mine to love," he said fiercely as he pressed the warm cloth against my sore flesh.

I stopped struggling. It felt so good on me, his touch gentle, caring. "You don't have to do that."

He smiled gently at me and lay on his side, facing me. "Yes, I do. It is my prerogative, my privilege as your man to take care of you."

I leaned forward and pecked his lips. "And you do it well."

His smile widened as he removed the cloth from between my legs and lay on his back, pulling me to him until my head rested against his chest.

I let out a yawn as I wrapped my arm around his chest.

"Sleep, my love," he whispered, brushing his thumb against the curve of my ass.

"Keep me in your arms."

"Always, this is where you belong," he replied and I fell asleep to the rhythm of his breathing.

20

CASSIE

I stirred and woke up deliciously sore from my love-making with Luca. He had taken me once more during the night and as I was a little less lost in my lust, I reassured him I was on the pill, not that he had seemed to care when he had let out a sigh of content once he was fully seated inside of me.

I stirred in the bed and pulled the cover tightly around me. I knew Luca was gone without even opening my eyes and I missed his body heat bitterly. Was it possible to be just that attuned to someone after just one night?

I finally blinked open my eyes and tried to see the clock on Luca's nightstand. I sat up in a jerk; it was much later than I anticipated and it had been years since I woke up that late.

Tesora. Come to the library. I have a surprise for you.

I sighed, getting out of the bed, and winced; yep I was definitely sore.

I grabbed my shorts and tank from the floor before padding to the first floor to my room, praying to God I would not meet Dom on my way.

We kicked him out last night and I knew he was going to tease me until next year if he saw me do the walk of shame to my bedroom.

I took a hot shower which did wonders for my sore muscles before dressing in leggings and a red plaid dress shirt.

I froze when I reached the library and heard a familiar giggle coming from the gap in the open door.

My heart jumped in my chest; I could hardly believe it.

I heard the giggle again.

"Jude?" I asked with incredulity, opening the door.

He was lying on his stomach in front of the fireplace, reading a book while Luca was sitting in his leather chair looking at him with a small smile.

Jude's head jerked up at the sound of my voice.

"Cassie!" He jumped from his spot on the floor and ran to me, wrapping me in his usual crushing hug.

"How?" I asked, hugging him back. "How?" I asked again, looking up at Luca who was looking at us from his spot in his chair, a bittersweet look on his face.

"I've been working on that for a while." He stood up and walked toward us. "It's only for a day," he added quickly. "I was trying to get him to come for your birthday but I got sick and..." He shrugged. "Happy belated birthday."

"This house is amazing, Cassie. Luca gave me a tour. I love it!"

Jude beamed up at me, and it was like having my carefree little brother again.

I removed his overgrown bangs from his eyes when he broke the hug. "How long have you been here?"

"About two hours but Luca said you worked hard and you were tired, so we let you sleep," he added before going to retrieve his book on the floor.

I looked at Luca as my cheeks tainted red.

"How are you?" he asked and I knew exactly what he meant.

"Perfect," I replied, my cheeks turning even redder.

He gave me a side-smirk full of male pride and I couldn't help but shake my head at the silliness of the moment.

"Jude was telling me how much he'd love to live here," Luca continued, coming to stand beside me, brushing the back of his hand against my cheek tenderly.

I turned toward Jude who was studying us

273

thoughtfully. "You would like to live here? With Luca and Dom?"

"Is Luca your boyfriend?"

"Yes, is Luca your boyfriend?" I swirled around to see Dom leaning on the doorframe, a mocking grin on his face. "What?" he asked, raising his hands in surrender. "I need to make sure I've been kicked from my home for a good reason."

I grimaced at the memory of Luca kicking him to the curb last night. I sent a helpless look to Luca who shrugged it off.

"I'd like to hear that answer too."

I sighed, concentrating on Jude's again. "Yes, he is."

Luca grabbed my hand, intertwining our fingers together.

"Are you okay with that?" I asked with apprehension. Jude was not great with changes or new people and me being with Luca and moving him here were big ones.

Jude rested his book on his lap, studying Luca silently.

He finally nodded. "Yeah, it's cool. I like Luca." He looked back down at his book. "Plus, he said he'll give me a library and will buy me a dog if I move in."

I looked up at Luca with my eyebrows arched.

He winked at me. "I never said I was above bribery."

I chuckled, leaning against him.

"When am I moving in?" Jude asked, keeping his eyes on the book he was reading.

"We're going to New York in a few days to see a lawyer. We'll work as fast as we can," Luca told him.

"We're going to New York."

I nodded. "Yes, I want you to meet my friends, see there's a life outside of..." He waved his hand dismissively.

"That was my idea," Dom piped in.

Luca glared at him, but I frowned. If Dom suggested it, he had to have a reason.

Luca leaned down and pecked my lips. "Why don't you stay with your brother for a while? I need to work for a bit." He looked toward Jude. "Your brother told me how much he loved burgers; Devlin will bring us back fast food for lunch."

I nodded taking a seat across from Jude, knowing that while he was engrossed in his book he wouldn't be interrupted, but I didn't mind. I loved him just the way he was.

"So how was your evening? Amazing, I bet," Dom teased, coming to sit beside me.

I looked up at him and he wiggled his eyebrows at me suggestively.

I rolled my eyes but remained silent.

"I've got to admit, I was a little annoyed to be sent out with the village idiot, but when I saw Luca coming down this morning whistling and with a spring in his step, I knew he was cured of his case of blue balls, making my night in the car almost worth it."

I quickly glanced at my brother who was humming to himself; he was completely gone.

"New York? Why?"

It was Dom's turn to look around. "I think we're getting there. There's one loose end that didn't disappear. The first doctor, he's in New York," he whispered.

"Okay…"

"Luca will have to go see Matteo or Benny. He won't take you there."

"And I'm grateful for that."

"The hospital is hiring. I need you to go for the interview, make your way over to his office as an overzealous attempt to get the job."

"Okay, and how do you come in?"

"You're causing a commotion, distracting them. I get the office all by myself while the perv's trying to calm you."

"What are you looking for? Dom, it's been two years."

He shrugged. "Account details—anything. Money leaves traces."

"Fine, whatever helps." I pointed at my brother. "He will be fine here, right? Despite everything."

"You mean our lives?"

I nodded. "I don't think he's made for it."

Dom looked at Jude. "You'd be surprised at how much a smart mind can do, and this one... He is scarily smart."

"He is."

"But no, Luca won't let this life taint him unless he wants to. Luca *is* a protector no matter what he thinks of himself. He will not let anything touch him or you... And the same applies to me."

I gave him a warm smile. "I know, you're like the big brother I never had."

"Uh-huh... Does it mean I need to have the talk with Luca?" Dom rested his forefinger on his chin. "You know, treat her well or I'll shoot you in the kneecaps kind of talk."

I rolled my eyes. "I'd like to see you try."

Luca came back a little after that and every time his eyes locked on me, I felt a little shiver going down my spine.

"I just spoke with the lawyer. We'll go there on Tuesday, just to give him the time to get all the papers ready for us."

"Perfect, thank you."

Luca walked closer to us and stood beside Jude. "Hey, Jude?"

Jude kept on reading as if nobody had talked. I peeked at the spine of the book—Arsene Lupin again. He was in his own world; nothing would distract him now.

Luca rested a gentle hand on his shoulder, startling him.

Jude blinked and looked up at Luca.

Luca smiled down at him. "The food's going to be here soon. Why don't you go with Dom in the big library upstairs and pick up some books to take with you?"

That did the trick because Jude jumped up from his seat and closed the book with a loud thud.

"There's a big library?" He looked at Luca with wide eyes.

I loved how my brother didn't regard Luca differently. I'd been worried at first when I'd imagined these two meetings. Luca was tall, muscular, and on top of the scars, he did have a dangerous air about him.

I was not sure how my brother would respond to him; he was awkward with strangers at best... And yet Jude had been accepting of him immediately.

Dom shook his head. "Getting kicked out yet again," he muttered, but the grin on his face showed he didn't mind in the least.

"I can take any book I want?" Jude asked as if he couldn't believe it.

Luca ruffled his hair. "Of course, whatever you like." He looked up at Dom and told him something in Italian.

Dom nodded and stood up. "Come on, Jude, let's give the lovebirds some privacy."

I watched them go and closed the door behind them before turning to Luca who was looking at me with such intimacy, it made my stomach twist.

"I need to learn Italian."

He nodded, walking closer to me and stopping just a breath away. "I'll teach you." He rested his hands on my hips. "I enjoy teaching you. But I won't hide anything from you; just ask."

"What did you just tell Dom?"

Luca leaned down and brushed his lips against my cheekbone. "I told him to keep your brother away from the top shelves; those are not books for him. But they are books you and I can explore."

My nipples hardened at the lustful thoughts entering my head at his proximity.

Luca closed the little distance between us and pulled me to him, resting his hands on my backside.

"How are you feeling today?"

"Good, a little sore but I don't mind it."

Luca brushed the shell of my ear with his lips. "You're still feeling me deep inside you, aren't you?"

"Yes," I admitted, pressing my thighs together.

Luca kissed the side of my face before pulling back reluctantly. "You're moving in my room today. There's plenty of space in my walk-in."

"It sounds a lot like an order."

He frowned. "I don't mean it to be, but I thought you understood that you were mine now and I intend to share your living space and share your bed every night. There is no alternative."

I hated to admit it, and the feminist in me probably screamed with indignation, but his alpha, dominant attitude thrilled me in ways that I never would have guessed.

I rested my hands on his shirt over his pecs and rubbed gently. "Of course I will."

He grinned. "*Brava.*"

"Thank you for Jude—it means the world to me." I looked up at him. "You, fighting for him, means more than I can say."

"There's not much I wouldn't do for you, Cassandra, except maybe let you go. You made a deal with the beast now, and I'm keeping you."

I stood on my toes and kissed his neck. "That's a good thing because I'm not going anywhere whether you like it or not."

"Is it supposed to be a threat?" he asked, arching an eyebrow in amusement.

I shook my head. "No, it's an oath."

The rest of the day went like a dream. I showed the garden to Jude and watched him play chess against Dom and Luca. He crushed them both and instead of being annoyed at being beat by a ten-year-old boy, the men were proud of him.

I could see it now, our life here. The family we'd be building soon and I couldn't wait for this life to begin because I trusted Luca to keep the darkness at bay.

He might have been a villain in his own narrative, but he wasn't, not in my story.

No, Luca Montanari was my hero.

21

LUCA

Saying I was happy was an understatement. I'd never thought it was possible, even before the accident, before I deserved nothing but penance, I'd never thought I had deserved a gift as precious as Cassandra West.

The loving, soft, forgiving, kind Cassandra West. She was the polar opposite of me and yet she completed me so perfectly.

I'd once told Carter that I had never done anything to warrant meeting a good woman and yet I got the best of them.

I woke up every morning expecting her side of the bed to be empty, to realize that it had all been a trick played by my alcohol-ridden brain to torture me a little more, but no, every time I opened my eyes in the morning I saw her, fast asleep beside me, her beautiful pink lips slightly open, and every morning I thanked whoever listened for giving me this invaluable gift.

"You don't mind, do you?" I asked her after we settled our bags in the New York hotel room. "I can take you if you want," I added quite reluctantly. I was not so keen on the idea of her meeting Benny, but I didn't want her to think I wanted to keep her hidden either.

She turned toward me and scrunched her nose on an adorable grimace. "If he's anything like your cousin Savio, I'd rather pass…no offense."

I laughed at that. "Like father, like son. I don't blame you." I pointed at the door. "And you get to spend some time with your girlfriend Dom and you girls can do whatever you like. Shopping and stuff."

She rolled her eyes. "I'll go get a dress for dinner."

I nodded. "I won't be long, I promise, and then you and I can have a little fun before we go to Carter's house."

She turned toward me, suddenly serious again. "How are you feeling about seeing your friend again after so long?"

This woman really could slay me; she saw right through me no matter what.

I knew I was supposed to reassure her, tell her that I was not bothered. I was the capo, nothing was supposed to touch me—at least not publicly—but she was my Cassie, the woman I swore to respect and to keep my walls down with. I was not going to be my father or any other man of the outfit. I couldn't be vulnerable but with her, I was going to be because she deserved the real Luca.

"I'm nervous," I admitted. "And mostly embarrassed, I've not been kind. He has tried time and time again to be there for me and I rejected any attempt. I just discarded him out of my life... Except for Dom, Carter was my only friend and I know it was the same for him."

She nodded. "Yes, but true friendship can come back from that. And they were pleased to have us over for dinner tonight." She grabbed my hand and kissed the back of it. "I'll be here for you, the whole time."

I squeezed her hand; she was my anchor.

I was reluctant to separate from her even for a short period, but I had to go see Benny.

Now that Cassie decided to be mine, I would need Matteo's support and to get it I had to take my place back, which based on what I witnessed, was more than overdue.

I took a deep breath, stopping at the back door of Effeuillage, the strip club we owned on the edge of the city's bad area. I didn't tell Benny about the visit; I wanted to surprise him.

He had thought that giving a strip club a French name would give it some class, but it hadn't fooled anyone. It was still a seedy club with washed-up dancers way past their prime.

When I tried to open the back door, a guard all dressed in black stepped in my way.

"No trespassing."

"I'm here to see Benny."

The guard stayed in front of the door, his glower deepening.

"Do you know who I am?" I had to give the guy a chance to rethink his actions before I broke his leg. "I'm Luca Montanari."

"Unless the capo tells me to let you in, I'm not letting you in."

I let out a chuckle. "Okay, the capo is telling you to let him in. I am the capo."

The guy gave me a half-grin. "Sure you are."

Yep, that guy wanted to die but he was lucky I didn't have the time to start a fight today.

I picked up my phone and dialed Benny's number.

"Where are you?" I asked as soon as he answered.

"Gianluca? I'm at the club."

"Your goon..." I looked at the guy in front of the door. "What's your name?"

"Fabrizio."

"Fabrizio is not letting me in. He said the capo ordered him... Ironic, don't you think?"

Within a couple of minutes, the door opened by a breathless Benny. I'd not seen him in over a year and Lord, he seemed even shorter and fatter than in my memories... He could be Dany Devito's body double.

I chuckled under my breath. That was a joke Dom would appreciate later.

"Ma cazzo!" He barked at the guard. "He's my nephew!"

"And the capo of the famiglia," I added calmly.

"Not really, but he shouldn't have stopped you! You're family," he added, his thick mustache twitching to the side, a clear sign of his nervosity.

I frowned. "Yes, Benny, really."

He wiped his damp hands against his black dress shirt and motioned me in.

I grimaced as soon as I walked in, thanking God I had not taken Cassie with me. It smelled like cheap alcohol and sex in this dump.

I shook my head and followed Benny to his office.

"Why did you come?" he asked as soon as he closed the door behind him.

I looked out of the one-way windows of his office to the stage where a stripper with saggy breasts and a thong moved for the handful of customers under a less than flattering red light.

I shrugged, keeping my eyes on the room. I kept my back to him on purpose; he needed to be reminded of his place. "You've been asking me to come for a while now. Didn't you mean it?"

"Of course I did! Gianluca, you're my nephew."

I finally turned around, putting my hands in my

pantsuit pockets. "There seems to be a misunder-standing between the ranks. People seem to think you're the capo."

Benny's nostrils flared. "I am."

"You're the *acting* capo. One word difference true...but a *whole* different meaning."

"Savio said you have a girl now." He cocked his head to the side. "I'm happy for you. I thought those scars would prevent it."

I nodded. "She doesn't seem to mind them." And with the way she was always kissing them, I dared to think she loved them as much as she loved me.

"Every woman would mind, Gianluca; if she says she doesn't, she's lying."

"But we all lie, don't we, Uncle Benny?"

He put his hand on his desk and tapped his fingers in quick succession. "What is it? Are you taking back your seat? Is it what she wants you to do?" He shook his head. "You didn't want that spot anymore; don't settle back in a lifestyle of hate for a woman."

"I'm not doing it for a woman."

"But you are doing it? What about your promise?"

I pointed at my chest. "What about *my* promise? What about yours? The one you made to uphold our values and do what's the best for the family."

He slammed his fist on the desk. "I've always done what's best for the family! I'm doing things your father was too scared of doing."

"Too scared or too sane?"

Benny shook his head. "Is that it? Now that the man is dead you'll defend his actions. I've not forgotten how much you two were fighting, about everything."

I sighed. This man was way too far up his own ass to see the truth about his actions.

"I have followers, you know. Things won't be as easy as you think."

I was taken aback by his boldness; my uncle was usually all bark, no bite—sending bigger dogs to fight his battles like a scared little girl.

"Are you *threatening* me?"

"No, Luca," he muttered.

Ah, backtracking. That was more like Benny.

"You gave me your spot; I deserve it. This is mine," he continued, almost whining.

I looked down at my watch. "I came as a courtesy, family reunion, and all that shit." I sighed. "I'll see you later."

"Luca!" he called after me as I opened the door. "What are you going to do?" he shouted as I kept on walking out of his miserable club.

I'd let him keep it in the end, let him be the king of his seedy kingdom as long as he stayed out of my way and didn't approach my woman.

My phone beeped as I reached the alley outside the club. I took a deep breath. Who would have thought I'd enjoy the smell of a city's alley? To be fair, everything was better than the pungent smell of this club.

I sighed, looking down at the photos on my screen, and frowned. Fuck, my day of confrontation was far from over, and I was positive I'd enjoy this one a lot less.

When I walked back into my room, a little of my dark mood faded when I saw Cassie standing there, a big smile on her face, visibly so happy to see me.

And despite my annoyance I couldn't help but smile back; this woman owned me.

"I found a dress for tonight. It's so pretty." She reached for my hand and stood on her tiptoes to give me a chaste kiss.

"Nope, this won't do," I replied, pulling her closer to me and deepening the kiss, leaving us both wanting and panting. I wanted to make love to her right now, but I had a score to settle and it couldn't wait.

"Where's Dom?"

"He's in his room." She pointed at the door. "I think I killed him with all the shopping."

I nodded, watching her putting bags away.

"Did you have a good afternoon? Did you do anything interesting?"

Her step faltered and she turned around, a faint hue on her face. "No, not really."

I sighed. She was a terrible liar, and the fact that she lied to me? It did break my heart a little.

"I'm going to see Dom, but I'll be right back to take a shower and get ready."

"Is everything okay? Did things work out with your uncle?"

I nodded. "Yes."

"I'll wait for you, we can shower together. Save some water." She blushed so deeply it made my heart squeeze in my chest with all the love I had for her. She was not yet used to flirting with me, at asking for what she wanted.

"No, go ahead," I told her a bit more abruptly than I ought to. I was more annoyed with her than I anticipated.

She jerked back and looked down, trying to hide her pain at my rejection.

I should have left it at that; that's what a capo should have done, but I was weak for her, and no matter what she did...as terrifying as it was to realize, I didn't think there was a sin she could commit that I would not forgive.

"Tesora, if I get in this shower with you, there won't be any dinner at Carter's house. I'll take you every way I can until neither of us can move."

"Oh." She gave me a side-look. "Maybe...maybe I'd like that."

I growled, looking heavenward. "You're killing me. I'll be right back," I added, turning around and leaving the room before I had a chance to reconsider my choice.

I knocked on Dom's door and as soon as he opened the door, I punched him so hard I was sure I'd have my knuckles bruised.

He fell on the floor with a pained growl. I took the opportunity to walk in and close the door behind me.

"What the fuck, Luca!" he barked, sitting up on the floor, bringing his hand up and touching his busted left eyebrow. He looked at his fingers coated with blood. "That's for lying to me, you fucking asshole, and for making her lie to me too."

Dom stayed seated on the floor but reached for the towel on the bed and pressed it on his eyebrow.

"What? Nothing to say?" I asked tauntingly. "Did you think I was that stupid, *amico*? She is a terrible liar and you—" I snorted. "You were too happy to stay behind today. And I know how loyal she is—the only person she would lie for is you."

"How did you find out?" He winced, pressing the towel a bit harder on his eyebrow.

I snorted. "Please give me more credit. I had you followed. What did you do at the hospital with my woman?"

"It's complicated."

"Uncomplicate it then!" I pointed an accusing finger at him. "You made her lie for you!"

"Oh, fuck right off, Gianluca. That girl is loyal to you to a fault. The only person she would lie for is not me...it's *you*!"

"The only reason she'd lied to me is for *me*?" I nodded, pursing my lips. "You must think I'm a special kind of stupid."

He sighed. "It all started the night of the ball. I didn't, well, no, I did have an allergic reaction but I caused it on purpose."

I arched my eyebrows in surprise; that was not something I had expected.

"Cassie caught me and wanted to run tell you the truth so I had to get her involved, and once I told her what I suspected, she wanted to help and didn't take no for an answer."

"Help you do what?"

"Prove that you didn't have an accident that night, that it was intentional. Prove that you weren't drunk and that these deaths are not on your conscience."

That revelation had the effect of being punched in the stomach. I sat down heavily on the chair in his room, looking at him like he was someone else.

"You think—" I stopped. I couldn't believe it was even possible. Could I erase this black mark from my book? "No." I shook my head. "Nobody would have ever hurt Arabella or my mother."

"Correct." He nodded. "But as you probably remember, they were not supposed to be there that night. They were supposed to leave for the estate early, but you had that big fight with your father and your mother decided to stay. It was you and your father that were supposed to be in that car—not them."

I rested my forearms on my thighs and looked down at my hands I had believed for years were covered in my family's blood. "Who would do that?"

"You know who, Luca. He wanted the spot for as long as I can remember."

I shook my head, still looking down at my hands. "Benny and Savio are idiots. Thick and obvious, they would have never managed to pull off something like that."

"Unless they had help."

I looked up. "Who?"

"The Armenians?" Dom shrugged. "Maybe they made a deal with them; they're stupid enough to."

I cocked my head to the side, pondering this. It was not impossible.

"Why did you go to the hospital today?"

"The writing in your medical file was different, the pages color didn't fit. Cassie found a few unusual things in it so we went there. She was the diversion and I broke into the file room."

"I see... So let me get this straight. You involved my woman in a potential murder plot against me by putting her in harm's way."

Dom winced. "Okay, it sounds bad when you're saying it like that."

"You know why? Because it fucking is!" I shouted.

Just the thought of Cassie being hurt caused me so much pain I could hardly breathe.

"Luca—"

I raised a finger to stop him. "Her involvement stops now, understood?"

Dom nodded, at least having the decency to look sheepish.

"Did you find evidence?" Please say yes.

"Some, not as much as I'd like."

I stood up, straightening my pants. "I'll arrange a meeting with Mattco tomorrow; you'll tell him everything you know, and we'll take it from there, understood?"

"Yes." He stood up too and grimaced when he saw his reflection in his mirror.

"And you keep her out of it! No more putting her in unnecessary danger or I swear to God..." I didn't need to finish that threat. "I'll see you in the morning."

"I love her too, you know," Dom said as I reached the door. "Not as you do, but just as deeply."

I turned my head to the side, keeping my hand on the handle. "I know you do. It is the only reason why you're still standing."

When I walked back into the room, Cassie was wrapped in a towel, freshly showered, and drying her hair.

She gave me a questioning look in the mirror,

following me silently with her eyes until I reached the bathroom.

I met her eyes in the mirror and smiled at her. *Ti amo*, I mouthed.

Her shoulders sagged with relief. *You too.* She mouthed back and just like that, we were okay.

I toweled myself dry after my quick shower and walked into the bedroom with the towel around my waist, and the lusty glint that appeared in her eyes made me feel like a superhero. I still couldn't believe I deserved her.

"Zip me up?" she asked, turning toward the mirror.

I came to stand behind her and brushed my knuckles over her spine, making her shiver.

"Your skin is so soft," I whispered before leaning down to kiss the back of her neck. I loved when she wore her hair up; her neck was so beautiful and delicate.

She sucked in a breath as I brushed my lips up and down the column of her neck. I peeked in the mirror and noticed her nipples were erect with desire.

"Tonight," I promised—or warned—as I zipped her up. "You look stunning," I told her as I studied her little black and silver cocktail dress she was wearing with the necklace I had given her. She never took it off and that made me happier than it should.

She swirled around and rested her little hand on

my scarred cheek. "You always say that," she teased with a smile.

I wrapped my arms around her and kissed her. "Because it's always true."

She rolled her eyes. "Even when I just woke up in my oversized pajamas? Because you say it then too."

"Especially when you wake up in these oversized pajamas! It means I get to take them off and eat that sweet little pussy of mine."

She let out a startled laugh as she blushed. It was now a favorite game of mine. How many times a day could I make my woman blush.

"*Your* pussy?"

I scoffed. "Of course! I'm not sharing or giving it back. It's mine."

She caressed my cheek and I could see all her love right there, in her stunning green eyes. I would die for you, I wanted to pledge.

"Yes, it's yours," she confirmed before getting out of my hold. "Now get ready, Mr. Montanari; we're already running late."

When she sat in the car to go to Carter's house just outside of the city, I grabbed her hand.

"I know you lied to me," I said as gently as I could to show her I was not actually angry.

She tensed, throwing me a side-look.

"Dom told me the truth, about the investigation you two were doing. Just the thought of you being in danger." I shook my head.

"I— Don't be mad at Dom; it was my idea to get involved!"

Of course, leave it to her to defend him.

I sighed. "Maybe so but he knows how dangerous our world is. He should have known better."

"I wanted to help you."

I brought her hand to my lips and kissed it. "And you did but now please stay out of it. I need you to be safe and sound, okay? I can't look into it and worry about you at the same time."

"Okay," she said in defeat.

"I'm going to see Matteo tomorrow after the appointment with the lawyer and I will tell you everything."

"You promise?"

"I swear it."

She smiled, sliding closer to me and resting her head on my shoulder. "I'm glad I don't have to keep the secret anymore. I hate keeping something from you."

I turned my head and kissed her forehead. "And you're also *very* bad at it."

"It's okay. I'd rather be like that."

"Me too."

When we parked in front of Carter's mansion, apprehension ceased me. I released a shaky breath.

"It's going to be fine," Cassie encouraged me, squeezing my thigh gently.

I let out a humorless laugh. "Lord, you must think

I'm a freak. First, I freaked out at the ball and now, here." I shook my head. "I must look like a scared little boy."

"No, I see a strong man who is starting to heal and is trying to get his life back. This is not easy and I'm so proud of you."

I nodded. "Let's go."

As soon as we got to the big wooden door we were ushered in by a majordomo who took us to a small dining room.

Nazalie smiled brightly when she saw us and Carter had his usual scowl on but it didn't have to mean anything to him.

Nazalie rushed toward me and hugged me. "Oh, Luca, it's so good to see you again."

I returned her hug awkwardly, refusing to let go of Cassie's hand.

Carter approached us and gave a faint smile to Cassie before turning toward me.

"Luca, you've been missed." I knew Carter King was not big on displays of emotion, at least for anyone other than the petty curvy woman standing beside him, and I thought it might have been why we'd been friends for so long—we were the same.

I pulled Cassie closer to me. "This is Cassie, She's my…" I stopped unsure of how to put it. Girlfriend? That was not enough. Fiancée? A little presumptuous. Honestly, all I could think of was *mine*. She was mine…she was my everything.

Carter nodded. "I get it." He turned to Nazalie and gave her a soft smile. "She just *is*."

"Yes." I looked at Cassie. "She just is."

I turned toward Nazalie and my eyes locked on her swollen belly... "Isn't that the same as two years ago?"

She laughed, resting a protective hand on her stomach. "This is baby number three actually. Leo and Connor are sleeping upstairs."

"Jesus! Three?"

Carter grinned. "What do you want me to say? I really wanted a little girl and it took three tries." He winked at me. "Plus, let's be honest, I quite enjoy making them."

"Carter!" Nazalie gasped, slapping his arm playfully.

He pulled her to him and kissed the top of her head. "I also love seeing my babies grow inside her."

My eyes instantaneously connected with Cassie's flat stomach—yes, I could definitely see the appeal. I couldn't wait to see my Cassie carry our baby, that little part of us. My inner caveman was overexcited at the idea of impregnating her... But not yet, she was still so young. We had all the time in the world.

Dinner went much better than I expected and it was like falling back into a routine. Despite the two years that had passed, it was like we never really lost touch.

Nazalie and Cassie connected immediately and I

could see Carter was also fond of her—how could he not be? Cassie was an angel in disguise.

After dinner, Nazalie took Cassie on a tour of the house while I followed Carter to his office for a drink.

"So you're back?" Carter asked after extending me a glass of bourbon.

I nodded, taking a sip.

"That's good because your uncle is not the best at ruling this city."

"I know and I'll be taking over, but I'll remain in the Estate. Cassie loves it."

"And you love Cassie," he finished for me.

"More than life."

"It's sort of cathartic, don't you think? Finding *the* person."

"It's terrifying."

Carter chuckled. "Yes, but in the best way possible. She gives me a reason to keep on going."

"I'm sorry," I finally admitted, albeit reluctantly.

"Don't be. You did what you needed to do for yourself. I'm just glad to see you came through the other side."

"Cassie helped a lot. She accepts it all, the good and the bad."

"That's how you know you found the one."

"I fear one day she will wake up and just go, decide it's too much and just walk away."

Carter sighed. "That fear, I have it too, and it

never really goes away. Over two years in this marriage, three kids later, and some mornings I still wake up in awe to have her beside me."

"I'm going to marry her."

"I know you will." He shook his head. "I'm glad you're back, Luca; you've been missed… Not by me but you know."

I laughed. "Duly noted and for the record, I didn't miss you either."

"I wouldn't have dreamed of it." And just like that, we were back to our old friendship.

CASSIE

I nervously wiped my hands on my pants as Luca and I waited for that big-shot family lawyer to call us into his office.

Luca grabbed my hand and kissed the back of it. "Everything is going to be fine."

I forced a smile. "Yeah, I know, it's just...Jude, you know."

He nodded. "I do and I promised we'd get him back as soon as possible, and you know how I always keep my word."

"Yes, I know you do and I trust you, but this..." I pointed at the lawyer's door. "No matter what, a lot of it is outside of your control."

He gave me his cheeky grin that made my girlie parts quiver. "It's cute that you think so. Tesora, I'm using the legal route, for now, but should it not work." He shrugged. "One way or another, we'll get our boy back."

Our boy... It was little things like that that made me love him even more.

"Ms. West, Mr. Montanari? Mr. Gutsberg is ready for you."

We walked into the biggest office I'd ever seen with a whole panel of windows at the back giving a premium view of the city.

I glanced at Luca. How much was he paying that lawyer?

The lawyer stood and motioned to the seats across from his desk.

"Mr. Montanari, what a pleasure to see you again. Please take a seat. Ms. West." He bowed his head slightly before sitting at his desk in front of a pile of papers.

"Sorry for the delay in getting you in but I have excellent news. I was on the phone with the Family District Court and frankly, Ms. West, your lawyer did a very poor job in this case."

"I, um, I didn't have a lawyer, you see." I fidgeted on my chair, suddenly feeling like I let my brother down. "I didn't do anything wrong and I didn't have money so—"

Luca reached for my hand and squeezed it. "It doesn't matter, what is it?"

"A couple of people offered to take your brother

temporarily. A Mrs. Broussard and a distant relative —India Cassidy?"

I nodded. "Yes India is my cousin from Vancouver and Mrs. Broussard was our old maid. I was staying with her."

The lawyer rested his arms on his desk and looked up at me. "All that to say that you were dismissed as a suspect very early in the investigation. I suspect some laziness and a lack of collaboration to have played a part in this mess, but your brother should have been given back to you weeks ago."

Does— No, it could not be that easy. I was not that lucky. "Does it mean I can—"

"Have him back?" The lawyer smiled. "Yes, certainly! They made a mistake and are expediting the procedure. My assistant will be chasing daily but I suspect you will be able to pick up your brother in the next couple of days."

"Oh, this is— This is—" I rested a trembling hand on my mouth, the relief bringing tears to my eyes.

The lawyer smiled. "I understand and you are welcome."

Luca squeezed my hand again. "How do we go about adoption?"

I turned my head toward him. "You want us to adopt a child?"

He gave me a teasing smile. "Not right now, I rather we work on trying to make one."

I blushed crimson in mortification at him saying that in front of a stranger.

"I'd like to adopt your brother, take away the stigma his name is causing him."

"I see... Because Montanari doesn't come with any preconceived stigmas?"

He laughed. "Yes, it does, but at least it comes with the type of stigma that will keep him safe no matter what."

I turned toward the lawyer. "Is it doable?"

The graying man nodded. "Well, yes, it is doable, but the issue is that his parents are still alive and even if they are in jail, they still have parental authority. The only way that it would work is if—"

"They died?" Luca tried.

"Oh, for God's sake," I muttered. I sometimes forgot my man was Mafia.

The lawyer was not even shocked. I wondered how often he dealt with men like Luca.

"No, the simplest way would be to have them relinquish their full parental rights to you or..." He gestured toward me. "Miss West. You can then start the process of adopting Jude West."

"You'll be okay with that?" Luca asked me.

"Yes, but—" I sighed. "As you know, my parents are very bad people. If they know it will make our lives easier, they won't do it."

Luca smiled at me, and it had a predatory edge I'd never really seen before; that was Capo Luca in front of me. "Oh, they will, trust me." He turned toward the lawyer again. "Start all the paperwork; we'll do that soon."

"Perfect. I will get started." He turned toward me and swirled a pile of documents toward me. "If you could please sign the agreement of guardianship. I will be able to finalize the release of your brother in the next day or so."

I signed everything, still having a hard time believing the nightmare was ending.

When we reached the street, waiting for the car, I couldn't contain my happiness anymore and pulled Luca in a hug.

He hugged me back with a startled laugh.

"What is that for?"

"For Jude, for me, for everything."

"You deserve everything and then more, tesora."

"So what about the curse of my last name?" I asked teasingly as he was looking at me with an amused smile. "Are you going to adopt me too?"

He snorted, tightening his hold around my waist. "No, you, I'll marry, of course."

I was stunned. He'd just said that like it was the most natural thing to say, like it was evident and not the bomb it was.

I followed him numbly inside the car.

"Are you in shock?"

I turned toward him in the seat. "I just, you just said that."

He nodded. "I did. I said you were mine, Cassie. I thought you knew what it meant."

"Yes, no, I mean— Was that a proposal?"

"Absolutely not! Give me more credit, tesora. When I propose, you'll know."

I shook my head with a small smile. "What are we doing now?"

He sighed, looking at his watch. "I've got to go see Matteo with Dom about…"

"Okay. You'll be fine though, right?"

"Of course I will. I won't leave you for long. Maybe book a massage."

"Good idea." I didn't really feel like getting a massage, but I didn't want him to worry about me.

"It's all good, tesora. I promise." He grabbed my hand and kissed the back of it. "Let's enjoy it, things are going well. Tonight I'm taking you for dinner at *Vignaiolo*. What do you say?"

"Isn't it that super famous restaurant with a few months' long waiting list?"

"It is."

"How can you get a table?"

He shrugged. "The perk of being the owner I suppose."

"Oh…" I knew that Luca was powerful, rich, and scary, but I had not yet really dealt with this side of him. I was sure it would all take a little getting used to but I loved him enough to deal with everything to come.

When we made it back to the hotel, we went to Dom's room instead of ours, and Dom was talking with a guard I'd seen around the property a few times before.

Dom turned to me and winked. "How are things, princess?"

I shook my head with a small smile. "Things are good."

He nodded before looking at Luca. "Sergio will look after Cassie while we do our stuff; he's been briefcd. Hc's good."

"Sergio," Luca called him with his commanding boss voice.

The burly young man turned toward him. "Boss."

"You're going to guard her as if she were your life, do you understand?" His voice was calm but the coldness behind it was terrifying.

"Of course, Boss, she is safe with me."

"Good, good." Luca nodded. "Because you see, you guard her as your life because it's exactly what she is. If anything...*anything* at all happens to her, you die. Do you understand that too?"

The guy paled.

"He is joking," I blurted out. I didn't need that guy to be terrified the whole time.

Luca looked down at me like I'd lost my mind. "I am certainly *not* joking."

I turned to Dom who shook his head and mouthed 'Not joking' to me.

Okay then…

Luca sighed and looked at his watch again. "We better go now. Matteo is not good with people who are late."

Dom snorted. "Matteo is never good with anything."

"Just one minute," Luca said to the guys as he walked inside the room with me.

He pulled me to him until his forehead was against mine. "You'll stay put, okay?" he asked with anxiety rolling off him.

"Yes, of course." I rested my hand on his chest, over his heart. "Why are you so worried?"

He pecked my lips. "Because I love you, and because my heart lives in your chest, and I hate leaving you alone in the city with anyone other than me or Dom."

I wrapped my arms around his waist. "I'll be fine. I'll stay put. I'll get a massage and a facial and every-thing, and then when you come back, we're going to lock the door and have fun for a few hours."

He grinned, and the mischievous glint in his eyes made my lower stomach clench. "I'll hold you to that."

"I hope you do."

Luca let me go and walked to the door. "Sergio will be in front of the door. Just open it and ask if you need anything."

I nodded. "Okay, I love you."

His face changed from determined to tender. "I don't think I'll ever get tired of hearing you say that."

"Well, that's good then because I never intend to stop."

"I love you too."

I giggled. "I know."

"*Furbetta*," he muttered before leaving me behind.

Now that he was gone, I didn't have to hide my anxiety anymore. I was worried about him talking to Matteo. I didn't know much about him, but based on what Dom had told me, he was not a pleasant man.

I just hoped he'd believe Luca and Dom and deal with any further danger looming over him.

I decided to follow Luca's advice and booked a massage and used the time to call Amy and ask to speak with Jude for a little while.

He was just as happy as I was to come and live in the Estate. It was true what Luca had said; luck was finally coming our way.

I had just made myself a sandwich when Sergio knocked on the door. I looked at the clock; the masseuse was a little early.

I opened the door to find a breathless Savio.

"Where is Sergio?"

"He went downstairs with Dom," he said with panic. "You've got to come with me now. Luca has been hurt, it's bad."

My heart stopped, my breathing stopped, everything stopped as if time went completely still. Those words were the most terrifying I'd ever heard.

"Let's go." I started to follow him down the corridor to the elevators, my mind going a thousand miles per second, but suddenly it didn't feel right. Why wasn't Dom coming to pick me up?

I slowed down my pace, deciding to test him. "How did he get hurt at Carter's office?"

"I'm not sure, a lone shooter was waiting for him there," he added, pressing the elevator button.

Liar! I stopped walking. "Sorry, my bag, I need it." I turned around and rushed back toward the room just fast enough not to show I was running away.

Once the door was closed behind me, I could call Luca and—

Just as I was about to walk into the room, an arm tightened around my neck, so tightly it cut off my air supply.

"I wonder, where did I go wrong?" Savio whispered against my ear.

I gasped as I felt the sting of a needle in my neck and everything went dark.

23

LUCA

"Do you realize how ludicrous it sounds?" Matteo asked, leaning back on his black leather chair while playing with his Zippo.

Matteo's office was just like him and his soul...all made of black furniture and glass. His desk imposing, his chair so big, it was more like a comfortable throne.

I leaned forward on my seat. "Are you telling me you don't think Benny would be able to kill to be capo?"

Matteo laughed. "Oh no, Benny's totally able to kill for this. But he and his idiot son..." He shook his head. "They are not good or smart enough to get away with something like that."

"Maybe the Armenians were involved. He does seem like their little bitch now."

Matteo rolled his eyes. "The Armenians are opportunists; they would not have bothered with your uncle before he became the capo." He sighed. "What evidence do you even have?"

Dom was about to answer when my phone vibrated. I looked to see Enzo's name. I frowned. The kid hated to speak on the phone for obvious reasons; having him call me didn't predict anything good.

"Enzo?"

Matteo threw me an incredulous look like he could not believe I was answering a call in his presence.

"L-l-luca. I-I-I t-think S-savio and my f-father have done s-s-something b-bad."

"What have they done?"

"C-c-cassie."

I jumped from my seat and gestured to Dom to stand up.

"Are you home?"

"Y-yes."

"Fine. Dom is coming to pick you up. You stay there." I hung up. "Enzo said his father has Cassie."

Dom paled as his hands tightened into a fist. "He's dead," he growled.

I sometimes forgot how important she was also for him.

"Bring Enzo back to the hotel. We'll meet you there."

"We?" Matteo asked when Dom was gone. "You know I can't mettle, Gianluca; this is something happening in your own family."

I shook my head. "But what if I take him down? Will I be judged?"

"You will."

"But he has her! I love her. "

"Well… That's a plot twist… She is not your wife, Gianluca; you have not officially claimed her as yours. For the famiglia, she is nothing more than an unbound civilian who knows way too much about us. Benny will not be judged too harshly for his hastiness."

"She is not nothing; for me she is everything. Do you even know what love is?"

He tipped his mouth in disgust. "God, no! I thank God every day for protecting me from such a curse."

"Maybe you should thank your lack of heart."

Matteo pondered that. "Yes, that too."

I was not above begging him, not for her. "Help me and I'll step up, take my seat again and be a good little capo."

Matteo looked at me with his sadistic smile. "I'm afraid it won't be enough this time."

I understood the underlying message. He wanted to bargain. "What do you want?"

"I want a favor."

I nodded, every minute lost was a risk on her life. "I'll give you anything. Help me save her."

"Anything?" The glimmer in his eyes unsettled me. "Don't make promises you can't keep."

"As long as it's not Cassie or our future children —anything."

Matteo made a disgusted sound. "Children? Lord, no! Who would willfully want those parasites? God, keep your offspring." He fake shuddered at the thought. "No, I'll ask you for something one day and you'll have to say yes, no matter what it is and you're stepping up now. You are the capo again from this moment."

"Fine, yes, whatever."

"*Giuro.*"

"*Lo giuro sulla mia vita, sul mio nome, e sul mio sangue.*"

He stood up with a nod. "Let's go."

When we made it to the hotel, Sergio was in my room, his face swollen and bleeding.

"How?" I barked at him, not caring he was half dead.

"I didn't expect Savio to—" He croaked before leaning against the wall, holding his head. "I think I have a concussion."

"You'd be lucky if it's all you have." I scanned the room and stopped at the bar by the kitchenette. "You and I will talk when I get her back."

I turned to Matteo, showing him the necklace I'd

bought Cassie and the note that simply said, '*Step down and get her back.*'

"I'm going to kill him," I announced.

Matteo shook his head. "No, you won't; don't make him a martyr. Don't start a war within the famiglia. He'll get dealt with."

At this moment Dom arrived with Enzo.

"L-l-luca, it's not m-m-me," he said, looking around with wide eyes, his big glasses perched precariously on his thin nose.

Any other day I would have been patient with him, nice. Enzo was a good kid and he got enough shit from his own father and brother.

"Enzo, I know that but you need to choose a side now. Where are they?"

He looked around uncertain, throwing a worried look toward Matteo. He knew something, but he also felt guilty. He knew that no matter what it would not end well.

"Look at me!" I snapped.

Enzo turned to me, startled by my tone.

"Forget Matteo, he can't help you now. I'm the worst nightmare in this room. Now choose and choose well. Either you side with your father and brother who always have a kick in humiliating you or you side with your capo." I pointed at myself. "And his consigliere." I pointed at Dom who looked at me with clear surprise.

Of course, he was my consigliere; there was no man in the world I trusted more than him.

"Wow…" Matteo rolled his eyes. "That's another plot twist I never saw coming. You are so unpredictable. A true man of mystery."

"I-I'm with y-you, L-l-luca. Always."

I gave him a sharp nod. If he didn't speak now, I swear to God I would take him down too.

"My f-f-father has a s-secret warehouse on t-t-the docks."

"Address?" Dom demanded.

Enzo retrieved a little notebook from his inside pocket and extended it to Dom.

"F-f-first page."

Dom opened the notebook and looked at me. "Seems legit." He jerked his head toward Enzo. "You're coming too."

By the time we reached the warehouse, I felt like a predator in a cage, restless and starving, ready to spring and kill.

As soon as the car stopped, I rushed out of the car and charged toward the door, ready to go in all gun blazing.

I was just reaching the back door when someone grabbed my arm to stop me.

I snarled, swirling around to face Matteo.

"Stop, don't let your emotions take over. Let's take a minute."

I looked down at his hand gripping my forearm. "Be careful, Genovese; people will think you care."

He snorted. "Hardly, but I finally convinced you, a half-decent capo, to step up, and it's not to have you killed or exiled now."

"Priorities, right?" I asked mockingly.

"Always." He looked at the door. "I'll go in first, just give me a minute and follow…and don't forget your promise."

I looked back at Dom who shrugged and Enzo who was cowering on the wall.

"You stay here, Enzo, okay?" I tried to make my voice sound softer than before.

He nodded, a grateful look on his face.

"Okay, let's go."

Matteo retrieved his Beretta from his right side holder and attached the silencer he had in his pocket.

I looked at him with my eyebrows arched. Who walked around with a silencer in his pocket?

"What? I'm always prepared." He shot the lock of the door in a soft thud.

"I'm going to kill them," I muttered to Dom as soon as Matteo walked in.

"I know."

Dom and I retrieved our guns and walked behind Matteo. It was clear that they used this warehouse for a lot of things that were questionable from our family rules.

We walked silently following a dim light and muffled voices in the distance.

Dom nudged me with his arm and jerked his head to the left.

I looked to see a box with Russian writing on it. I could bet it was weapons. Benny was dealing weapons with the Russians or the Armenians... That man was even more stupid than I thought...or maybe not; he took the prize when he stole my woman.

"You shouldn't have taken her, Benny; it was not smart," Matteo said with a stern voice.

"I did it for us, Matteo. She knows too much."

I revealed myself from behind a shelving unit and came to stand beside Matteo, Dom taking his other side.

Benny tensed as I looked around and found Cassie on a chair in the middle of the room, her arms tied behind her back, her ankles attached to the chair legs. Her head was hanging down, her chin to her chest. Her beautiful red hair falling like a veil over her face, hiding what I longed to see most.

Savio moved behind her, his gun much too close to her for my liking.

"Picking sides, Matteo?" Benny asked, his frustration evident. "What happened to the simple observer role. As far as I know, I have not broken any rules. She's unclaimed."

Matteo shrugged. "And I'm just here...*merely* observing."

"Don't worry, Gianluca, maybe I drugged her a little more than I should have, but she's still breathing." Savio sneered. I didn't miss the unspoken 'for now.'

I will enjoy killing you.

"You took what was mine," I told Benny, trying to rein in my anger.

"Please, Luca, she is just a little girl—a maid to whom you told everything without swearing her to the famiglia. We don't like loose ends. I'm fixing *your* mistakes."

"Is that why you killed my family?"

Benny took a step back in surprise.

"W-what are you talking about?"

"My mother and sister? What monster does that?"

He shook his head. "This is insane! You have no proof. I'm not just anyone, Gianluca. I'm the capo!" he roared, the gun shaking in his hand.

"Acting capo, Benny. And not anymore—I took my role back. I never should have given it to you."

Benny looked at Matteo, his face so red it almost looked purple.

"Yes, he is the capo."

"And I have proof."

"You can't have proof!" he barked. "They were not supposed to be there! They were there because of you. You killed them!"

It hit me like a ton of bricks. He just admitted somehow that he had caused the accident intending to kill me and my father. He was the one who killed my family, the two kindest souls in the world in a power play, and I raised my hand, pointing my gun to his face.

"I'd think twice about it," Savio warned, standing behind Cassie, raising the gun to the side of her head.

"Where's your loyalty?" Benny spat at Matteo.

"What loyalty do I owe *you*?" He frowned, clearly annoyed by Benny's outburst.

Benny gave him a wicked smile. "Brother, brother, where are you? I'm standing right next to you," he sang.

I didn't have the time to realize what was happening until I noticed Matteo's gun from the corner of my eyes and Benny fell heavily to the floor, a clean shot right in the middle of the forehead.

Then I heard the cock of a gun and felt the shot on my side and I felt like I'd just died.

24

CASSIE

Noise? Water? Pain? Everything at the same time. My mouth felt so dry it was like I had cotton balls in it.

I moaned softly, trying to move, but my arms were stuck and suddenly I heard a deafening bang quickly followed by a second one.

I jerked back on my chair, wincing at the pain in my head and my body.

"Cassie, mi amore, open your eyes."

"Luca?" I tried to speak but my throat was so dry like I had swallowed sand.

"Cassie, please."

I was not familiar with such desperation in his voice.

I tried my hardest to open my eyes but my vision

was a little blurry. I could just see Luca's shape kneeling in front of me as his hands touched my legs.

"I feel weird." Why was I feeling weird? Why didn't I remember anything after the lawyer appointment?

"Luca?"

"Yes, tesora. I'm here, and I'm not letting you out of my sight again."

I felt someone tug at my hands and turned my head, startled.

Dom threw me a quick smile before working on my hands, untying them.

I looked up and noticed Matteo standing behind Luca and everything came back like a wave. Savio, the needle.

"Savio kidnapped me!"

I could see Luca's face more clearly now and the worry in his face, the deep frown between his eyebrows, the thin line of his lips.

"He did, sweetheart."

Matteo came to stand beside Luca, looking all kingly in his dark suit. He eyed me critically and extended a bottle of water to Luca before saying something in Italian.

Luca replied quite harshly to him before turning toward me. "Drink, it will help with the drugs' side effects," Luca said gently, still kneeling in front of me.

I nodded, trying to take the bottle but my hand was shaking too much.

Luca brought the water to my lips and I drank greedily, the cold water doing wonders to my achy throat. I had not even realized I had drunk the whole thing. until Luca discarded the bottle and spoke over my shoulder. "Can you get another one? Also, tell Enzo what happened."

Matteo was still eyeing me, and the intensity of his eyes made me uncomfortable.

"They didn't do that alone, you know that, right? The whole thing—it was too well executed." He spoke for Luca's benefit.

Luca sighed. "I know but that's a problem for another time."

Matteo nodded before taking the white pocket square from his dark-gray suit and extending it to Luca.

Luca wiped my cheek so gently it almost made me cry. This big man was always so tender to me.

"Blood?" I gasped when he folded the fabric to put in his pocket. I didn't feel hurt.

Luca cradled the other side of my face with his big hand. "Not yours, tesora." His eyes flickered to his side.

I followed his eyes and winced. I'd seen dead people at the hospital but this one was different. Savio was lying on the floor right beside me, his left dead eye looking straight at me as the other was completely gone by a bullet wound, his blood slowly soiling the concrete floor.

"Oh, Luca…" My eyes trailed off to the body a bit further to the dead Benny. "Are you going to be in trouble?"

His whole face morphed into so much tenderness. "Oh, anima mia," He let out a tired chuckle. "You've been drugged, kidnapped, and almost killed, and you worry about me?"

"Of course." I frowned, why was he so surprised? "I love you."

Matteo cleared his throat. "Sorry to interrupt the most touching moment in history," he started, clearly not sorry at all. "But we need to move now. She can't be here when the team comes and leave the kid to me."

"Kid? What kid?"

Matteo threw me an exasperated look. "Nothing of your concern and just to appease your mind. Gianluca didn't kill anyone. I took this one out," he said, pointing to Luca's uncle.

"And I killed Savio," Dom said, coming back with another bottle of water. "I could not let anyone hurt my OTH buddy, right?" He gave me one of his cheeky grins, trying to hide the real fear he just had.

"I don't even want to know what that means," Matteo huffed. "Grab her, take the car, and go."

Luca reached for me and carried me bridal style.

"What did Matteo say to you?" I asked as I wrapped my arms around his neck.

"When?" he asked before kissing my temple and sighing with relief.

"When he gave you the water."

Luca rolled his eyes. "Matteo is a little old-fashioned. He said that a capo knelt for no one."

"I see…"

"I replied that I would not kneel to anyone including him, but that the woman who holds my heart and tattered soul, was an exception to the rule."

I gave him a little smile and rested my head in the crook of his neck, feeling his warm skin, his light stubble, smelling his intoxicating aftershave; I've never felt safer than in his arms.

I kept going in and out of sleep all the way to the hotel.

"I'm going to order some food for you and some coffee. I'll help you take a shower now, okay?"

He called food service and walked me slowly to the bathroom. He turned on the water on the gigantic wall shower and as the luxurious bathroom started to lightly steam up, he removed my clothes and his with almost military precision and he took me with him in the shower, lathering me with the lilac-smelling soap and then washing my hair with such tenderness.

I leaned against his back as he massaged my scalp. "You're so good at taking care of me," I whispered, feeling so relaxed despite everything.

"You are good at taking care of me too; it's a partnership that we have, Cassie." He twirled me around so I could look at him. "It's you and me." He kissed the tip of my nose. "Always."

"Always."

He rinsed the shampoo out of my hair and made me sit on the tile seat in the shower as he washed quickly.

Once he was done, he toweled me dry and helped me into my pj's before taking care of himself and once he was dressed, he pulled me into his arms and carried me to the bed.

"Luca, I'm fine now. I'm not an invalid."

"You got kidnapped and drugged, my love. Let me take care of you."

I sighed but gave in. I knew it was just as much for him as it was for me.

He put me in bed and arranged the covers around me. "I'll be right back."

I relaxed against the fluffy pillows when Luca rolled in a cart full of food. "I was not sure what you wanted."

"Luca…" I chided before settling for the plate of scrambled eggs with toast.

He sat on the comfy cream armchair across the bed and looked at me, a glass of scotch in his hand.

"Marry me," he blurted out when I was halfway through my plate of food.

I almost choked on my toast. "What?"

"Marry me, tomorrow…just, marry me."

"Is that a proposal?"

He nodded.

"Of course I'll marry you Luca Montanari, but…" I shook my head. "We can't just get married right now. This is crazy; we barely know each other."

"Yes, we can. I requested a license this morning." He leaned forward on his seat. "I know you, I know everything that matters. Marry me—tomorrow morning. I don't want to leave New York without you as my wife."

"Luca, it is the fear of losing me talking. I—"

He shook his head. "I always fear losing you, tesora. Whether you are in danger or not. You're my great love, my *only* love. You are my chance of happiness and I realized that a long time ago. But I pushed these feelings away, buried them because I shouldn't have wanted you and because of the way I feel for you—fuck, woman, it scares me in ways I can hardly comprehend. You deserve a fairy tale, and this love we share, baby, it's not the fairy tale you want or you dream of."

"You are my Prince Luca; the dark armor doesn't scare me."

"I'm back on top of the food chain. I'm Mafia—it's dark, it's dirty. I won't be able to tell you everything and there are things you'll hear, you'll see that you won't like, that you won't agree with but I'll have to do them anyway. I'll be the darkness surrounding your bright light. But I swear to never smother it, never."

"Let your darkness embrace my light, Luca Montanari. I don't scare easily. Why can't we make our own fairy tale, you and me? It doesn't have to be Disney. It only needs to be us."

"We can have your fairy-tale wedding later if you want, whenever, wherever, but for now give me that. Cassie, I beg you, marry me."

"I don't want a fairy-tale wedding, not now, not ever. Yes, as crazy as it is, I'll marry you tomorrow."

Luca's face lit up like a child on Christmas morning, and just for that, I knew I made the right choice.

"Make love to me, Luca Montanari," I said once he removed the food from my lap.

He froze for a second, his eyes lighting up with a lustful glint. "You've been hurt, tesora. I'm not sure—"

"But I am." I removed my pajama top, giving him a full view of my erect nipples. "My mind is clear now and I'm craving your hands on my skin."

Luca's eyes raked over my chest, his face morphing from indecision to pure desire. I still could hardly believe the power I had over that man. How much he wanted me.

He removed his own pajamas and his magnificent body and semi-hard cock made my stomach flutter and my lady part clench at the thought of his big cock inside me.

I pulled back the cover and lifted my hips in a silent invitation for him to take off my pajama bottom. I knew how much he enjoyed stripping me.

He growled with appreciation and hooked his fingers on the side of my pants, taking them down slowly before throwing them on the other side of the room.

He straddled my legs and looked down at me like a predator ready to sprawl, looking for the most vulnerable part to attack. If only he knew—all parts of me were vulnerable under his heated dark look.

"*La mia bellissima fidanzata*." He beamed, brushing his fingers softly on my nipples.

My skin felt like it was on fire.

He leaned down and licked one of my nipples as a gush of wetness settled between my thighs.

He brushed his lips against my collarbone, the curve of my throat.

"I'm going to tattoo you with my lips," he murmured before nipping on my jawline.

I tried to squeeze my legs, seeking the friction I was dying for.

"What do you want?" he demanded, alternating between licking, nipping, and sucking at my skin.

"You," I let out breathlessly. "Inside of me."

He moved to lay beside me, never breaking the ministrations that were driving me insane.

"Inside of you?" he asked, letting his big hand trail

down my stomach. "Here?" he asked, cupping my pussy in a possessive gesture.

"Yes," I mewled, nudging my hips up and parting my legs more, giving his hand full access.

Luca sucked at my breast as his fingers parted my folds, testing my wetness.

He entered me with his finger, and I moaned, raising my hips once more, wanting his finger deeper... I wanted more, just more.

He let my nipple out of his mouth in a pop. "Always so wet for me, so hot and ready."

"Always for you."

"Only for me." I shouldn't enjoy the dark possessiveness with which he ordered that and yet I did. It pushed my desire to the borders of insanity.

I nodded, closing my eyes. "Only for you." I let my hand wander blindly until it wrapped around his steel-hard cock.

I squeezed, making him hiss and thrust in my hand.

"You're mine too."

"Yes, I'm yours. Always and forever."

"Make love to me."

Luca removed his finger and sucked it into his mouth as he settled between my legs, never breaking eye contact.

"You taste like my own personal ambrosia, tesora," he said as he thrust his hips slowly, rubbing his cock against my soaked heat.

"I will need to taste yours soon." I spread my legs wider and rocked my hips again.

Luca raised his hips, grabbed his cock, and entered me with agonizing slowness, keeping his eyes on me until he was fully seated in me.

I rested my heels on top of his ass and gripped his shoulders.

He made sweet, soft love to me, with long, slow, deep thrusts that I felt all the way to my heart.

He kissed me, caressed me, and murmured so many love words both in English and Italian with each thrust.

I felt him grow bigger inside me; he was close. He threw his head backward as he brought his hand down and rubbed my clit with his thumbpad, taking me right over the edge.

As my inner muscles squeezed tightly around his length, he shouted my name, shooting his own release deep inside of me.

He fell heavily to the side, leaving me empty, but he almost immediately pulled me into the warmth of his arms.

I rested my head on his chest, listening to his heavy breathing and heartbeat.

"I love you, Luca," I whispered, wrapping my arm around his torso.

His arms tightened around me. "You are my everything," he replied wistfully before kissing the top of my head.

I fell asleep, satiated, happy, and feeling safe in the arms of the man I loved, lulled by the rhythm of his strong heartbeat.

And I knew without a shadow of a doubt that despite everything that life would throw our way— Luca Montanari and I were forever.

LUCA

I woke up at dawn and looked at my fiancée asleep on the bed beside me.

"Fiancée," I whispered, letting my eyes trail down her slender neck and beautiful hair in the little light of the rising sun seeping through the gap in the heavy curtain.

I hardly believed that after everything I'd done, everything she'd been through with me, or because of me, she was ready to officially be mine.

I crawled out of bed as carefully as I could, made sure the curtains were perfectly closed, and walked out of the room, ready to start down the warpath to get as much as possible done before she woke up and could rethink anything.

She won't, she loves you, I repeated to myself.

I called Dom.

"Who died?" he mumbled sleepily on the phone.

"You, if you're not in my room in the next five minutes."

Dom walked in wearing sweats and T-shirt, a dark look on his face. "What the fuck," he grumbled. "You know with all the shit I helped Genovese to deal with, I barely slept. But you know as your consigliere…" He sighed.

"You are my consigliere. Did you ever think I would pick anyone else?"

Dom looked at me with incredulity. "I can't be. I'm the son of a simple made man; it's not like it's done."

I shook my head. "And yet you are. I told Matteo, it was validated. There is no man I trust more than you, Domenico. I trust you with my life and most of all I trust you with hers. You are not only my security, you are my best friend."

Dom cleared his throat and looked away. "What do you need?"

"I'm getting married today."

"Are you?" Dom turned toward me. "Does she know? Are you asking me for her hand in marriage?"

I gave him my middle finger. "I need you to help me."

He chuckled. "Of course. What do you need?"

"Go to our usual jeweler and pick up the engagement ring I ordered. Ask her to give you the matching wedding ring and a platinum band for me."

"You had an engagement ring made?"

I nodded. "A few weeks ago, when I went to New York. I've known she was the one from the moment I saw her appear on my screen."

"I've known for a while too." He rubbed his face. "What else do you need?"

"I need you to go see Matteo and tell him he needs to come to City Hall this afternoon with another member of the council. I need them to witness."

"Matteo? Really?" He grimaced. "I spent four hours with the guy after you left; it's plenty for a lifetime."

I sighed. "Dom, please."

"*Si.*" He rubbed his stubble. "What do you think it all meant, yesterday? Why did Matteo help?"

I didn't want Dom to worry, giving Matteo a blank promise as I did was stupid beyond belief, but it was born out of a desperation Dom couldn't understand.

"Matteo wanted me back on top; helping me get Cassie was the only way. If she had died—" I couldn't contain the shiver that went down my spine and the wave of nausea that hit my stomach at the mere thought.

Dom paled too, his hand tightening into a tight fist on the counter. I knew that the idea of losing

Cassie was just as unfathomable to him as it was to me.

"If she had died, there would have been no me left."

"And I would have killed them all," Dom added darkly.

I nodded, throwing a look toward the bedroom where my woman was still sleeping. We would both die for her and the thought reassured me somehow.

"I'll go deal with Genovese. Anything else?"

I shook my head. "No, Cassie doesn't want a big fuss."

Dom gave me a small smile. "I didn't expect anything less from her. She is all about simplicity."

"I still can't believe she chose me," I admitted.

Dom snorted. "I can't either, that woman is clinically insane."

I threw him a withering look. "Cazzo."

He chuckled, shaking his head. "You are not seeing yourself clearly; you never did. She sees *you,* who you truly are, and yes, you're not easy but you are a good man, the best of men. Did you really think I'd follow you in the depth of despair if I ever doubted you, Luca?" He gave me a small smile. "She made the right choice. I don't think she could ever find anyone who would be just as dedicated as you."

It was my turn to have a lump of emotion forming in my throat.

I cleared my throat. "You better go now; this

wedding will not happen by itself. I have to call Carter now. I have a few favors to cash out."

Dom glanced at the clock in the room. "It's six thirty."

I shrugged. "They have two infants; I'm pretty sure they're up."

Dom nodded. "Fine, I'll get ready and go. I should be back in the next few hours with the rings."

Dom turned toward the door, took a step, but stopped before turning around again.

"What do you think Benny meant when he sang?"

Ah, that, I did wonder the same thing but that also was a problem for another time. Did Benny know what I did? Who I killed in the name of brotherhood?

"It was the desperate words of a desperate man, trying to goad us to buy time." I waved my hand dismissively. "I have enough things to deal with. That was irrelevant."

Dom nodded. "Yeah, I think you're right." But I knew him well enough to know that he would not forget.

As soon as Dom was gone I called Carter and as predicted he was already wide awake, the sound of a wailing child in the background.

"Whatever it is, Luca, it will have to wait," he said as a way of greeting.

"I'm getting married and I need your help."

Carter was silent for a few seconds. "And you needed to say that now? Congratulations."

"I'm getting married today."

"Oh." Carter chuckled. "Worried she'll change her mind? I can't blame you."

I rolled my eyes. Why was I surrounded by assholes? *Because you're an asshole*, the little taunting voice replied.

Carter sighed. "What do you need?"

"You as my witness, your wife to help mine, and access to King's Mall."

"One sec—" The line went quiet as he put himself on mute. "Nazalie said yes."

I would have teased him endlessly about that before but now I knew better because what Cassie said went.

"Perfect. When can you be here?"

"Couple of hours?"

"See you then."

I ordered breakfast for Cassie and rolled it into the room. I opened the curtain halfway and looked at her in the bed, my heart squeezing almost painfully in my chest. Would this feeling ever go away? Would I one day be used to having her? I doubted it.

I sat carefully beside her and brushed my lips on her cheekbone, trailing down her cheek to her neck.

She sighed with content. "Be careful, Mr. Montanari. I might request this type of wake-up call every morning."

I chuckled against her neck. "What my queen wants, my queen gets." I moved from my spot on her neck and met her green eyes still full of sleep. "I brought you breakfast." I smiled. "The future bride needs to eat and get ready because her bridal team will be here shortly."

She blinked at me silently and suddenly I was frozen with fear. Did she forget about yesterday? Had the drugs played tricks on her? And the more frightening thought of all, did she change her mind?

"Cassie?" Lord, did my voice sound as scared as I thought it did?

"I thought it was just a quick wedding. You don't need to go to any hassle; all that matters is that I'm marrying you."

I let out a relieved chuckle. "Tesora, it's as much for me as it is for you. It's the only one we'll ever have —humor me."

She shook her head with a little cheeky smile on her face. "I love you, my sweet beast."

I pecked her lips. "Sweet only for you, *bellissima*."

I took a quick shower as she ate her breakfast and I went back to the living room to give her some privacy. The excitement of the day was starting to really get to me.

Dom was the first to come back.

"Matteo was a conceited ass about the wedding. He said to tell you 'another plot twist he never saw coming' but he'll be there at one with Romero."

I nodded. "Being an ass is Matteo's default mode."

Dom cocked his head to the side. "I thought it was a psycho killer."

I nodded "That too." I took the engagement ring from him and looked at it. It was just as beautiful as I had imagined. The ring was made of platinum, set with round black diamonds, emeralds for the stem, and a round, red diamond center stone for the rose.

"Is it a—"

"Red rose, yes," I confirmed. "A reminder of our garden."

"Look who's romantic."

"*Vaffanculo.*" I closed the red velvety box and looked toward our bedroom. "Carter will be here any minute; let him in please. I just need to have a word with my fiancée."

I went into the bedroom and once the shower stopped running, I waited until the door clicked open and I went down on one knee, the ring box open in front of me.

She stepped out, her wet hair in a tight bun, dressed in black leggings and a red flannel shirt.

Her eyes went wide at the position. "Luca?"

I smiled at her. "I know you already accepted but I wanted to make this right. "Cassandra West, I'm asking again. Marry me today?"

She laughed and rushed toward me. "Of course."

I stood up and placed the ring on her finger.

"A rose? Luca, it is so beautiful."

"I had it made especially for us." I ran my thumb

on the black diamonds. "My eyes." Then the emer-alds, "Your eyes." And finally the red diamond. "My eternal love for you…all born in a garden."

She grabbed my face and pulled me down to kiss me deeply. I was not one to relinquish dominance, but for her, I would.

Once we broke the kiss, both breathless, she grabbed my hand, intertwined our fingers, and walked into the living room.

"I'm getting married!" She beamed to Dom, showing him her ring.

"Nice! Who's the lucky bastard?"

"Asshole!" I muttered as Cassie rolled her eyes.

She let go of my hand and walked to him, pulling him into a hug.

"I have something to ask you actually. Would you give me away and be my witness? Except for Luca and Jude, you're the person who matters most to me and it would mean the world to me."

Dom looked away, his eyes carrying the glint of unshed tears. "I'm not crying, you're crying."

"I never said you were crying," Cassie replied gently.

Dom sniffled. "Shut up."

It was the moment Carter and Nazalie showed up.

Nazalie pulled Cassie into a hug. "I'm so happy for you." She turned to me. "I told you that you would one day get that happiness too."

I nodded, I remember that. She'd told me that on

her wedding day. "And I said I had not done anything to deserve it."

"This is a thing with love, Luca; it's not always something you deserve. It's a gift. You just need to be brave enough to seize it." Carter pulled Nazalie close to him and kissed the top of her head.

"Not that I want to be a pain, but I need to steal the future bride away if we want to be on time at City Hall."

"I'm coming with," Dom piped in. "I'm the maid of honor."

I threw him a grateful look, knowing that it would bring me peace of mind to have him with Cassie.

"I'll see you soon, Mr. Montanari." Cassie smiled at me before pecking my lips with a chaste kiss.

I watched her go, trying to smother the wave of anxiety at seeing her leave my sight.

"What happened?" Carter asked as soon as we were alone.

I turned toward him. "What do you mean?"

"You love the woman, that much is clear, but why get married now? It was not in the cards two days ago."

"It was always in the cards, but I almost lost her yesterday and it was enough for me to realize that waiting one more day would be wasting my time. I want her as my wife so why wait. Time is precious, and so damned fucking short, Carter."

He nodded. "Good answer." He looked at his watch. "Okay, time to go and get you a suit. I won't fail at my best man duties and let you get married looking like a tramp."

I picked a dark-blue three-piece suit with a white shirt and matching tie. We stopped at Carter's gentlemen's club for a glass of expensive bourbon and a nice cigar—his version of an express bachelor party —before taking a shower there and changing into my suit.

We arrived at City Hall at the same time as Matteo and Romero exited the car.

"Matteo." I bowed my head to him. "Romero." I I maintained eye contact, daring him to challenge me. Romero was an older member of the council; it was probably the reason why Matteo chose him as a witness. Nobody would doubt Romero's words and he was too old to hold any kind of petty grudge.

"Luca Montanari. I'm glad to see you. I didn't expect that your nuptials would be the first time we met again," Romero said, cocking his head to the side. "Can I assume that an heir is in the making?"

Ah, yes, pregnancies had been the number one reason for shotgun weddings within the family and I'd fuck Cassie bare from the first time, without knowing she was on the pill.

"Not impossible," I said evasively. It was true enough and this would reinforce Cassie's position as my wife.

Romero chuckled. "The message is clear. I'll see you in there. I have a judge to see for a minute or two."

Matteo chuckled once Romero was out of earshot. "Better for him to believe you got her pregnant than to know how pussywhipped you are. I understand."

"No, you really don't."

He raised his hands in surrender, a mocking smile on his face. "No, I don't, and seeing you I'm even more grateful."

"So what are we doing with…you know."

Matteo looked straight ahead, burying his hands in his black pantsuit pockets.

"Benny and Savio have been killed by the Albanians. They tried to steal from them." Matteo shrugged. "Traitors die. The kid is free; he's working for me now. Quite a step up. He's grateful enough to keep his mouth shut."

I nodded. "Thank you."

"I didn't do it to spare your bleeding heart."

I looked at Carter who was waiting at the top of the stairs, knowing better than to eavesdrop on this conversation.

"But we still need to figure out wh—"

"Get married, Luca. Enjoy your wife and new life for a while. Impregnate her, make sure the stray you're adopting will follow the rules, and then come see me; we'll deal with that then. For now, I have a lot of cleaning to do. *Capisce?*"

"Understood."

Matteo nodded, throwing me a side-look. "Go get married, Gianluca; you are such a blushing bride." He went up the stairs slowly, laughing at his own joke.

I went up the stairs after him and joined Carter.

"Is everything okay?"

I sighed with a nod. "As okay as it will ever be."

Carter jerked his head toward the doors. "Let's go. Nazalie just texted me; they'll be here any minute."

My stomach squeezed with anticipation at the thought of getting married.

Carter and I walked into the room where the clerk was already waiting. Matteo and Romero were sitting at the back of the room.

A couple of minutes later Nazalie walked into the room. She winked at me and sat in the front row, and then the door opened and my breath stalled as my heart skipped a beat.

My angel walked in, dressed in a simple flowing floor-length silky cream-colored V-neck dress, the sleeves made of cream lace with red roses on them.

Her hair was up in an intricate hairdo with a few red roses in it. She was just breathtakingly beautiful. I saw a flash from the corner of my eyes, but I couldn't care less. Nothing short of a nuclear incident could make me avert my eyes from the most beautiful woman I had ever seen.

She smiled so brightly at me; her eyes shining with unshed tears, she almost slew me.

I wanted to fall on my knees and thank her once again for saving me, for loving the beast, and making him human once more.

For bringing me back to life when I thought all hopes were lost...for just being her.

She stopped beside me and turned to face me.

Dom removed her hand from his arm and put it on mine.

"Don't fuck it up, *idiota*," he whispered teasingly before going to stand on Cassie's side.

I brought her hand up and kissed it.

"Cassandra, you are so beautiful." I knew she could hear the awe in my voice and see it in my face.

She blushed, looking down at our hands. "You are quite dashing too."

The clerk proceeded with the ceremony and I just repeated my part as a good boy, while being lost in my now wife's eyes.

Cassie would have to swear allegiance to Matteo just after the ceremony. She will repeat the words of the oath I'd taken almost twenty years ago. She would kiss his ring and she would be induced as my wife.

"If you don't mind, I'd like to say a few words," I told the clerk.

"Umm, yes, but there are oth—"

"Five minutes," I ordered.

"Y-yes, of course," he muttered, realizing it had not been a request.

"Cassandra Montanari, my soul, my life, my heart. From the start it has not been easy. Our love developed in the most unlikely circumstances. You fell for the most unlikely man. You became my everything, Cassie, my love. You make me stronger and you helped me from losing my mind. You've made this life beautiful; you gave me a purpose—the one to be the man who deserves you every day…" I brought my hand up, cradling her check. "I thank God for you, for your love, and I'll make sure I'm worthy of it even during the darkest moment."

She sniffled. "I promised not to cry but I don't know what more to say except, *Lo giuro su Dio e sulla famiglia. Il mio cuore, il mio amore e la mia lealtà sono tuoi. Ora e per sempre. Faccio questo giuramento col sangue, nel silenzio della notte, e sotto la luce delle stelle e lo splendore della luna. Tutti i tuoi segreti saranno miei, tutti i tuoi peccati saranno miei, tutto il tuo dolore sarà mio. Sono tuo completamente.*"

I took a sharp intake of breath and looked at Dom over her shoulder. She'd not just given the general loyalty oath. No, here, in the middle of the room and in quite a decent Italian, she had surrendered her life to me, making us one.

Dom smiled and nodded his head in a 'you're welcome' gesture. That, right there, was the most beautiful present they could have given me.

"Cassie, you know what you just—"

She stood on her tiptoes and kissed my lips to stop me. "I swear it on God and the family. My heart, my love, and my loyalty are yours. Now and forever. I'm taking this oath in blood, in the silence of the night, and under the light of the stars and splendor of the moon. All your secrets will be mine, all your sins will be mine, all your pain will be mine. I am yours completely." She repeated the oath in English. "I know what I promised, Luca, and I surrender to you, in every way."

That sent a message to my cock as a flash of her on her knees settled in my brain. It was so not the time and place.

I kissed her a bit too deeply for the occasion, but I didn't care. She was Mrs. Montanari and for the first time in what seemed like forever, I was looking forward to what the future would bring.

Who would have thought it would take a five one fierce redhead to save the beast?

EPILOGUE

CASSIE

Six months later.

I settled a bit more comfortably on the lounge chair and despite the PSF 50 sunscreen and enormous umbrella giving me shade, I could feel my pale skin heat up.

I adjusted my sunglasses and scanned the blue sea of the Bahamas, looking for my husband.

We had to delay our honeymoon for a while. First, because Luca had a lot of cleanup to do and we wanted to make sure that Jude was completely settled at Hartfield before leaving him behind with Dom.

Luca had managed to get our parents to sign over their parental authority, and I had not cared how he did it. The adoption had been finalized a little over a month ago, and Jude was as happy as I had been to leave the name West behind and become a Montanari.

My brother loved Luca and Dom and neither seemed to mind his little quirks and OCDs. If I had not loved them by then, I would have by now.

Jude loved the house, the library, and the private school Luca got him in.

I lost my train of thought when my husband came out of the water in his black swim shorts, his black hair wet and curling, his big muscular sun-kissed chest covered with droplets of water that I wanted to kiss away.

Luca had rented us a beach villa for two weeks, with access to a semi-private beach, and I saw how the neighbors looked at Luca. With his massive frame and striking scars, he was terrifying, but for me, he wasn't and hadn't been since that one night in the library.

When I looked at him all I felt was love, peace, and a healthy dose of lust.

Luca leaned over me and kissed me, sending some blissfully refreshing droplets of water on my skin.

"How's our boy doing?" he asked, sitting on the lounge chair across from me.

"Which one?"

He chuckled.

"He said Dom is teaching him to fight and he also

said we need to stop calling him and babying him." I smiled at him. "You've been calling him behind my back too, haven't you?"

He shrugged. "I'm worried. He is still so young."

"Dom is great with him; they are having fun."

Luca grunted. "The boy is eleven; he doesn't need fun. He needs structure."

I laughed at that. "Look at you, being the strict father figure."

"You like that, don't you?"

"I do, maybc you can punish mc too."

"Don't push me, woman…" He reached over and trailed his hand up my leg. "Or I swear I'll take you right here and give the neighbors a show."

I let out a breathless laugh, getting way too hot under his touch, almost forgetting what I wanted to say.

"You enjoy being a father?" I asked him.

He frowned. "Yes, I told you, I love Jude; he is such an easy kid to parent."

I nodded. "It's good, you've got about seven months of training left."

"It's nice to—" He froze, his eyes settling on my stomach. "Seven months?"

"Uh-huh."

"Does it mean that—"

"We're pregnant?" I rested my hand on my stomach. "Yes, we are."

Luca fell on his knees beside my chair and kissed my stomach before kissing me.

"Our baby…tesora." He kissed my stomach again, making me shiver.

"You're going to be the best father, Luca. I can't wait until I see you carry our baby in your arms."

"I'm going to love you so much, baby," he said to my stomach, caressing it. "Be good to mama, okay?"

I rested my hand in his hair, caressing it softly.

He turned his head to face me. "I can't wait to see your body grow to accommodate our baby. Just the thought of you as a mother. I'll keep you·safe, both of you."

"I know, my love. I never had a doubt."

I squealed as Luca stood, taking me in his arms. "Luca, what are you doing?"

"I'm going to make love to my future baby mama. Do you have a problem with that?" he asked, already walking toward the house.

I laughed. "No, of course not. I can't get enough of you."

"Same here. Thanks again for saving me, belissima."

I brought my hand up, cradling his cheek. "Thanks for letting me save you, my beast."

He growled, making me giggle.

"You woke up the beast, Mrs. Montanari; now is the time to pay up."

And I happily paid the price that night as he made love to me insatiably in our bed.

Luca Montanari, Mafia boss, beast, unfeeling man for some. Husband, lover, friend, and father for others. A contradiction of a man but most of all...mine.

The End...for now.

AUTHOR'S NOTE

Thank you so much for reading Luca and Cassie's story. I hope you enjoyed it as much as I enjoyed writing it.

Also, if you have it in your heart to leave a little review, I would be really grateful.

A few questions are still unanswered and there's a reason trust me – It is a series of three books and it will all be answered. Each book will concentrate on a different sexy Mafia man and his strong heroine.

Make sure to check **Twisted Knight**, the standalone sequel of **The Cosa Nostra** Series. It will be Dom's book and quite darker than Broken Prince! You don't want to miss it and finally find out what Dom's kink is 😊. It will be released **July/August 2021**.

If you are intrigued by Carter and Nazalie, you can read their story in **The Dark King** which is available on amazon for $/£0.99 and you can read it for free on KindleUnlimited.

I wanted to thank my Street Team for always promoting my work. I appreciate you girls much more than you think.

I also wanted to thank my betas – Jolien, Liz and Ashley for your enthusiasm about this series – It means a lot.

All the Best,

R.G. Angel xx

ABOUT ME

I'm a trained lawyer, world traveler, coffee addict,
cheese aficionado, avid book reviewer and blogger.
I consider myself as an 'Eclectic romantic' as I love to
devour every type of romance and I want to write
romance in every sub-genre I can think of.
When I'm not busy doing all my lawyerly mayhem,
and because I'm living in rainy (yet beautiful) Britain,
I mostly enjoy indoor activities such as reading,
watching TV, playing with my crazy puppies and
writing stories I hope will make you dream and will
bring you as much joy as I had writing them.
If you want to know any of the latest news join my
reader group R.G.'s Angels on Facebook or subscribe
to my newsletter!

Keep calm and read on!
R.G. Angel

ALSO, BY R.G. ANGEL

The Patricians series
Bittersweet Legacy
Bittersweet Revenge
Bittersweet Truth
Bittersweet Love (Coming soon)

The Cosa Nostra series
The Dark King (Prequel Novella)

Standalones
Lovable
The Tragedy of Us
The Bargain